DANGEROUS
OBSESSION

J.M. JEFFRIES

Genesis Press Inc.

Indigo Love Stories

An imprint Genesis Press Publishing

Indigo Love Stories
c/o Genesis Press, Inc.
1213 Hwy 45 N, 2nd Floor
Columbus, MS 39705

All characters in this book have no existence outside the imagination of the author and have no relation whatsoever to anyone bearing the same name or names. They are not even distantly inspired by any individual known or unknown to the author and all incidents are pure invention

Copyright© 2003 by J.M. Jeffries
Dangerous Obsession

ISBN 1-58571-109-8
Manufactured in the United States of America

First Edition

Visit us at www.genesis-press.com
or call at 1-888-Indigo-1

—∽∿∽—

Marco slid his arms around her. She closed her eyes and breathed in his scent, a mixture of plain old soap and something lemony. "I'm heartbroken. He's ruined a lot of things for me." She thought about her parents. Maybe they hadn't done her a favor by shielding her the way they had, but they had always had her welfare in mind. They had understood her and were patient with her. Never condemning her, yet never allowing her to give in to her fears. With their deaths, Sawyer wiped out her support system.

DEDICATION

Jackie: As always, Ingrid, my light at the end of the tunnel. For Lily Elizabeth, welcome to this world. To the Wild Women Writers may success, adventure, and passion be yours.

Miriam: To Parker, thank you for your enduring faith in me. To my children, Miriam and Jeff, your love sustains me. To my grandson, Frederik, welcome to the world. To my son-in-law, Peter, I'm glad your part of the family. To the Wild Women Writers, many more trips to places foreign and exotic.

PROLOGUE

Arizona Desert

Lily Alexander ran. Her side hurt and her lungs burned with the need for oxygen. Her legs felt like lead. The rocky ground cut her bare feet, but she couldn't afford to think about the pain. She couldn't stop. Not now. Not yet. Not with him so close behind her.

Sweat popped out on her skin, then dried to a sticky film. She had to get away. The thought was a litany in her mind. *Keep running. Keep running.* Running meant escape. Escape meant survival. Once she stopped, she would never start again. Then she would be dead.

Five days ago she'd been in her dorm room studying for finals, but one simple phone call had changed everything. Now, she was running for her life.

She tripped and went flying, hitting the ground with hands out-stretched. Pain vibrated through every muscle. The skin on her knees burned. Sand filled her mouth.

She tried to still her hoarse breathing. Could he hear her? How far behind was he? Glancing behind, she saw only blackness, knowing he was near. She could feel him. Galvanized by her fear, she pushed up and scrambled to her feet.

Ahead, the lights of the highway shone. Cars zoomed along the ribbon of asphalt. If she could make it to the highway, she might have a chance.

"Lily," a voice called out to her. "Come back to me. I won't hurt you. I promise."

Sidestepping one boulder and scrambling over another, the flouncy white chiffon dress he'd forced her to wear caught and almost jerked her to a standstill. Then the fabric ripped and she floundered forward again.

She couldn't fail. She knew if she were caught again, death was certain. Tears streamed down her cheeks, blood oozed from the cuts on her hands and knees, but she reached the embankment, and scrambled over a wooden fence. She ran onto the road and stopped, swaying back and forth, unable to continue. Here she waited, for death or life, depending on the whim of fate.

She gulped air and prayed a car would stop. A pair of headlights wound around a curve in the road and approached. Lily could only lift her hands in a gesture of supplication.

Brakes screeched. A whoosh of air brushed her as the car skidded to a stop. A glance over her shoulder showed a reddish moon, and a dark figure silhouetted against it. She smiled. "I beat you," she yelled, though her triumph felt hollow.

He turned, and disappeared behind the hill.

A car door slammed. Lily turned. A flashlight blazed in her face, blinding her.

"Lady," a man's harsh voice demanded. "What are you doing?"

"Help me," Lily pleaded, raising her hands. In the harsh glow of his flashlight, she saw the blood dripping down her fingers.

He stared hard at her. "Are you Lily Alexander?"

She nodded.

The flashlight pointed to the ground and she saw that the car wasn't just a car, but a police cruiser. The man wasn't just a man, but a cop. "The whole state has been looking for you."

She started laughing and the laughter turned to tears. She slid to her knees. The cop knelt down beside her and draped his jacket around her shoulders. Helping her to her feet, she embraced him. "You're safe now."

"I'm safe," she whispered. "I'm safe."

But she shuddered knowing she'd never feel safe again.

CHAPTER ONE

Twelve years later

Marco Jackson sat at his desk, an opened file folder spread across the surface. He doodled, his pen waltzing across the paper forming cartoon drawings of a Great Dane in a Phoenix PD uniform, as he studied a colored photo of a severed arm tossed in a trash can outside of a posh Mexican restaurant.

The arm belonged to Eunice Cameron, matriarch of the mighty Cameron clan. The thin white limb had fingernails painted a bright red. They were broken; testament to her struggle to survive. Purple bruises spotted the white skin. Since no blood had been found on scene, everyone assumed the victim had been dismembered elsewhere and the parts disposed of into various trash receptacles throughout Phoenix.

The coroner's report stated the arms were cut pre-mortem. No wonder she had struggled so hard. A shiver ran through Marco, he couldn't imagine watching himself being hacked up one piece at a time. All he could think of was this was a gruesome way to die. Doing someone this way involved a lot of hate. He wrote Eunice's name on his doodle pad circling the block letters several times. Then he drew a picture of a knife with blood dripping from the end.

Marco flipped through several more photos, each one detailing the grisly demise of Eunice Cameron. The wealthy window of a billionaire businessman who had pre-deceased her by ten years, she had been left with a posse of greedy relatives and two rapacious stepchildren.

A door slammed. Lieutenant Cher Dawson entered the squad room, a mug of coffee in one hand and a newspaper in the other. She looked calm and unruffled even though she was late. Twenty minutes late to be exact. Marco resisted looking at his watch.

The Lieutenant had been tardy almost every morning for the last month, ever since her wedding. In that time, she'd changed, and in Marco's opinion, not for the better. The hard-edged woman he'd grown to admire and respect had softened. She'd even changed her image.

Today, she wore one of her bright outfits, a cherry red pants suit and diamond earrings big enough to gag an elephant. If his sister, Elena, had been with him, she would have identified the designer. But Elena had left the force for marriage and motherhood. Marco still missed her.

Love might cause a person to forget how to read a clock, but to buy a whole new wardrobe? Thank God, Marco hadn't been that lucky yet. Not that he hadn't had enough prodding from his Italian-born mother, to whom children and grandchildren meant everything.

"Morning, Jackson." Dawson glanced around the empty squad room. "And where is everybody on this glorious spring morning?" She folded the paper and planted her butt on the corner of his desk. She sipped her squad room coffee-hot, black and out of the downstairs pot that was never cleaned.

"Whitaker and Greyhorse are in court. Bradley called in sick. Martinez is down in the evidence room. That new guy, whose name no one seems to know, hasn't shown up yet." The Cold Case Unit had scored a lot of publicity in the last few months with the solving of two high-profile crimes that had given Dawson the authority to recruit some extra bodies for the unit.

She smiled. "Along with that unnamed new guy, I stole Victor Chavez away from hate crimes. He's starting next week."

Marco high-fived her. Chavez was a real coup, dedicated and hard-working, and he knew where the office was. "Right on, boss."

Crime was down in Phoenix, which gave the Cold Case Unit another added benefit. The Lieutenant could pick and chose whom she wanted in the unit and she had done exactly that, ransacking some of the other units that had been forced to downsize.

She laughed. "What are you working on?" She perched over him like a condor.

He held up one of the photos for her to see. "Do you remember the Cameron murder about five years ago?"

She made a strange face. "The rich chick who got cut up and her parts tossed all over the city."

"That's the one." He stashed the photo back in the folder. "I'm thinking of having a go at it."

"Really?" Cher glanced through the folder, skimming the information. "Everyone thought the ugly step-kids did the deed because she wasn't dying soon enough to suit them."

"That's the theory, but no one's been able to pin it on them." Marco leaned back in his chair, feeling like the cat who had just lunched on the canary. He was going to crack this baby right open. "Until now, that is."

She pointed at him. "You have a lead?"

"Nope. I'm just being self-confident." He put his feet on the desk. He liked being in Cold Case. He could choose the case he wanted to work on and spend as much time as he wanted in pursuing the leads. He wouldn't be as lucky as Wyatt Earp Whitaker, who had a knack for sifting through the most ordinary, boring evidence and finding the one clue someone had overlooked that would lead him, through an inspired moment of deduction, to the perpetrator. Marco was more tenacious, more linear in the way he worked an investigation. No big flashes of inspiration for him; dogged determination was his modus operandi.

Dawson whacked him on the ankle with the newspaper. No one could treat her squad room like a home except her.

His boss may have changed on the outside, but where it counted she still was made of titanium steel. "Sorry." He dropped his feet to the ground.

"That is one stone-cold 'who-done-it.'" Cher closed the file and handed it back to him. "No one could prove the step-kids killed her, but neither is there proof someone else did the deed. So what's the fascination?"

Marco noticed she left a big red lipstick mark on the white coffee cup. Before her marriage, she hadn't even worn makeup and now she was all done up. Her smooth mahogany skin looked so perfect, Marco wouldn't have known she wore war paint until Elena had made the same observation at Dawson's wedding. "Sex. Drugs. Money. Hacksaws. What else does a guy need to develop an interest?"

"Okay, it's a start, but it's also spring. When a young man's fancy turns to..." She glanced out of the window at the cloudless blue sky. "So tell me, how's your love life?"

Marco stifled a groan as the stench of her burnt coffee spiraled around him. He didn't like the detour this conversation had just taken.

"Are you seeing anyone?" she persisted. "Are you dating? Have you had your tires rotated lately?"

A hot flush rose up his neck. Talking to the lieutenant was like talking to his mother, even though she was barely three years older

7

than he was. Since Dawson had married her college sweetheart, she was suddenly concerned about everyone's happiness. He wanted his old, miserable, sharp-tongued boss back. "My love life is fine." *And none of your concern.*

"Just checking." She smiled and slid off his desk. She turned toward her office. Just before she reached the door she faced him again. "Do you know who L.B. Alexander is?"

"No." Though the name did ring a bell. He'd heard it before, but no particular memory surfaced to attach itself to the name.

"True crime writer. Damn good, too. She's done some consulting for the department a few times. A few years ago she wrote a book about the Cameron murder. Maybe you should talk to her. She might have something you can sink your teeth into. She lives just south of Phoenix in the old Rancho Del Mar sub-division. Give me a second and I'll write down her address and phone number for you." She opened the door to her office and disappeared inside.

Marco frowned as he reopened the file again, amazed that the lieutenant remembered police business at all, considering how active her social life was with her new husband. He'd even heard on the office grapevine she was seeing a fertility specialist.

He couldn't imagine her with a baby. A baby! The irony almost caused him to laugh. She already had a daughter, but the girl was almost grown. What could Dawson be thinking of, starting a family at this time of her life? Especially when she'd just been told she might be in line for a big promotion.

Marco stroked his chin. He was trapped by people in love. First Elena had traded her career for love, marital bliss, and dirty diapers. Now Dawson was about to do the same. All this love stuff was enough to make him turn in his badge and take up life as a lone prospector out in the desert hunting for the Lost Dutchman Mine.

Marco had inherited Elena's position after Dawson strong-armed him into leaving the homicide unit and working for her. He'd accepted because he wanted a slower pace, and the time to give each case his total attention. He liked solving mysteries. They were like jigsaw puzzles. All the pieces were there, they just needed someone to put them in order and make sense of them. The Cold Case Unit suited him.

Dawson returned, and handed him a piece of paper with an address and phone number written on it. "This is L. B. Alexander's private number. Don't spread it around."

Marco reached for the phone. "I'll call her."

"Don't bother with the phone call. She's home. Just go and see her. The number's in case you get lost."

He grimaced and stood. So he had a small directional problem. Big deal. He usually ended up where he intended to be even if his detours took him through some pretty interesting neighborhoods. "First, I'm going to talk to the coroner. I'll contact her after lunch."

Dawson smiled. One thing that hadn't changed about her, the predatory gleam in her eyes when she had somebody just where she wanted them. "Go get me a killer, Jackson."

"Will do, Boss."

Marco braked his department-issue car in front of an eight-foot wrought-iron gate attached to a brick fence.

L.B. Alexander lived in an old community on the southeast side of the city. The fifties-era community consisted of authentic adobe homes situated on twenty-acre lots and twisting roads that could cause a person unfamiliar with the area to get lost in a major way.

Through the bars of the gate, he could see a sand-colored adobe house standing on a rocky knoll that gave it a 360-degree view. The sprawling ranch appeared to have sprouted wings from the original design with two extensions that jutted out at right angles from the original structure. Nice digs, he thought. Writing must pay well.

One of L.B. Alexander's books lay on the seat next to him. From the portrait on the back of the cover, he'd been surprised to learn L.B. Alexander was a beautiful woman with a wealth of tight, curly black hair, an aristocratic face and skin the color of Belgian chocolate—his favorite kind. Her full ruby lips smiled up at him like she had a truck full of secrets. Those lush lips begged to be kissed. She had a long neck like a swan. He couldn't see the rest of her, but his imagination said she had to be hot all the way down to her toes.

He'd glanced over her book while eating lunch. Her terse, hard-edged writing style had reminded him of the Dashiell Hammett books he'd pilfered from his father's library when he'd been a kid. He had loved those books, and even though his whole family was in law enforcement in some manner, those books had decided his own fate.

He'd known he'd be a cop, too, just like his older brothers. His dad had been the best, and after a distinguished career, he'd retired from the force and gone on to television stardom as the ornery captain of an elite unit of Phoenix street cops, making more money in a season than he had as a thirty-year veteran on the force.

A keypad and an intercom stood to one side of the wrought iron gate. Marco pressed a button, and after a few seconds a disembodied voice answered. "Hello? Please identify yourself." The voice was sultry and hot, yet it gave no mental image of the owner.

"I'm Detective Marco Jackson, Phoenix P.D. My commanding officer, Lieutenant Cher Dawson, suggested I discuss a case with L.B. Alexander."

"Finally." The voice sharpened with excitement. "What took you so long?"

He heard a click and the gate rolled to one side, allowing him entry onto the grounds.

———✺———

Lily Alexander wiped the perspiration from her face as she turned off the treadmill and stepped down. She did a couple of stretches to cool down after her workout. "Natalie," she called to her secretary.

A tall, bird-like woman appeared a few seconds later. "Yes?" Her voice was breathless and chirpy as though she had been a sparrow in a previous life.

"I want you to call the fish guy." Lily pointed to her five hundred gallon, saltwater fish tank on the south wall separating her home gym from her office. "I think my sea anemone is dying."

Lily spent most of her time in these two rooms and had wanted them as pleasant as possible. Four years ago, her mother had decorated the rooms with straight-back mission style furniture, brown leather Morris chairs, and hand-woven Navaho rugs in vibrant reds and blacks. Lily had made few changes except to add her parents' portraits to the walls. She knew Regina and Lowell Alexander had had high hopes for her, their only daughter. She had hung their portraits across from her desk so she see them daily and remember them. Having the portraits near made her feel protected and loved.

Natalie Gould opened the notebook that never left her hand. Her dark red-brown hair bobbed around her pale elfin face as she wrote quickly. She was the most efficient secretary Lily had ever had. She didn't talk much, and was good with details.

"What else, Boss?"

"Finish correcting the galleys that my editor sent. Call my agent; tell him the new manuscript is almost done, and that I'll have it in the mail by the end of the month."

"Which new manuscript?" Natalie asked in her precise, chirpy voice. "The mystery, or the non-fiction on the Clarksville murder?"

Lily rolled her eyes. "The non-fiction." Lily finished her stretches. "I may never finish my mystery. Making up stories isn't as easy as I thought it would be. I'll be working on this one for months yet. Also, call the grocery store and tell them I don't like the generic macaroni and cheese they sent instead of my usual brand. I can tell the difference. If the manager gives you any lip, remind him that I can make other arrangements. Home Bound, Inc. contracts with several other grocers in the area. Find out who they are."

Home Bound, Inc. was a company that arranged for the services to come to her. Originally designed to accommodate agoraphobics like Lily, the company had branched out to encompass anyone who was homebound for any reason.

"Very well." Natalie scribbled in her notebook.

"One more thing."

Natalie looked up. "Yes?"

"Cut Ralph Davidson a check, and include a letter terminating him from my employment. The damn private eye hasn't done anything in the last three months and I'm not paying him one more cent so he can feed off of my gravy train." Lily didn't like having to fire Ralph, but *he* worked for *her* and too often he acted as though she worked for him.

Natalie added the last directive to her notebook. She raised one eyebrow. "When I'm finished with the letters and phone calls, I'm going to get some lunch. What do you want? Chinese or Italian?"

"Surprise me." Not that Natalie would. Left to her own devices, she always stopped at The Peking Palace. She was as predictable as she was efficient.

The buzzer rang signaling someone was at the gate. Lily activated the intercom. "Hello? Please identify yourself." A deep, almost magnetic voice identified itself as Marco Jackson of the Phoenix Police Department. "Finally. What took you so long?" Lily pressed the button that opened the gate. She turned to Natalie. "Did you hear that? After all this time, the police department has finally decided to believe me. I've told them a dozen times my father didn't kill my mother and then himself. They were murdered." She could hardly contain her elation.

"You don't really know what he wants." Natalie, always the cautious one, urged more wariness.

Lily disregarded her secretary's words and rushed down the long hall that linked her office with the front of the house. Through the beveled glass window inset on either side of the heavy wood door, she saw a beige sedan stop and a tall man get out. He stood for a moment shading his eyes with his hand and staring at her house. A well cut suit draped his tall muscular body. The stark white shirt and navy tie offered a masculine contrast to his honey-colored skin. Close-cropped black hair framed his head.

Then he sauntered up the cactus lined pathway toward the veranda. *He had a nice walk. A cop walk. Cocky and self-assured, the kind of walk that let a woman know he was all man.* A tingle went through her. She almost didn't recognize it. Hell it had been a long time since a guy's strut made her get all excited. A heated flush danced on her skin.

Lily spotted a paperback book in his right hand and recognized her photo on the back cover. *How utterly charming! He had been interested enough to check out her credentials. That spoke volumes about him.*

This guy was thorough. A man to get the job done. He was exactly what she needed.

He was lean with broad shoulders and a rangy build. For a second, she thought he was a white man, but he turned his head and she saw the broad nose and full lips. *He was a brother.*

She opened the door as he stepped on the porch. A blast of Arizona heat warmed the entryway. "Detective Jackson?"

A flicker of surprise crossed his handsome face. "You're tiny."

She grinned. *What an interesting opening line.* She hadn't heard that one before. "I like to think of myself as a statuesque midget."

He smiled revealing even white teeth. "You're not tall enough to be a midget."

Wow! She was a sucker for a man with a good dentist. "I'm five foot one. I'm not Mini-Me."

"Mini-Me?" He looked confused.

"Austin Powers." Even as isolated as Lily was from the outside world, she'd managed to see the movie. The video store had sent it over in her weekly order. "Didn't you see the movie?"

He shook his head. "I don't have the time for too many movies."

"Obviously not." *What kind of man didn't watch movies?* "And people tell me I need to get out of the house every once in a while." She opened the door wide and stood aside for him to enter. "Don't just stand there, please come in."

He studied her for a second or two more, his expression blank as he entered the cool foyer.

Detective Jackson had his cop face on. Good. She hoped he had his cop brain with him, too. She closed the door and flipped the lock. "Come to my office." Lily led the way down the long hallway past the living room, dining room and kitchen. His black leather shoes slapped against the highly polished boards of the wood floor.

In her office, she directed him to a chair and went to the storage closet, pulling out the cardboard box she'd been filling for the last two years. She dropped the box on her huge oak desk. "Here's all the evidence I've been able to compile." She pulled out a bulging manila file folder and shoved it at him.

He didn't reach for the file, but his eyes narrowed as he seemed to study it. "Did my Lieutenant call you?"

Lily settled the folder on his lap. *Cher would never call; that would spoil her sadistic control over the situation.* Though she had to admit, Cher had gotten a little softer lately. "Why would she?"

He was cute, but dumb. Phoenix P.D. wasn't taking her too seriously if this was the best they had to send her. She'd have a long talk with Cher over this bozo. At least her friend had finally sent someone. Beggars couldn't be choosers.

Detective Jackson pointed to the box. "Because you have everything ready for me."

Was this guy sitting on his mind? "I've been trying to prove my parents were murdered for over two years."

Detective Jackson scratched the back of his head. "Your parents were murdered?"

As she yanked out the ballistics report on the murder to show to him, her heart sank. "Tell me that's why you're here?"

What cruel joke was Cher playing? No, Lily couldn't give up hope, but she felt the ribbon of fleeting illusion deserting her. He hadn't come to help her.

He shook his head. "Sorry, but I don't think we're both on the same train tracks here."

The papers rattled in her hand. "So tell me, Detective Jackson, what train track are you on?"

"The Cameron murder." He held up the paperback book with

Eunice Cameron's smiling face on it. "Lieutenant Dawson told me you'd written a book on the investigation and that I should talk to you. She said you know everything there is to know about the case, and you would be more than happy to help me in any way."

Lily began to shake. She didn't need to ask, but she felt compelled to do so anyway. At least she would have the confirmation. "You're not here to investigate my parent's murder?" How could she have raised her hopes so foolishly again? As the cops told her before, all she had were theories with absolutely no evidence to support them. Cher hadn't sent this man to help her. At least he had the decency to look sorry.

"I don't know anything about your parents' murder, Ms. Alexander."

She didn't care. As regretful as he might be, she wanted him gone. "Get out!" She stuffed the ballistics report back into the box. The tears she had not shed in a long time burst over and dripped down her cheeks. "Just get the hell out." Why did she always expect so much? She brushed the tears away impatiently, annoyed with herself that she'd shown weakness in front of him.

He held up the book. "But I need your help."

Rage rolled in her stomach. "If you want to know what I know about the Cameron murder, read the damn book." She wrestled the heavy box to the closet and shoved it back on the shelf, then slammed the door. When would she learn? "The step-son and the step-daughter did it, and good luck bringing them home. They're living the high life in Fiji. So save the city a few bucks and quit while you can. You'll never prove they murdered their step-mommy without a confession, and they are so knee-deep in rum and dope, I doubt they know what day it is. So I don't think they're going to be much help to you."

She stalked to her office door and stood rigid with anger, waiting for him to leave. She wiped the tears from her cheeks angry that he'd seen her cry. She seldom gave into to her tears. Grief accomplished nothing. Revenge was another matter.

He hauled himself out of the chair. "I'm sorry we seem to be at cross-purposes. Can't I change your mind?"

"What do you think?" If the department didn't care enough about her parents, why should she bother to help them? Tapping her foot angrily, she tried to control her fury. At the moment, she felt like a fool.

Detective Jackson opened his mouth as though intending to say something, but then didn't utter a word. He made his way down the hall.

Not until the front door closed and she heard his car start, did Lily dare leave her office. Hurrying to her bedroom, she slammed the door, then stripped off her sweaty exercise clothes. What she needed was a nice hot, soothing bath. The water would remove the memory of what just happened in her office. All of her hope had disappeared. Maybe she should just give up and move on.

She entered the cool serenity of her bathroom. The sea green and pale china blue soothed her almost immediately. The wood floor was cool under her bare feet. She turned on the shower and listened to the splash of water against the handmade tiles on the walls. After she lit several vanilla-scented candles, she began to feel a modicum of calm returning. When she felt centered, she stepped inside the shower stall. Warm water cascaded over her body, soothing her.

Lily scrubbed her skin with vanilla scented soap. Just when she thought she'd regained control, her body began to shake so hard she thought she would break apart. She stood under the water until it turned to ice, forcing back gulping sobs.

All those phone calls she'd made over the last two years, and the police still hadn't believed her. All the hope she'd nurtured over the past months drained away with the water. Her parents' murderer would never be brought to justice, would never be punished. Grief numbed her. If the police weren't interested, she'd have to continue on alone. Not a problem, she'd already been alone for two years. She could go on.

Out of the shower, she dried herself with a huge ivory towel. The line to her personal telephone rang as she dressed herself. Was Detective Jackson calling to apologize? Answering it, she heard nothing but the distant sounds of street traffic ... and breathing. Soft breathing. In and out in a subtle manner that made her skin crawl.

He was there. Her parent's murderer. She could just hear the soft intake of his breath over the noise of a car horn. His name was Joe Sawyer and he was the same man who'd abducted her so many years before. Her testimony had sent him to jail and since his parole, Sawyer had been stalking her in a campaign of terror designed to bring her to her knees. A campaign that had started with her parent's murder. He was a clever man. So clever that he had hoodwinked the police into accepting his innocence by showing them that he was reformed and that Lily was nothing more than a high-strung filly who probably needed a shrink.

The few times the police had taken the time to investigate her complaints, Sawyer had been able to prove his whereabouts with unassailable alibis. During each incident Sawyer, the supposedly reformed criminal and newly appointed deacon of the Little Lambs of God Evangelical Church, had been in the full view of his flock of homeless people at a local shelter.

She didn't care where or how he was able to hide, she would get him. "I'll stop you," she promised softly. "I'll find a way."

He laughed faintly and hung up.

For a long time, Lily stared at the phone in her hand. Gradually her resolve returned. If Joe Sawyer thought she was helpless and stupid, he'd better think again. She'd stop him. She'd put an end to his reign of terror even if she had to kill him herself.

CHAPTER TWO

Marco felt a mild disappointment that the Eunice Cameron case wasn't going to go anywhere. Poor Eunice. Her murderers would probably remain unpunished. They'd been clever, but even clever murderers make mistakes and he figured they would too eventually. In the meantime, his initial excitement was replaced by curiosity over Lily Alexander's remarks about her parents.

Marco sat in the bowels of the basement storage room. Dust surrounded him making him sneeze, and occasionally he'd swear he heard the squeaking of rats as they played deep in the shadows. If one thing in life bothered him, it was rats.

He sat at a long, industrial steel table. Spread out in front of him was the file containing the whole story detailing the past of Lily Burdette Alexander. The story wasn't a pretty one and sympathy for her washed over Marco.

At twenty-one, only a few weeks shy of graduation, she'd been abducted from her dorm room at Arizona State University. She was missing for five days. Every state police agency, including the local office of the FBI, had searched for her until she'd turned up on Highway 412 near Eagle Trail Mountain in a frightened, and confused state. She'd been tortured, and severely beaten.

The composite drawing of her abductor she had given to the police had eventually led to the arrest of an ASU student named Joseph Anthony Sawyer, who had been questioned in the disappearance of another student a year ago when her battered, lifeless body had been found on the outskirts of Phoenix. Nothing had come of the investigation and he'd been released.

But with Lily's testimony of how he'd abducted her, tortured her, Sawyer had been convicted of felony kidnapping and assault to do bodily harm. Beautiful, petite, fragile Lily had stood up for herself and refused to be victimized any longer.

Knowing the personal and emotional toll of such a decision, Marco had to admire her. Any victim of a violent crime needed courage to face the perpetrator in court. He wondered if that one traumatic incident had propelled her into her career of crime writing.

After leaving her house, Marco had stopped at several bookstores and bought copies of the remaining seven books she had published in the last twelve years.

He sat in the car and skimmed them, admiring her careful attention to detail and the logic behind her resolutions. She would have made a great cop. She had the persistence and determination cops needed.

In one case, she'd uncovered evidence that freed a man from death row only months before he had been scheduled to be executed for a grisly double murder. Her work on the case was instrumental in bringing the real killer to justice and had brought her to the attention of police forces around the country.

Because of her capable deduction methods, Marco knew he had to seriously consider her contention that her parents had been murdered. She would never have made such statements if she wasn't sure of what she was talking about. Because of her conviction, he had sequestered himself in the storage room that housed the thousands of files on closed investigations, and searched for the box containing the reports on her parents.

When he found the files on her parent's murder-suicide, he realized that he vaguely remembered the case. Though at the time, he'd been deeply involved in his own puzzling murder and hadn't paid much attention. But he recalled the talk around the squad room and how one detective on the case had called Lily Alexander nothing more than a hysterical, delusional female. Having met her, Marco didn't think Lily was hysterical or delusional. From the knowledge exhibited in her books, he deduced that she knew exactly what she was talking about.

Walter Innis, the detective who had caught the case, was one of Homicide's legends. His report stated a clear murder-suicide with no indication of anything unusual. Marco had worked with Innis a few times when he had been newly assigned to Homicide and respected the man. Although Innis was still with the department, he was now assigned to the Governor's Violent Crime Task Force.

Marco read the files and an elusive quality in the pages jumped out at him. The more he read, the more he felt something wasn't right. Though the evidence pointed directly to a murder-suicide and the investigation had been by the numbers, his palms started to sweat.

When his palms began dripping, he knew something was really off. Marco couldn't pinpoint exactly where the problem existed, but he could feel it. The more he read, the more he believed that the crime sounded like an example in a textbook, too calculated and too perfect and less than what it truly appeared. *Everything was so right it felt all wrong.*

At the back of the file was a list of Lily's calls to the police department. She had been in contact with every office who would talk to her from the media department to the Chief detailing her concerns. She'd made over forty calls in the last two years.

Marco wondered if Innis had ever bothered to call her back. Innis was not a patient man. For all his deductive skills, he was inclined to simply make inspired guesses. And he wouldn't like being pressed into a deeper investigation by Lily Alexander when he was satisfied his conclusion was the correct one. Especially when the evidence didn't support the theory.

Marco should talk to Innis? But what would he say? That he had a feeling! What did he have beside sweaty palms to make him think that this murder-suicide didn't feel right? He couldn't go to Dawson with his sweaty palms theory. She'd drop kick him out of her office once she'd stopped laughing.

Sweaty palms were not enough to re-open a case.

He sat back, analyzing his reasons wondering if his interest in the case evolved from his interest in Lily Alexander. True, Lily Alexander was a very attractive woman. The photo on the back of the books didn't even begin to do her justice. Was he letting a personal feeling get in the way of his professional duties? No, he was too good a cop for that. He prided himself on his professionalism.

Yet something continued to gnaw at him. Maybe he needed to do some discreet checking to satisfy his curiosity. He'd never have to talk to Lily unless something came of it.

Marco's father would help. Even though retired, the former Homicide captain liked to keep himself in the mix. Daddy Jackson liked to keep his skills sharp. Being a cop had helped him with his acting. Marco would ask his dad to review everything just to put his own sense of uncertainty to rest.

His cell phone rang. He answered on the second ring. "Jackson."

A baby cried in the background. "Talk sense to me," Elena Jackson North said.

He smiled at his sister's abrupt greeting. "What's up, sis?" He began doodling as she spoke. Whenever he needed to clarify his thoughts, he doodled. The image of a baby with a diaper attached to his sister by a ball and chain began to take shape on his notepad. He doubted she really felt restricted by the baby, but sometimes when he looked at his married brothers Angelo and Roberto, he felt as though parenthood was a strangling affair.

"I'm drowning in baby spit." Elena's voice didn't sound complaining, more matter-of-fact. "Don't get me wrong, I love being a mom, but I need some intelligent conversation. You're my last hope."

"Thanks. That makes me feel special. Where's your husband?" Elena had married Reardon North, one of the nation's foremost football quarterbacks, snatching him from the eligible bachelor's list to the consternation of thousands of unmarried women with big dreams.

"In Boston," she grumbled. "He left yesterday for his family's annual financial shindig. He'll be gone for two weeks and I'm so lonely."

Marco put his pen down and closed his notebook. "Why didn't you tag along?"

"And spend two weeks with the Dragon Lady? Are you nuts? She hates me."

Marco winced. He'd only met Reardon's mother, Harriet North, once, and he still hadn't thawed out, but he did give the woman the benefit of the doubt. Maybe she was just naturally reserved. The Jackson family *en masse* was hard to take. Any big family took a bit of getting used to. "She doesn't hate you."

Elena sighed. "She hates me. I can't do anything right. If Daniel cries and I pick him up, I'm spoiling him. If he cries and I don't pick him up, I'm neglecting him. If the wind blows, it's my fault."

Marco chuckled. "Sis, don't be so paranoid. You're not a cop anymore." Marco heard an even more dramatic sigh on her end. He knew his sister was happy, but he suspected every once in a while she missed being on the force. Nothing ever quite took the place of being a cop.

He didn't know if he would ever be able to leave even if the graphic novel he'd been working on panned out. He'd just die on the job of old age.

"Just remember dinner on Sunday. It's your birthday and the bash is at my house because our mom said so. You can tell me all about what you're working on."

Maybe he could get her to help? Her insights were always razor sharp. "I'm working—"

"No!" She interrupted him. "Don't tell me. Save it for Sunday."

"Fine." The last thing he wanted to celebrate was another birthday when he would have to endure his mother's sighs and pointed comments regarding his unmarried state at the grand old age of soon-to-be thirty-four. He added wrinkles to his doodle face.

She laughed. "I heard through the grapevine that Carlo is bringing a date. Can you believe that? And we all thought he had decided to become a virgin again."

He groaned. How his little sister knew all the Jackson men's business was beyond him. Must be a chick thing. "Don't talk about things like that. I know I'm your brother, but I'm still a guy. I don't want to know what you know about the big 'it'."

"You mean sex?" Her voice was teasing and light.

"Elena," Marco growled. Raising his head, he saw the desk officer staring at him. "Stop it," he whispered in the phone and turned his back so the nosy guy couldn't hear him. "Stop talking about the 'S' word."

"When was the last time you had any?"

Life was a conspiracy. Dawson, his mother, and now his baby sister. "Not you, too." He ran sweaty fingers across his equally damp forehead. *Did everyone know he wasn't seeing any action lately?* "Dawson asked me just this morning if I was knocking boots with anyone."

"Are you?"

"No, I'm working."

"You know that old adage. All work and no play makes a Jackson a dull boy."

"Listen, I'll see you Sunday." He said goodbye and clicked off his phone. He stuffed the phone in his pocket and stood. Gathering up the files he saw the desk cop smiling at him—the guy had heard every word. Now his lack of a love life would be broadcast all over the department within the next thirty minutes. A heated flush climbed up his neck. First he was raked over the coals by an irate, but extremely sexy, midget, then his baby sister had to get in his business. He should have stayed in bed.

Still burning with embarrassment, Marco headed toward the stairs. A good grisly murder could make a guy forget about anything, even his kid sister demanding the intimate details of his personal life.

Sorry, Eunice, he mentally apologized. But the Alexander case, though closed, gnawed at him. He needed to talk to Dawson. If she gave her okay, he would put the Cameron case on the back burner and give the Alexander file a deeper look-see. And do something brave and noble to get back into Lily Alexander's good graces.

He stopped abruptly. Why the hell should he care if she was mad at him? Like he'd ever see her again. He blew out a long breath. He really did need to get a life away from the department.

He hiked up the three floors to the Cold Case Unit. He spotted Dawson sitting at her desk reading reports, her face drawn into a frown. Whitaker studied a computer screen. Marco glanced at the screen and found that he was playing solitaire. Marco didn't particularly like Whitaker. The man was a loose cannon with no respect for authority, or the rules. He played by them, but just barely. On one hand, Marco detested Whitaker's open defiance of policy, but on the other, he envied Whitaker's ninety-five percent clearance rate. Whitaker didn't just skirt the line between right and wrong, he sauntered up to it, then re-drew the boundaries to suit him.

The tall Navaho, Jacob Greyhorse, was just leaving. This was a man Marco admired. Two weeks ago, Greyhorse brought in a preppie rich kid suspected of killing his girlfriend and sat with the guy in the interrogation room for three hours without saying a word. The suspect finally broke down and started crying like a baby, spilling his guts. Along with his confession of the murder, the jerk had also divulged his participation in a country club drug ring the police didn't even know was operating in the city.

Greyhorse was a thinking man's detective. Reserved and soft-spoken, the tall Navaho had infinite patience and an incredible capacity to open windows into the souls of the most twisted individuals.

Marco's suspects confessed because he made himself into their best friend. Back in the day when he was with the regular Homicide unit, his fellow detectives called him the "The Shrink" because he could make a suspect feel like he understood their pain. Once they opened up to him, Marco had them.

He knocked on Dawson's door. "Can I get a minute?"

She looked up from a folder she'd been reading. "Come on in." She set the folder aside.

Marco noticed she'd taken off her suit jacket and the white blouse looked perfect next to her dark skin. He went inside and sat down.

She smiled at him. "Did you get me an autograph?

He squirmed in the large chair, feeling like he was back at St. Martin de Tours Elementary School facing Father Shamus, the Grand Inquisitor. "You neglected to ask for one." His palms started sweating again.

She leaned forward, planting her elbows on the large steel desk. "You're not the smart Jackson, are you?"

"The midget lady handed me my butt because I was there on the wrong case. I don't need lip service from you, even if you are the boss."

Her left eyebrow rose. "A little sensitive, are we? You need a date. Better yet, you need an easy date."

Marco wiped damp palms on his pant leg. "Somewhere in that statement is some sexual harassment."

Dawson held up her left hand showcasing a boulder-sized diamond ring. "Trust me, you're safe."

"I wasn't concerned about my virtue." He was worried she'd mangle his ego. But then again, if she did, he'd know where he stood.

"I'm blushing. Now back to the point. How badly did your meeting go with L.B. Alexander?"

He paused for a moment to think about how he was going to form his next comment. "L.B. Alexander is a very interesting woman."

Dawson smiled. "Now there's an ambiguous statement if I ever heard one."

How much did Dawson know about Alexander? "She lives in a house with more security than the CIA training center. What gives?"

"Did she tell you about being stalked?"

Now that was interesting. "We didn't get that far." He'd barely escaped alive.

Dawson shrugged. "She's rich and attractive. And she writes about true crime. She's made a few enemies along the way. Assuming she truly is being stalked and not imagining it." An odd look filled Dawson's eyes.

Marco felt compelled to defend Lily. An aura of fear surrounded her, and after reading her parents' file, he didn't think she was imagining anything. "Do you think that is a fair assessment, considering what happened to her?"

Dawson shrugged. "I have nothing but respect for the lady. I just wanted to see your reaction."

"Excuse me." He felt as though he'd failed a test.

A strange expression crossed his boss' face. "You know she's agoraphobic."

He'd never heard the term. He doubted he could even pronounce it. "What's that?"

Dawson explained. "Fear of the outdoors. Has massive anxiety attacks at the thought of standing outside with nothing but sky overhead."

Marco didn't know what to say. He didn't know anyone who couldn't go outside. Maybe she was a nutcase. *A beautiful, sexy nutcase.* "She never goes outside? Ever?"

Dawson nodded. "Not even to get the newspaper."

Leaning back in the barrel shaped chair, he thought of a million questions he wanted to ask. "How does she do her research for her books?"

"She wasn't always that way." Dawson steepled her fingers. "Until her parents died, she'd go out occasionally to do her research, appear on a few TV shows, but she's always battled the problem. Her parents helped, but since they were murdered, she's completely retreated from the world." Dawson frowned.

"How come," Marco asked, "you know so much about her?"

"Lily and I are tight. We go back a lot of years. She's been a big help with my stellar rise in Cold Case ."

Rubbing his chin, he tried to figure how anyone would know something Dawson didn't. No wonder Dawson wanted to get him to Alexander's house. It was payback time. "Is she why we suddenly have four new detectives?"

She pointed a finger at him and pretended to shoot. "In a very roundabout way."

"What gives?"

"Lily has the most inspired gift to find the most trivial pieces of information that can sink an aircraft carrier."

Now he was dying to know. "I'm interested." What other secrets resided behind the beautiful eyes of Lily Alexander?

Dawson gave him a smug smile. "Does this mean that you've abandoned the Cameron case in favor of something else?"

He nodded. "Nothing to go on."

She simply smiled.

Marco shifted in the chair. He had the distinct feeling he'd been manipulated. "You saw an opportunity and sent me out there on purpose. She showed me a ballistics report and crime scene photos. You gave her the copies of the paperwork, didn't you?"

Her eyebrow raised ever so slightly. "Did you dust the report for fingerprints?"

"Was I supposed to?" Dawson invented methods of sneaky he hadn't heard of yet. He knew if she looked into the case, it would be considered favoritism, a big no-no according to the department regs, but if he chose to work on the case, no one could say jack-diddly and she hadn't broken a rule. Oh she was good. Very, very good. She hadn't changed that much after all. Deep down inside, she was still her old cranky, manipulative self. He felt relieved to know that she hadn't totally abdicated her position as the meanest woman on the force.

She smiled at him. "Then you can't prove I've done anything against departmental policy. Except wait for the right opportunity to send a detective to her house and give him a chance to be a hero."

"Tell me something."

"Yeah?"

He narrowed his eyes and stared at her. "I've gotten convictions on thinner evidence than that. What makes you think you won't get busted?"

Again she smiled, a knowing look in her eyes. She had him. "What are you going to do?"

Marco thought for a moment and then chose his words with care. "I don't know why, and I don't know if I'll find anything, but something about her parent's murder just isn't right."

"How do you know this?"

He hadn't planned to reveal his scientific sweaty palms method, but held up his hands. "The sweaty palms are always a dead giveaway."

She touched her sleek dark hair. "I know what you mean. When something's not sitting right with me, the hairs on the back of my neck stand up."

"You don't have a problem if I put the Cameron case aside and take a look at Lily's parents' file?"

She gave a long, dramatic sigh, then straightened the papers on her desk. "Well, Jackson, you know the policy is to allow Cold Case detectives to investigate whatever strikes their fancy, but I really don't want you to waste your precious time on a loser case and I'm afraid the Cameron case is a dead end."

Marco's chest rumbled with laughter. "I'm feeling kind of manipulated."

She smiled. "That's how I work."

Marco pushed to his feet, aware that Dawson's okay gave him enough reason to revisit Lily Alexander. His body hummed with the thought of seeing the luscious Lily again.

"Jackson." She stopped him at the door.

"Yeah, Boss."

"Catch me a killer."

Lily hung up the phone and polished off her morning cup of coffee. The call had been from her best friend, Cher. Just like her pal to wait until the next day to pass along the good news. A smile crept across Lily's face. Cher was sly. She was good at being sly.

Lily had herself a detective. A good-looking one at that. She hoped he was as smart as he was pretty. She heard herself sigh. A warm tendril curled in her stomach. She almost couldn't wait to see the sexy cop again.

Biting her bottom lip, she wanted to giggle like a schoolgirl. Then she felt silly, and mentally scolded herself. She didn't have time for romance. She didn't need love, she needed justice. Maybe, just maybe, if she could put her past behind her she would be okay and have a life again.

Lily pushed away from the table and retrieved the box containing all the information on her parents' murder, setting it on her desk. She would be needing this, after all.

The intercom buzzer went off. Someone was at the front gate. Lily paid no attention knowing Detective Jackson wouldn't be this early. He was the only person she wanted to talk to. Natalie could get the door, and take care of whoever was making a nuisance of themselves. Lily went back to organizing her files, anticipating the handsome detective's return sometime today.

Boy, had he thrown her for a loop. Lily always had a weakness for tall men. Marco Jackson reminded her she was still a woman. A very lonely woman. She wasn't sure if she liked being reminded of what she couldn't have anymore.

After a few minutes, she heard the front door open and close then Natalie's high heels clicking on the tile floor as she headed toward the office.

"A package for you." Natalie put the small brown box on Lily's desk.

Lily ordered almost everything she needed off the Internet, from catalogues or through Home Bound Inc. The Net was a haven for someone like her, and she utilized it to it's full potential. "Who delivered the box?" She searched for a return address, hesitating to open anything before knowing who sent it.

Natalie shook her head. "Just a messenger. Nothing unusual."

Lily reached for a pair of scissors and slipped the sharp point of the shears along the tape. "Did I order anything recently?" She flipped open the flaps of the box and saw shredded newspaper. She started pulling the paper out. Something reddish-brown and dry resided in the depths of the box. She grabbed the object, and drew it out of the box. Whatever it was it felt soft and spongy. Freeing the item of the clinging paper, she realized it was a heart. A human heart. She held a human heart in her hands. She screamed and dropped the heart into the box.

"What's the matter?"

Lily couldn't talk. Her chest tightened. She started hyperventilating. Clutching her throat, she gasped for air. Her heart raced as though it would explode out of her chest.

Natalie approached the desk and then jumped back.

"Can't ... breathe!" Lily screeched through strangled breaths.

Natalie raced around to Lily's side of the desk and yanked open a drawer. She pulled out a small brown paper bag. She positioned the bag over Lily's mouth and nose. "Breathe. Slowly. In and out. Slowly. You can do it."

Lily gripped Natalie's slender wrist, hanging on for dear life. She turned away from the heart on her desk. Staring at her aquarium, she went through the routine of controlling her hypersensitive emotions. She picked an object to center on. *Focus on the fish. Focus on the fish.*

Her gaze narrowed in on Leo, her lionfish. His brown and white body flickered in the water as he raced back and forth from one end of the tank to the other. *Hello, Leo. How are you today?*

She breathed in and out of the bag. She listened to the rhythmic crinkling of the bag and the ragged tone of her breathing. *You're looking good, Leo baby.* The pain in her chest eased.

When the attack ended, she turned and found Natalie still staring at the heart. "Call 9-1-1," Lily ordered.

Natalie raised the phone, a trembling finger poised over the number keys. Then she punched in the number and in a faint voice asked for help. She listened for a moment and then gave the address. She hung up the phone. "There's something else in the box."

"What?" Lily leaned back in the chair afraid to move.

Natalie handed her box.

Lily reached in and drew out a grainy photo of Detective Jackson waiting in his car at her front gate. The photo was stained with crusty blood. A yellow post-it note with a message neatly typed on it was attached to the edge of the photo.

Lily, you've always had my heart. Now you have his.

CHAPTER THREE

Marco flipped through the coroner's report, a cup of lukewarm coffee in front of him. The cramped office had an eerie feel that clung to the plain furniture and bleak white walls. He found himself staring off into space thinking about Lily Alexander. Not her case, but the woman herself.

After going into the complete file of what had happened to her and her parents, he understood why she hid from the world. No one should have to go through what she suffered.

Marco had seen the ugliness of the world up close and personal but he couldn't fathom how Lily's slender shoulders had borne the weight of the evil that nearly destroyed her life. Marco wanted to make things right for her. He wanted to give her justice.

A technician, wearing sanitary green pants, shirt, and a shower cap, poked her head in. "Detective Jackson, you have a phone call. Line four."

"Thanks, Rhonda." Marco pushed thoughts of Lily to the back of his mind as he punched the line button on the phone and lifted the receiver. "Jackson."

"Get your butt over to Lily's now." Dawson's voice crackled with tension.

The detectives in the unit called this edict a command performance. Right now he was in the middle of something big and he couldn't be subjected to Dawson's whims. "But—"

"Now," Dawson snapped. And hung up.

Marco closed the file. He tucked the paperwork under his arm and headed out the door. Through the long glass window, he saw the coroner in the examination room, hunched over a fresh body. He knocked on the glass window. The older man looked up. Marco pointed at the door and the man buzzed him in.

Inside was the stench of antiseptic, blood, and surprisingly enough, pizza sauce. He held up the folder. "Doc, mind if I borrow this?" He'd make a Xerox of everything and return the file later.

"Yeah, just make sure I get everything back."

Since his patrolman days, Marco had nurtured a very friendly relationship with Dan Early, the Phoenix coroner. Doc Early had had his hand in every death in the city for the last forty years. He'd seen it all, done it all, and best of all, he never forgot a case he'd worked on. The man was better than a room full of files. Marco could pretty much get anything out the guy he needed, from his personal notes, to first in line to get his bodies sliced and diced.

Marco never forgot the coroner's birthday, or the names of all of his kids. His mama raised him right and his daddy taught him how to be a cop. "Will do." Marco glanced at the body on the stainless steel table. The dead guy was dirty with a long, mangy beard and filthy hair that hadn't been cut or washed in a decade. Marco pegged him right away as one of the city's homeless. "What happened to him?"

"A cop found him last night near the railroad tracks out on Interstate 10. No heart. Looks like it was ripped right out of his chest."

What an ugly way to check out. He never liked checking out the fresh 'deads'. "At a time like this, I don't miss being in Homicide."

"Yeah, I know what you mean." Early pointed to the pizza delivery box on a round stool. "Wanna slice? Double pepperoni."

Marco's stomach roiled. "No." Some things he never liked, and eating in the examination room was one of them.

The doctor shrugged. "Suit yourself," he said as he helped himself to a slice.

Marco lifted the folder. "I'll get your paperwork back to you in a day or two."

Doc Early nodded and adjusted the microphone over his mouth.

Marco tucked the folder under his arm, and headed out to his car. Dawson hadn't said what kind of emergency, but he switched on his lights and siren.

———— ~m~ ————

As he drove up the dirt road, he found the gate to Lily's house standing wide open. Lining the driveway were two squad cars, the crime scene team's van, and Dawson's brand new silver Jaguar XJ6 convertible. What was going on?

Marco flashed his badge at the cop guarding the gate. "What's happening?"

"I just got here myself, but Dawson is on the warpath. You better get inside."

Marco parked behind the Jag, got out and hurried into the house. The place was in an uproar. He could hear Dawson barking orders from the direction of Lily's office. Her secretary, hurried down the long hall as fast as her sensible shoes could carry her.

Entering the office, he saw Lily sitting on a black leather sofa, a paper bag clutched in one hand. She was tear-stained and sweaty. Dawson sat next to her, embracing her and whispering in her ear. One of the uniformed officers stood over a cardboard box.

Lily lifted her head as he approached. Her eyes rolled back, and he thought she might faint.

Dawson patted her shoulder. "I told you, Jackson is okay. He's too difficult to kill."

What were they talking about? "Why wouldn't I be?"

Dawson inclined her head toward the box. "Go and take a peek."

He joined the photographer who was snapping photos of the box, which contained a human heart residing in a clear plastic bag. Next to the bag, he spotted a picture of himself in his Chevy Caprice at Lily's gate. He read the attached note and turned back to Lily and his boss. "I know where this heart came from."

Both women stared straight at him. "What do you mean," Dawson demanded.

"Just before I left the coroner's this morning, he had a guy on the table missing his heart."

"Any I.D. on the victim?" Lily asked.

He was glad to see she was perking up. "A homeless guy, by the appearance of him." Marco reached into his pocket to call the Homicide unit and let him know they had found the victim's heart. The cell phone was turned off, and he realized why Dawson had phoned the coroner's office directly and not his cell phone. After he talked to the lead detective on the homeless man's case, he hung up and squatted in front of Lily. He wanted to comfort her. He put his hand on her knee and heat shot up his hand. He moved his hand away, uncomfortable with the raw sensation. "How are you doing?"

Lily stood, almost knocking him over. "Fine! I just can't take this anymore. I know who killed that man. Why can't you people catch him?"

Dawson pulled her down. "You need to relax."

Marco stood to put himself out of Lily's way. He didn't think his dignity could take it if she knocked him on his butt in front of half the force. "We'll get this all straightened out. Right now, I'm worried about you."

Lily jumped to her feet. "I'm fine, I just need to get out of here." She brushed past him and headed out of the office.

His arm throbbed where she touched him. He pivoted to watch her rush away. His instincts screamed for him to chase her, but his head warned him not to.

Dawson rolled her eyes. "Go with her."

Hesitating, he felt ridiculous. He needed to treat her as he would any other victim.

"Now." Cher growled.

Marco followed Lily down the hall. She walked like an old woman, shoulders stooped, head down. She braced herself against the wall with one hand. "Ms. Alexander. Lily. Do you know who killed that man?"

Lily stopped and turned. She nodded her head the springy curls bouncing around her face.

"Tell me."

She grabbed his arm. "Come with me."

The heat of her touch penetrated through his jacket. His heart began to race. He was helpless to stop her and followed her down a long hall that spanned the length of her house. He had to get his emotions under control. Marco realized she could take him anywhere she wanted to at this moment.

She stopped in front of a set of double doors.

Frayed yellow crime scene tape hung on the hinges. She let go of his arm and he breathed a sigh of relief. With her touching him, he couldn't seem to concentrate on doing his job. "Who killed that man?"

She took a deep breath. "Joe Sawyer."

"Joe Sawyer! The man who..." He didn't even want to think about what Lily had gone through twelve years ago.

"Yes, the man who abducted me." Her voice was matter of fact. "He murdered my parents and now he killed that poor man." She fumbled with the door handle and opened the door.

Her words just hit him. *Murdered her parents?* How did she know? "What evidence do you have?"

Lily turned to face him. "Because I escaped. I beat him. I fought back. If not for me, he'd probably still be hurting women. But I stopped him and now he's paying me back."

Marco stared into the room. He'd seen the crime scene photos and knew that this was the room where her parents had died. Breathing deep, he smelled the dust and stale air. A small streak of light showed between the drawn drapes. White paper cutouts of two bodies lay on the floor. "Why do you keep the room like this?"

"Because the evidence is still here that will prove Joe Sawyer killed them." She walked across the pale tile floor and drew open the drapes. Dust motes swirled through the air.

"Lily, you had one of the best homicide detectives working on this case. What do you know that he didn't?"

With tears in her chocolate-brown eyes, she said, "I know my parents."

He saw the deep pain in her and resisted the effort to comfort her knowing she would reject his offer. He also saw her steely determination. For a few seconds, he couldn't breathe. He could feel the heat of desire all the way down to his feet.

Marco hadn't been this attracted to a woman in a long time. It didn't matter that she was a case he was working or that some people would think her crusade was crazy. She tempted him. These feelings had to cease and desist. Now.

Shaking his head he refocused on the job at hand. "None of us wants to think our parents are vulnerable. The reports stated that your dad had terminal stomach cancer."

"My father would never have killed himself. He would have done everything he could to get five more minutes of life. He wasn't a quitter. And more importantly, he loved my mother and me more than anything else in the world. He would never harm her or me."

In her long blue tee shirt and black leggings, Lily looked more like a teenage girl instead of an internationally known writer. More than just petite, she seemed fragile as if a good breeze could knock her down, but Marco sensed her resilience. Tension radiated from her slim body.

"I hear that all the time," Marco said, "but that doesn't stop people from one moment of insanity."

She shook her head. "My parents would never have violated this house."

"How do you know?" He could have recited chapter and verse every person who'd ever told him that same thing. But in the end, what a wife or daughter had insisted wasn't a suicide almost always was.

Her small breasts rose and fell rapidly as if she were trying to control herself. "I have suffered all my life from panic attacks and anxiety. My parents refused to let me succumb to my fears. They made me go out and take part in life. They would never violate the sanctity of this house. They understood how important this house is. It's my haven. My security. My sanctuary. They would never have done anything to contaminate it. I need this house to keep me sane. I haven't left it since their funeral. And I'm not leaving now, Detective. Ever."

Checking the angle of the body cutouts, he wished he could divine some overriding clue to end this case now so he could get away from the subtle spell she was casting over him. "How do you know Joe Sawyer is the murderer and not some lunatic fan? Or someone else who is just plain crazy?" Her unshakeable belief had already swayed him, but his training demanded he play the role of devil's advocate.

Her fear was gone. "Joe Sawyer owes me. I took away the two things he loved the most: I stood up to him in that shack and deprived him of his fun. Then I faced him in court and denied him his freedom. Trust me, the murders of my parents are nothing but vengeance. He lost control of me and he intends to make me pay. He's not going to stop until he's destroyed my life," and in a whisper she added, "or killed me.

Marco knew what was in her mind and in her heart. Sawyer's fixation on a vendetta made him want to protect her. "I pulled his records and he'd been out for a whole year before your parent's death. Why do you think he waited that long?"

Before she answered, she beckoned to him and left the room. He waited as she closed the door and checked the lock. She leaned back against the dark wood. "Sawyer is not a stupid man. If he had done anything right after being granted parole and released from jail, he'd be the first person the cops would question. Instead he waited and took the time to establish himself in the community. He became a deacon in his church, he found a job, and married a very nice lady. For the last three years, he's been a model ex-con and a productive member of society. He's fooled just about everyone, including the cops. But not me." Her voice was fierce and the look in her eyes was intense and angry.

He wanted to believe Lily so much he ached. But he couldn't. He knew in *her* head she wasn't lying, but before he could do anything he had to have tangible proof. "People change."

She shook her head. "Not Joe Sawyer."

Lily couldn't believe she had told Marco Jackson so much about her past. She'd come close to baring her entire soul, but something stopped her from completely opening up. The only person she'd ever confided in was Cher, but even then only to a limited degree.

Marco was different. He seemed to really care. He listened to her as though she wasn't a whacko out for revenge. The fact warmed her heart. With him, she didn't feel so crazy and obsessed. But she knew he couldn't help her either. As big as his broad shoulders may be, she didn't think he could be her champion. The case was closed: the verdict murder-suicide. No matter what Lily might feel, she couldn't change the department's mind. All the evidence pointed in one direction and the only counter-proof she had was a gut feeling that meant nothing to anyone but her.

The telephone in her parent's bedroom rang. She ran down the hall, Marco close behind. She was worried that Natalie or one of the cops would answer the call. She pushed open the door to her bedroom and grabbed the receiver. For a second there was nothing but silence, and then a soft strain of music filtered through the wires.

"*Killing me softly with his song. Killing me softly.*"

"What is it?" Marco asked, although he was already sure he knew the answer.

She handed him the phone. He listened for a few seconds and stared at her. She took the receiver from him and hung it up. "That was Joe. He's toying with me."

"We can stop this."

"How? You can't prove anything." She pointed to the display on her caller ID box. "That phone number is out in the middle of nowhere and more than likely is a pay phone."

"No one's been able to trace the calls to him?"

"I've tried everything. I even have a friend with the FBI and she can't get anywhere. All I have left to do is hope he makes a mistake before he kills me."

"I'll catch him."

She ran both her hands through her hair. "Are you boasting?" Even as she asked the question her heart did a funny little flip-flop. Could he help her? Was he the one to end the terror?

He lifted his chin. "Sawyer made this personal when he sent you a dead man's heart with my picture attached."

Lily crossed her arms over her chest, surprised to see the anger on his handsome face. "One of the things I'm sure you learned in the Academy is never let a case get personal."

"You're taking it personal."

"I'm not a cop."

His seductively full lips narrowed to a straight line. "I know a personal threat when I see it. I have two options. I can either let this ride, or I can cut this guy off."

"Which way are you leaning?"

The corner of his mouth lifted in a cocky grin. "I'm leaning toward cutting him off."

Her entire body trembled. "You don't think I'm crazy."

"Nope." His low voice soothed her and gave her new hope.

The rest of the day passed in a blur for Lily. Neither Cher nor Marco Jackson would leave. The officers tracked dirt all over her floors. Her housekeeper was going to have a fit. Once the fireworks had ended, Natalie fell apart and had to take the reminder of the day off. She was great in an emergency, but once the crisis ended, Natalie folded.

All Lily wanted was for everyone to leave her alone. Her cats were in hiding and she'd never find them in this huge house. She wanted to draw a bath for herself and sit in the bubbles with candles on the sides and a full pint of Ben and Jerry's Chocolate Chip Cookie Dough Ice Cream.

By mid-afternoon, Lily finally pushed Cher and Marco out the door. Cher had offered to stay with her, but Lily had firmly told her no. That hunk of a husband she just married would have a fit. Lily was desperate for peace and quiet. Finally, the house was empty.

She went to the bathroom and started the water running in the bathtub. Every time she passed a phone in the house, she glanced at it. Finally, she pulled the cords out. If only for a few hours, Joe wouldn't be able to get to her.

Just as she put her foot in the bath water, the doorbell rang. Who the hell was that? No one had buzzed her from the gate. For a second, she froze, trying to think who could be at the door. Joe Sawyer. She grabbed her robe. She was suddenly aware of how alone in the big house she was.

The doorbell rang again. Lily's heart pounded, and her mouth went dry. Her Glock 9mm was in the nightstand drawer. Quickly, she opened the drawer, checked the chamber to make sure the gun was loaded and headed toward the front door.

A dog barked. Lily's hand tightened on the butt of the gun. Had Sawyer brought her some macabre present?

She peered through the beveled glass window and saw Marco Jackson standing on the front porch. A motorcycle with a sidecar stood on the circular drive.

Lily shoved the gun into the pocket of her robe and opened the door. "What the hell are you doing here?"

Marco had to make this sound good. He gave her what he hoped was his most winning smile. "Lieutenant Dawson has put you in protective custody."

She glared at him. "And you're my jailor."

Pointing to his black and white spotted dog, he forced his smile wider. "No. Harley, here, is the jailor."

"What the hell is it? A Shetland pony?"

"A Harlequin Great Dane."

Lily put her hands on her hips. "You brought your dog?"

"Usually, I dump her at my sister's but Elena has a new baby and is sort of busy. So I brought Harley along. I didn't think you'd mind. She's good company and good protection. You have lots of land for her to roam."

"I have cats and my cats don't like dogs."

Marco put his finger to his lips. "Sh! Harley doesn't know she's a dog." He looked around. "Where's Natalie?"

"She was pretty rattled. I told her to go spend a few days with her mother in Tucson." She looked around him and her eyes widened at the sight of his two suitcases. "Are you planning to drag this case out until Christmas?"

He glanced over his shoulder at his luggage. "No. It's just kind of dumb for me to go back and forth between here and the office and have to stop at home each time for clean clothes."

"I don't need a bodyguard. If I thought I did, I'd hire one."

Marco shook his head. "You don't understand. Dawson assigned me to be your bodyguard. If I don't keep you safe, she is going to skin me alive." Among other horrible things. Marco still vibrated with the force of Dawson's threats. If anything happened to her, Marco would be dog meat.

Lily's lips twitched. "So you decided honor was better than

death."

He grinned. "I have season tickets for the Scorpions this year. A private box. I have a reason to live." He gave her a wicked wink.

"Forgive me." Her voice held a hint of sarcasm. "I had no idea season tickets for a football team was something to be so cherished."

Damn, but she was a feisty one. He was going to like her. He could tell already. "No sweat." He inclined his head toward the door. "Are you going to let me in?"

"Do I have a choice?"

He shook his head. "Nope." He picked up his computer case and an overnight bag.

Lily stepped aside. "Welcome to my home."

He didn't miss the caustic undertone in her voice. "Thanks."

She reached into her pocket, removed a handgun, opened the clip and slid it out. She put the clip and the handgun back into her pocket.

A hot babe with a big gun. Hot damn! Could this investigation get any better?

CHAPTER FOUR

"Were you going to shoot me?" Marco asked eyeing the semi-automatic pistol warily.

"I didn't know who was at the door. Natalie is the only one with the code to the security gate."

"She gave the code to me." He had to be grateful she hadn't shot him. He sensed that Lily had more strength in her little body than she knew what to do with.

An angry glint darkened her brown eyes. "Natalie had no right to do that without consulting me."

"Maybe she's concerned about you."

"Maybe she should mind her own business. I really should shoot Natalie first, but I don't think I'm smart enough to cover up a double murder.'""

Marco stroked Harley's massive head. "We're here to help you, so rein in your inner bitch."

"My inner bitch? What about yours?" Lily pointed at Harley who regarded her with wide-eyed curiosity. They were practically nose-to-nose.

"Touché."

"What kind of cop brings a dog on a stake-out anyhow?"

For a second Marco didn't know what to say. Cher would hand him his ass if he didn't keep her best friend safe. "Harley may be a slobbering, lay on the couch, watch ESPN type of dog, but she is trained in protection. Give me your hand."

"What?"

He held his hand out to her. "Give me your hand."

Lily put her hands behind her back. "No."

Marco reached behind her and grabbed her hand. For a second he was amazed how soft her skin was. And how warm. His heart kicked into double time. He thought about letting go but didn't. Carefully he brought Lily's hand around and pushed her small fist against Harley's nose. Harley sniffed. Then Marco rubbed her hand against the dog's cheek. "Protect."

Lily relaxed her fingers. The dog licked Lily's hand and sniffed up and down her fingers and wrist. Then she licked Lily's hand again.

Lily dragged her hand away. "Ugh!" She wiped her hand on her robe. "What did you do that for?"

Marco patted the Great Dane's head. "Because now Harley will never hurt you and she will die to protect you."

"What is Harley going to do, sit on Sawyer when he shows up to kill me? Or drown him in drool?"

Marco smiled. Damn but she had a smart mouth. She was sexy as hell. "Let me tell you a little story about my Harley. I was watching my niece at the park, and somehow I got engrossed in the sports page and a little lax on my duty. Some guy tried to snatch my niece and by the time Harley was done with him, he was no good to no woman ever again."

"Ouch!"

"Now Harley knows you're part of her pack. And among the Jacksons that's a life-long commitment."

Lily eyed the dog. "Bless her little heart."

If it wouldn't have been an unmasculine thing to do, Marco would have sighed. This woman gives nothing up.

Lily licked her lips. "You're not going to leave are you?"

"Nope." Marco couldn't stop staring at her luscious mouth. "Cher Dawson will hurt me." Hurt was not a strong enough word.

"And you follow orders like the good worker bee that you are, don't you?"

"That's what I'm talking about."

Lily pursed those full lips. "Since I'm forced to deal with you and Sea Biscuit here, let me show you where you're going to stay. And when you get back to the office today, you tell Cher Dawson that I know everything there is to know about her, and don't think there won't be a reckoning over this." She whirled and led the way down the cool hall.

"You know what, Grasshopper." Marco couldn't stop the grin from spreading across his face. "I don't think the Lieutenant is quaking in her shoes over that threat." Like anyone could be afraid of the big, bad midget. Scary, maybe, but he'd never call her midget to her face.

He picked up his luggage and followed her. She had a nice behind. She swayed with a graceful swing of her hips, and Marco felt himself go hot. He could imagine her image draped across a canvas painted in vibrant shades of brown. His fingers ached to grab his sketchpad and draw her. He had to stop those salacious thoughts right now. She was a victim. He had no business thinking anything other than the solving of her case.

He couldn't afford a repeat of Katherine Dix. That case had nearly destroyed his career. She'd fallen in love with him while he'd been working her father's homicide, and truth be told, his own feelings had run deep. Deeper than anything he'd felt before for a women, but he'd lost his objectivity and almost soured the case.

Lily was work and he couldn't afford to let her be anything more.

She opened the door to a spacious room with a four-poster king-sized bed against one wall. The design was Spanish with the dark wood and the almost overwhelming sense of size. The room was almost as large as his whole house and a lot more opulent with the dark furniture and the Navaho rug on the floor.

Marco had gone from sharing a bedroom with all his brothers, bunk beds and no space, to his bachelor pad. Admittedly his house was Spartan—no pictures on the wall and garage sale furniture. His one concession to comfort had been a big-screen TV. He didn't need much else. A couch was a couch. He was stashing his money for retirement so he could concentrate on his art.

He set his suitcases down. Harley padded to the bed and sniffed underneath. "This is living. I don't think I've ever been on a stake-out before that came with such luxury."

"I do my best."

Marco winced at her cynicism. "Time out. I'm not the bad guy."

She rubbed her forehead. "I know. The last couple days have been rough."

He grabbed her by her shoulders and heat radiated up his arms. "I'm not going to let anything happen to you." Big mistake. He should not have touched her again. "Sawyer may be a smart crook, but we're smarter. You and I will hogtie him and make him pay."

She tilted her head up at him. "You don't think I'm crazy?"

"Crazy like a fox, Grasshopper."

"Don't call me that. I'm not a green, crunchy bug that my cats drag in. And most of time, they're missing a leg."

He laughed.

And so did she. Marco hugged her. If nothing else, maybe he could convince himself that she was like his sister. Though the deep heat that spread through him told him he was going to have to work hard to make his hormones rethink their position.

51

Beatrix Hunter sat at her desk feeling elated and triumphant. She'd done it. She'd out-maneuvered Cher "Barracuda" Dawson and managed to get herself assigned to Cold Case.

She ran her hand across the top of her empty desk and mentally decorated it with her orchid plants and family pictures. The light was good in the squad room; her orchids would do well.

She glanced back at Cher Dawson who stood at the water cooler talking to Jacob Greyhorse. Dawson hadn't been too thrilled to have Beatrix in the unit, but she hadn't made any comment other than to give her a long, thoughtful look. And Beatrix was being very careful not to call any attention to herself.

She wriggled her butt in her chair. She couldn't prevent the smile that crossed her face. She was a real detective now. Real police. No more Officer Friendly for her. She could wear a gun, sensible shoes, and she didn't have to be meticulously groomed every minute of every day for the rest of her career. She let out a big sigh of relief.

Closing her eyes, she leaned back in her chair and heard that unsatisfying squeak of pretend leather and springs in need of oiling. That was okay; she'd bring her own chair in.

"What the hell are you doing, Hunter?" Cher Dawson said. "I don't want you making yourself too comfortable. You're not gonna be here long."

Beatrix forced herself to remain calm. "Good morning, Lieutenant Dawson. You look lovely this morning." And the Lieutenant did look nice. Since she'd married an old flame, she'd changed from the surly, take-no-prisoners cop to something a little more glamorous.

Beatrix could appreciate the image change. Not that Dawson hadn't looked good before, but now she was stunning in her dark blue Donna Karan suit and handsome Prada pumps. She was obviously enjoying the fact that she had a very wealthy husband.

Dawson frowned. "Before we run out of witty repartee from your Swiss finishing school, I have an assignment for you."

Beatrix held up her hand. "Excuse me, but I believe that one of the most important elements of Cold Case is that your officers can pick and choose their own cases to work on."

Dawson frowned. "Hunter, you've come into my unit directly from being Officer Friendly. What experience do you have in a homicide investigation? Much less one that's been sitting on the back burner for decades."

"I have a little bit of experience," Beatrix admitted with more cheer than she actually felt. She had already helped with two headline grabbing investigations and felt that she knew her way around a lot more than Dawson realized.

"My point exactly. You have a little experience. I'm not going to let you screw with my reputation simply because you have the skills to bull-shit your way into my unit."

"I appreciate your honesty," was all Beatrix answered though she felt some resentment that Dawson so easily discounted the help she had been in the past.

Dawson leaned over her. "This is how we play in my sandbox. I'm turning you over to Marco Jackson and he's going to turn you into the murder police."

"Why Jackson? Why not Whitaker. He has the best clearance rate." *And Whitaker wasn't too bad looking with his bad boy image and his perpetual smirk.* Beatrix wouldn't mind working with him, though it seemed to her that he solved cases too easily.

For the first time, Dawson smiled. "Believe it or not, Hunter, I *do* like you—a very little bit." She held up her thumb and forefinger spaced a bare centimeter apart. "I wouldn't wish Whitaker on my worst enemy."

Beatrix was surprised. "Really? You like me?" *Don't let Dawson's comments go to your head, Beatrix.*

"You have a sense of style and your persistence makes up for your lack of experience." Dawson smiled. "I can mold you."

Beatrix felt a flash of annoyance. "You make me feel like one of my mother's prize Bichons."

"What?"

"Little white dogs that looks like a puff of cotton. Not that I mind being compared to them. Mother likes them better than most people." *In fact her mother liked her dogs better than her daughter. She'd been told so often enough.* She shut her mother out of her mind. *Don't go there*, she sternly lectured herself.

Dawson frowned slightly. "I don't consider you a show dog. You're a detective! No matter how you managed to wrangle a spot in Cold Case, when I'm done with you, every police department in this country will happily snap you up."

Beatrix was surprised. "You're training me in order to get rid of me?"

"If you learn your lessons well and you bring me results, then I'm keeping you." She handed Beatrix a sheet of paper with an address on it. "This is where Marco is. Go talk to him."

Dazed, Beatrix resisted the impulse to salute. She'd joined the department because the society life her parents wanted for her wasn't particularly appealing. She needed to feel useful, to make a difference. Her trust fund—thank you Grandma Claire—gave her the opportunity to pick and choose what she wanted to do.

She'd spoken to a police recruiter when she'd been at ASU who'd encouraged her to look at law enforcement. From that moment on, she'd found her purpose. "Thank you, Lieutenant."

Dawson glared at her. "Don't disappoint me."

"I won't." Beatrix grabbed her purse and started for the door.

"Hunter," Dawson called out.

Beatrix turned.

Dawson grinned. "Find me the bad guy."

Beatrix gave a bright smile and gave Dawson a thumb's up sign and headed out to door to her car.

—✠—

Marco Jackson met Beatrix at the door. "Come on in."

He swung the door wide and she walked inside and tried not to be impressed. Just the drive up from the wrought iron gates had left her breathless. No imitation adobe house for whoever lived here. The adobe walls were the real thing. The house spoke of old money and class.

Double doors, almost nine feet high and carved with traditional Mexican designs, opened to a gracious entry. Stained glass windows cast rich colors on the wood floor. Vases of flowers sat on tables filling the air with gentle scents. The house was cool and comfortable.

Hunter did a complete three hundred and sixty degree turn unable to believe that Marco Jackson could be so lucky. "Jackson, what are you working on?"

"Welcome to the A-Team assignment, Hunter." He led her into the living room which took her breath away.

Mission furniture—the real thing—was situated throughout the huge room. A vibrant Navajo rug covered the wood floor. Exposed wood beams added interest to the high ceilings. A large picture window opened onto an enclosed desert garden that had been meticulously arranged to give the effect of the desert without actually being outside in the desert.

Whoever decorated this room had a nice eye. It projected both style and warmth-a far contrast to Beatrix' mother's home which was so elegant and filled with expensive objects d'art, which was neither warm nor inviting. Beatrix had always been afraid to move for fear she'd break something.

"I think I've been drafted into bodyguard duty." Jackson pointed at a leather Morris chair facing the desert garden.

Beatrix sat and waited. A Great Dane suddenly rose from behind a Mission style sofa and trotted over to her to lay its heavy head in her lap and look up at her with huge droopy eyes. "Hello there." She patted the animal's head. Though she liked dogs, she found the large ones a bit intimidating.

"That's Harley," Marco said.

Beatrix simply smiled. Her mother wouldn't consider this animal a dog, but a beast of burden. She smoothed her skirt over her knees with shaking hands. "So what's my part, Jackson?"

"I need you to be my legs."

"You have legs." She stared pointedly at his legs.

Jackson grinned. "Didn't Dawson explain to you what's going on?"

"Just that I need training in detective work." She smothered the tiny resentment she'd felt at her boss' high-handed statement. Beatrix knew Cold Case was an elite unit and only the best were allowed into the inner circle, but she had confidence in her ability. In fact she'd already had a case picked out. That Dawson had short-circuited her still rankled. "And she seems to feel you're the one to do the training."

"Probably because of my infinite amount of patience."

Beatrix raised an eyebrow. "I thought it was your sparkling wit."

She was flattered in a way because Marco was one of the best detectives. His performance had always been above board. His exploits in homicide were legendary. In a way, she knew that Dawson felt she was worth training or she would never have been assigned as his partner.

Jackson burst out laughing. "You know, Hunter, you're okay."

Pride filled her. For the first time since she'd been assigned, she felt as though she would be able to contribute something worthwhile, something more challenging than her Officer Friendly persona, or holding press conferences as a media officer where reporters asked questions she had trained herself to evade. "So what do you want from me?"

Marco seemed to think for a few moments. Harley padded over to him, put her head in his lap and gazed at him with adoring eyes. He stroked her ears. "First, let me explain what's going on."

Beatrix listened as he quickly recounted L.B. Alexander's history and the current problem. Beatrix had read a couple of L. B. Alexander's books and had no idea the author lived here in Phoenix. "Do I get to meet her?"

Marco nodded. "Yeah, but right now I want to clarify a few things with you. Then I'll introduce you. First off, I want you to do a victim profile of Lily's parents. Find out everything you can about them. No matter how inconsequential."

"Why not ask Ms. Alexander?"

Marco held up an index finger. "This is police lesson number one. Lily knows her parents better than anyone, but she will only give details she thinks are important. She may even hide information because nobody wants to have their loved ones seen in a negative light, which means everything she tells me will be biased. A good detective needs all the details, no matter how trivial. Cases are solved on details. Interview the people who knew her parents."

"I could be doing that for five months. Can't you just tell me the right questions I should be asking these people, to cut down on the time?"

Jackson frowned at her. "Part of your job as a detective is to be intuitive. You have to feel your way around and find your own style."

She pulled a brand new notebook out of her purse and flipped it open. She wrote 'find my style' as the first entry.

"And while you're doing that, find out what you can about an ex-con named Joe Sawyer. Talk to everyone except him."

"Don't want to make him nervous just yet?"

"Bingo." Marco gave her a wide smile.

When he'd concluded his instructions, he took her toward the back of the house where she was introduced to L.B. Alexander and immediately liked what she saw.

Lily met her curious gaze with a direct look of her own, then assured her of her full cooperation in the investigation of this case.

With that Beatrix found herself being escorted toward the front door. As she drove out the gates, she was already planning how to put into action Marco's requests.

Lily closed the door and locked it. She leaned back against the cool wood for a moment, almost too tired to move. The last few days had drained her. She wasn't used to having so many people in her house, fussing around her. She needed some quiet time.

She headed back toward her office and found Marco on her computer. "Detective Hunter seems very nice."

"She's a rookie, but she'll do." Marco tapped at the keyboard.

Lily took a closer look at the computer monitor and realized Marco was viewing a website she was familiar with. The site was devoted to the understanding of agoraphobia, and Lily had participated in chats with other people like herself. They were her main support group now that her parents were dead. She didn't know whether to be flattered or annoyed. She settled on curious—it was safer.

Marco Jackson aroused thoughts in her she'd rather keep buried. In this little stretch of time, his easygoing masculinity reminded her that she was still a woman. A very lonely woman. She didn't like that at all. She liked keeping the real world at a distance. Marco Jackson's presence in her home was unsettling, to say the least.

"If you want to know about agoraphobia, just ask me. I'll tell you what you need to know."

He glanced back at her over his shoulder, a light in his eyes revealing a bit of disbelief. "Don't you get bored staying home all the time?"

"No. Only boring people get bored." At least, that was what her mother used to say. Her mother had insisted on what Lily called her 'no whining' policy. "I have my work and I have my toys."

"Toys?" Marco looked curious. "Like what?"

"Let me show you." She started toward the door, beckoning to him, a little thrill vibrating up and down her spine.

Marco followed her toward the back of the house, his solid footsteps echoing down the hall, his subtle masculine scent reminiscent of a weekend skiing in Telluride. Clean, fresh woodsy. Free. Marco Jackson smelled like freedom.

Lily ran a shaky hand over her mouth. My goodness, she was practically drooling like his big stupid dog. Her eyes turned heavenward. Save me from my libido. She threw open double doors and led him into her media room. She grinned at his face awe-struck face.

He walked into the room. "I have seen the Holy Land."

Four recliners faced a projection screen which took up half the wall. A second wall was lined with shelves filled with thousands of videotapes and DVDs.

Her father had decided that Lily needed to be exposed to as much entertainment as possible and had collected every movie he could find, along with every music CD. Lily added to the collection religiously with each new DVD as it came to market.

Opposite the shelves, she opened a row of cabinets to show the two hundred-disc DVD-CD player, the digital cable box, and the state-of-the-art Bose speaker system.

She opened another set of louvered doors on the back wall to show him the tiny galley tucked into what had originally been the closet.

The refrigerator was completely filled with sodas and fruit juices. The bar was stocked with every alcoholic beverage, a variety of wines, and a cabinet in a corner that held all the snack food any man could possibly want, including an industrial size popcorn popper usually found in theaters.

Marco walked around the room, peering at the movies and the music CDs. "I could live in this room."

She nodded. "Exactly." She opened a CD box, slid the CD into the player and turned it on with the universal remote she kept on a stand next to the one chair that belonged to her exclusively.

Her father's favorite musician blasted out of the speakers and she smiled at the look of pure delight on Marco's face.

"Coltrane," he said. "A Love Supreme." He looked as though he had died and gone to heaven.

"Very good." She turned off the music and turned on the TV to flick through several of the channels that the digital satellite dish on her roof provided. "I have every channel known to woman. If you want to watch soccer from Venezuela, it's a snap of the fingers. Or a kinky Italian game show, I have it. Or nude newscasters in Russia, I can get that, too." She pushed a button on the remote and a soccer game appeared. Then she switched to a game show and then to the BBC and finally to the Comedy Channel where some comedian took a pratfall, and the audience erupted into laughter.

"Let me correct myself, you know how to be at home."

"Home is all I have." She was thankful her parents had understood that. Though they had done their best to encourage her to live as normal a life as possible, they never treated her as though she were an invalid. Not that she was disabled, but they understood the debilitating elements of her agoraphobia.

He turned to her. "Why is that?"

"I have nothing else."

"For a woman who studies crime, you should know not to be evasive with a cop. Makes me think you're guilty."

Surprised, she tilted her head to study his handsome, boyish face. Funny, she hadn't noticed the small scar on his upper lip. Not that it marred the perfection of his mouth. Hell, it just made him look sexier. "Guilty of what?"

"Of not wanting to share your life."

This guy was all about asking questions that made her feel naked. "No deep, dark secrets in my past. I'm an open book. When I was abducted, everything about me was in the newspapers. When Sawyer went to trial, everything was in the newspapers again. When my parents were murdered, everything was in the paper a third time. My life is public domain." The reporters left no stone unturned.

He studied her. "But I want to know what wasn't in the newspapers."

As if anything had been left unsaid. "You know what the newspapers didn't tell you. That I like Gene Kelly and Audrey Hepburn movies. That I took ballet lessons because at one time I wanted to be a dancer. Once sold more cookies than anyone in my Girl Scout troop and received an award for it."

"My mom loves Gene Kelly," he mused. "She made us all take dance lessons." He launched into a soft shoe, twirling around the room as though he were Fred Astaire. He was so sexy! His willingness to make a fool out of himself just to get a laugh made him totally endearing. How could she resist a man like him? He almost made her feel that life was worth something.

When he stopped dancing, Lily went to the last unopened cabinet and flung it open. In the very center was a framed copy of the first issue of the X-Men signed by the great man himself, Stan Lee. Surrounding the comic book was every X-Man figurine and as many related products as she could show. "And last but not least." She pointed at her collection proudly.

Marco stared at the shrine, positioning both hands over his heart. "Be still, my heart. You're an X-Men fan."

"To the core."

Marco smiled. "You know a man's soul."

"I do?" What she knew about men could be written on a postage stamp with room left over to copy the entire Bible in ten different languages. But she didn't tell him that. Let him believe she had more knowledge than she actually possessed. "You and I are just big kids at heart."

He smiled broadly at her. "Marry me?"

Lily was momentarily silent. Her mouth went dry. Panic swamped her. She shook her head. "Yeah, I'll marry you and maybe you can get Wolverine to be your best man. And I'll have Storm be my Maid of Honor."

"Cool." The big, boyish grin on his face made him look ten years old. "We'll need a license. I'll have to contact Wolverine and you'll have to contact Storm. Night Crawler can officiate. And Professor Xavier will provide the music."

She laughed and stepped away from him putting distance between them and the tension radiating through her. He was dangerous. He made her feel things she didn't want to feel. He made her remember that a whole world existed outside her front door. "Does Cher know about your proclivities?"

"Very few people know the real Marco Jackson." He winked at her and made a face that told her it was all a game.

Marco's cell phone rang and he pulled it out of his pocket. "Jackson," he said and listened for a few seconds. "I'll be there ASAP." He disconnected. "Natalie's in the hospital."

CHAPTER FIVE

Marco parked his motorcycle in a slot reserved for cops and placed his helmet in the storage container and locked it. He slapped a Phoenix P.D. on duty sticker on the front of the handlebars and raced toward the emergency room doors. They whispered open and the strong smell of antiseptic and pine cleaner almost made him gag. He hated hospitals.

He stopped at the reception desk, IDed himself, asked for Natalie and was directed to an examination room down the hall.

He spotted Detective Tom Stone talking to two uniformed officers. When Marco approached, Tom nodded at the two officers left who turned and left.

Tom Stone had been with Violent Crimes for almost five years. Marco and he had crossed paths a couple years before when one of his victims had turned into a homicide. Since then, they'd had a beer or two a couple times and seen each other at charity functions.

"How is Natalie Gould?" Marco asked.

Tom shrugged. "The doctor is with her now. If I hadn't found her clutching your business card, I wouldn't have known who to call."

"Tell me what happened."

Tom glanced at his notebook. "We received an anonymous 9-1-1 call. When the officer discovered her, he radioed the paramedics and then reported that her apartment had been broken into and was pretty thoroughly trashed. I went out to investigate. The officer on the scene told me Miss Gould was badly beaten, apparently with a wooden baseball bat that was left at the scene. The doctor will have to tell us the extent of her injuries, but if I'm any judge, she's going to be in the hospital for a long time."

"I'm glad you got to her as quickly as you did."

"I heard you were transferred to Cold Case. Is this Miss Gould involved in a case you're working now, or from when you were still with homicide?"

"Current case." Marco gave Tom a quick rundown of Lily's case and Natalie's relationship to Lily.

Tom Stone wrote a few details down. When he finished, the doctor came out. "We're prepping Miss Gould for surgery."

"When can I talk to her?" Tom Stone asked.

The doctor shook his head. "Not any time soon. Her jaw's broken in several places and will need to be wired shut, she has internal injuries, two broken ribs, and the fingers on both hands have been broken. That lady took a lot of abuse."

"Any sexual trauma?" Tom asked.

"We checked, but nothing showed. Was this a domestic?"

Tom Stone shook his head. "We're still checking into that, doctor. Thanks for the update." Tom dug a business card out of his jacket pocket and handed it to the doctor. "Call me when you think I can talk to her."

The doctor pocketed the card. The door behind him opened and a medical technician wheeled Natalie Gould out. Natalie's bruised eyes were closed and Marco felt as though he'd been punched. Beaten was not the word he would have used. Brutalized was more like it.

"Know anyone who would want to hurt Miss Gould this badly?" Tom Stone asked Marco.

Marco watched the retreating Gurney disappear into an elevator. "I might have a guy. He's long shot"

"Long shots pay big."

"My thoughts exactly. Let's go check him out."

—〰—

Joe Sawyer stood inside the door to his tiny house wearing brown pajamas and rubbing his eyes. He was a tall, skinny man with thick black glasses and dark blonde tousled hair. He had a nondescript appearance. One that allowed him to blend in. To be invisible.

On the surface Marco had a hard time believing this nerdy guy could be responsible for so much evil, but what he had done to Lily was nothing less than depraved. He wiped his damp palms on his pants. A rage built in him twisting his gut. He needed to muzzle this guy soon.

"Can I help you?" Sawyer asked in a fuzzy voice, his eyes unfocused and glazed.

Marco showed his badge. He forced himself to control the strange fire in his belly. This case had become personal and Marco knew he his emotions were guiding him when he should remain neutral. "I'm Detective Jackson and this is Detective Stone. We'd like to ask you some questions."

"Is something wrong with Anna?" A frantic expression crossed his face.

"Is Anna your wife?" Tom Stone asked.

Sawyer nodded. "Yes."

"Nothing is wrong with Anna," Marco said.

Sawyer frowned. "What is this about then?"

Marco slipped his foot in between the door and the jam. Damn but he was itching for a showdown. "Mind if we come in?" Marco asked.

"I was sleeping, but I guess not." Sawyer stood aside and allowed them to enter a dim living room. Sawyer opened the drapes to allow some light inside and Marco could see that the room was extremely tidy. The furniture was old, but well cared for. Each surface gleamed with polish.

"If nothing's wrong with Anna," Sawyer said, "why are you here?"

Stone moved to one side boxing him in. "Where were you this morning around seven a.m.?"

Sawyer shrugged. "I was just getting off work."

Marco shifted his position moving closer to Sawyer who inched away. "What do you do?"

Sawyer didn't twitch. "I work for a janitorial company."

Flexing his fingers Marco stared straight at him. "What's the name of your company?"

Sawyer frowned. "Keep-it-Klean. All with Ks. If one of our customers complained, you need to take it up with my boss."

Stone hitched his jacket back revealing his pistol. "Who's your boss?"

Sawyer's eyes slid from Marco to Stone. "Matt Nettle."

The guy was calm. Too calm. Almost too perfect. As if he had rehearsed his reactions. Marco eyed him. His palms started to sweat again and he knew that all of Lily's suspicions were correct. Somehow, Sawyer was guilty of murdering her parents, and of stalking Lily. How he knew, he couldn't say. Marco just had a gut feeling. He resisted the need to wipe his palms on the sides of his thighs.

If Marco intended to free Lily from this bastard, he had to start breaking down the man's control. "Your boss can verify you were at work at seven?" Stone asked.

"My time card can."

"Anybody can punch a time card." Stone circled the edge of the living room. He glanced at a stack of magazines and then at a pile of mail on a side table.

Sawyer smiled at Marco. "You're right, but I would never ask anyone to cheat for me. That would be unethical."

Marco wanted to smack the smug expression right off the bastard's face, but he had to stay cool. He couldn't allow his judgment to be clouded by his need to protect Lily. Lily had gone through too much at this man's hand. Marco would end it. He didn't know how, he didn't know when, but Sawyer's playtime was over.

Stone shook his head. "Can I get a glass of water?"

Sawyer's mouth dropped open for a second. "I guess so." He walked toward a hallway and Stone followed after a quick backward glance at Marco.

Marco grinned. Stone had given him a moment alone in the living room to see if he could snoop anything out. Never knew when a criminal might get stupid. Though something told him, Sawyer wasn't stupid.

Marco walked around the small living room. One wall held a couple dozen photos. One was a wedding photo of Sawyer and a woman. The woman was unremarkable in a plump sort of way with dark brown hair and a round, bland face. She was so different from Lily. Marco was puzzled over Sawyer's choice of a wife. Her expression was neutral, no character showed. Even her gray suit seemed devoid of life.

Lily overflowed with fire. How typical of Sawyer to marry a doormat he could control, while lusting after a woman of substance. The wife was meant to give Sawyer credibility and mislead the cops into thinking Sawyer was now a man with normal responsibilities. An average Joe with nothing more on his mind than his next mortgage payment. Marco wasn't fooled.

As he moved down the row of photos, he realized that except for the wedding photo, no others included the wife. The rest of the photos were of Joe standing at a pulpit with an open Bible in his hands, or in front of a church shaking hands with people. And one where he was being baptized in a pool, his hands together in prayer and his face transported with something Marco didn't recognize. He studied the last photo intently for a moment. Sawyer was trying to give off the aura of the newly converted, but there was a sly droop to his mouth that told Marco the whole thing was an act.

Marco paused at a bookcase to study the row of books. Sawyer was into Christian books. One book lay open with a small silver cross artfully draped over the open pages just waiting for some poor slob who didn't know his butt from a hole in the wall to write Sawyer a free pass to heaven. Yeah, Marco thought, some guy goes to prison and he finds God. The only problem was they usually left God behind at the door to freedom.

Everything was cookie cutter perfect. Lily was like this to some degree, but Marco knew the familiar comforted her and gave her control. With Sawyer there was an element of fake about it. Joe Sawyer had a history of violence. Nobody walked way from that kind of past. Marco needed to talk to Joe's parole officer.

Because Marco found nothing laying around screaming 'I'm guilty' he walked down the hall toward the kitchen alert to the layout of the house. Two doors on one side of the hall opened into two bedrooms. The first bedroom was the master with a double bed neatly made. The second room had been turned into a den with a computer and desk on one side and a day bed pushed against the opposite wall.

He wandered into the kitchen where Sawyer stood against a counter adding ice to two large glasses of water. He handed one glass to Stone and offered the other to Marco. Marco accepted the cup, but didn't drink.

"You said you were sleeping," Marco said to Sawyer.

"I was."

"The beds are made."

"I sleep on the sofa sometimes." Sawyer gave a little chuckle that sounded a mite too forced. "I have mornings when I'm too tired to go to bed and my wife works really hard to keep the house clean. So I just sleep on the sofa."

"You weren't too tired to put your pajamas on."

Sawyer shrugged. "Good intentions, Detective. By the time I brushed my teeth and said my daily prayers, I just couldn't force myself those last few feet to the bed."

Good intentions, my ass. He'd probably spent his early morning stashing his bloody clothes until he had a chance to get rid of them. "The sofa doesn't look comfortable."

Sawyer grinned. "Trust me, Detective. After all those years in prison, anything with a little cush is comfortable."

"You were in prison?" Sawyer sounded so honest, Marco almost believed him. "A fine-upstanding man of God like you?"

"Detective, that's what this is all about? I realize I'm still on parole and you have the right to come in here and make a mockery of my life any time you choose. But I would like to know where this conversation is going because I need my sleep. I like to spend time with my wife before I go to work." He winked. "If you know what I mean."

Stone leaned against the counter. "Where is your wife?

"She's working. She's the secretary at our church. The Little Lambs of God Evangelical Church. Over on 25th street. You should drop in some time. Everyone needs God in their life."

"Right." Marco's good Catholic mother would have a stroke if she found out he'd even thought of attending a different church.

Stone's eyebrows rose. "Do you know a Natalie Gould?"

Sawyer's brow creased as though he were thinking deeply. "No. Is she a member of my congregation?"

"Do you know Lily Alexander?"

A remorseful expression worked its way across Sawyer's face. "Regretfully, yes. Lily Alexander has made my acquaintance. Something I deeply regret."

Marco forced himself not to smile. *Let the game begin.*

"What do you mean?" Stone arched his bushy eyebrow.

"Before I understood the laws of God, I was a law unto myself. I was an evil man. A wicked man, and I did wicked things."

If the man bursts into a sermon, Marco thought, he would shoot him. "What was this evil, wicked thing that you did?"

Sawyer's eyes went flat. "My psychiatrist tells me not to talk about it anymore. That's in the past and how I live now is what is important. I've atoned for my mistakes. I paid my debt to society and Miss Alexander. I have no idea who Natalie Gould is and whatever happened to her, I had nothing to do with it."

"Who said anything happened to her?" Tom Stone gave a tiny smile.

"You wouldn't be here if she were safely where she was supposed to be."

"She's Miss Alexander's secretary." Stone put down his glass. "She was attacked this morning in her apartment."

"I'm deeply sorry for her pain." He closed his eyes and mumbled a prayer. "Thank you, God." He smiled at Stone and Marco. "I need to pray for her. Gentlemen, I'm sorry this is a waste of your time. Miss Alexander has never forgiven me for what I did to her and I understand. I pray for her daily. But I can't help you. I know nothing about what happened to Miss Gould. One of the stipulations of my parole is that I stay away from Miss Alexander."

"How's that going for you? Parole, I mean."

Sawyer smiled. "It's a part of my salvation and I accept that."

Marco had to get out of there. Sawyer's contrition grated on him. Marco took out a card and handed it to Sawyer. "Here's my card. If you think of anything, give me a call."

Marco opened the front door and stepped out into the hot morning sun. Another day, another scorcher, he thought as they walked toward the car. "How would you like some help on this case?"

Stone shrugged. "I'm ten cases deep, and my wife and I are trying to plan our vacation in the next week and a half. I'm all about using some help."

Marco took out his cell phone and called Beatrix Hunter. He gave her the particulars of what happened so far and asked her to check out Sawyer's parole officer and the janitorial service where he worked.

~m~

Lily huddled on the sofa trying not to think about Natalie. "Do you think she's going to be all right?" If the news was bad, would Marco call or tell her in person? She believed so. He was a straight-up kind of man. Lily suspected there was little or no guile in him. She liked that despite the fact that he'd invaded her life—dog and all.

Cher Dawson set a cup of tea down in front of Lily. "Marco will call when he can."

Lily cradled the tea in her hands. Knowing Marco was her champion comforted her. He would make Sawyer leave her alone. He would kick Sawyer out of her life.

Thin spirals of hot mist rose to dampen her face. She inhaled the aromatic herbal smell. She hated feeling so vulnerable and out of control. In her house, she should be all-powerful, not a sniveling mass of Jell-o. "Damn, you've gone domestic." Marriage had changed Cher, removing the hard edge that Lily was most familiar with.

Cher chuckled. "I'll cut you some slack because Natalie is in the hospital. But next time, I'll...." her voice trailed away the threat unsaid.

Lily loved Cher. She had met Cher ten years ago while researching a book and that one encounter had blossomed into a strong friendship.

Cher sat down in an over-stuffed leather chair and pulled her feet up under her. "What do you think of Marco Jackson?" Her voice was a shade too casual as she lifted the cup of tea to her lips.

Lily lifted an eyebrow. He made her feel soft. Dependent. Out of control. All the things, she tried to avoid. But he was sweet and funny. And he loved the X-men. "He has Harley, a big vicious dog, a gold earring in one ear, and has a high-stress profession. Oh yeah! He screams 'bad boy.'" As though on cue, Harley rose from the rug where she'd been sunning herself by the French doors that led to the small enclosed garden and resettled at Lily's feet.

Cher simply smiled. "There's something to be said for a bad boy."

Lily stared at her friend. "And how would you know? You married Mr. Perfect."

Cher rolled her eyes. "The man cannot hang up a towel to save his ass."

"You make it sound like towel dysfunction is a reason for divorce?"

Cher shook her head. "For the kind of sex he gives me, I can let the towel situation slide."

Lily laughed. "You are so obscenely happy, you make me ill."

"Sick with jealousy?"

"Sick with nausea."

Cher sipped her own tea. "I recommend married life."

"Let me give up a light laugh here."

Cher set her cup down. "Lily, you're pretty, you have a nice house and money. What man wouldn't want you?"

Lily tapped her head. "Mental problem here. How am I supposed to go out and meet a man? I can't leave the house?"

"Stop saying that about yourself," Cher said. "You make it sound like you should be in the mental ward."

"Sometimes I wish..." Lily let the words trail off. She wanted a lot of things. The list was way too long to even contemplate.

"If you don't like your life, change it. Get in your parent's car and drive down to a gas station. Hell why keep it around and make Natalie run it around the block once a week. Use it."

Lily had kept her parents' Volvo in hopes that one day she'd be able to drive it, but the best she'd been able to do the last two years was to stand in the garage door and look at it. "I just can't seem to conquer this little problem I have with open spaces."

Cher glanced at the ceiling. "How many degrees do you have, sweetie?"

Lily held up three fingers. She had a Bachelor's degree in political science and two Masters—English and History.

"Then use that big brain. You are the captain of your destiny, girl."

"It's not just the car, it's other things."

Cher smiled. "I've just set you up with one of the hottest pieces of man-flesh in the city. Make your voodoo priestess grandma proud. Brew up a love potion. Dance naked under the moonlight. Do whatever your mother's Haitian relatives do to get their groove on."

Shocked, she found herself laughing. She tried to imagine herself dancing naked in the moonlight, but the image bogged her mind. "Marco's all right."

"Excuse me. All right. Trust me, if Luc hadn't come back into my life, I would have been tempted to jump that pony and ride him to the finish line."

Jealousy surged through Lily. The emotion scared her. She didn't want any woman making a claim on Marco. "I don't want to know this."

"Me either." Marco walked into the living room. He rubbed his eyes. Harley jumped to her feet and trotted over to him. He absently patted her head.

Cher's head whipped around. She put down her cup and picked up her purse. "Okay, I've said enough. I think I better get back to the station." She kissed Lily's cheek and grabbed Marco by the lapel of his jacket. "If this ever gets out ...."

"Say no more, boss." Marco raised a hand in a Boy Scout salute.

Cher left, the front door slamming after her.

Lily waited for him to say something, anything. She'd been gossiping about him. Her own emotions were in turmoil and for a second she wondered if Marco had any tender feelings for Cher. The thought made her sick to her stomach. And worse it made her feel guilty. No, Cher was happily married.

"I feel kind of cheap, now." Marco took off his jacket.

Lily's flesh burned. "I'm embarrassed."

"Don't worry." He loosened his tie. "I'll mark that down as the girl version of guy talk."

Lily took a deep breath. She couldn't drag her gaze away from the graceful motion of his long tapered fingers. He had beautiful hands. For a second she wondered how those fingers would feel on her skin.

Her lips went dry. His invasion of her life made her realize how empty her existence was. "How is Natalie doing?"

Marco sat next to her on the sofa. The teasing light in his eyes disappeared. He was going to relay some bad news. He'd been a homicide cop and was probably getting up the courage to tell her that Natalie was dead.

"Don't sugar-coat anything. Just tell me."

"Natalie's in bad shape."

Relief flooded her. Natalie wasn't dead. "How serious?"

He gave her a comforting smile. "She's going to be a guest of the hospital for a while."

Lily bit her lip. "What if ..." She shuddered. "What if he goes back to finish the job?"

"I arranged twenty-four/seven protection."

"Thank you." Lily stared at her clenched fists. Her champion. He would do no less then protect her and those she cared about. For the first time since she received the news about Natalie she felt tension ease within her.

"Do you think Joe Sawyer is the one who hurt Natalie?"

"I don't doubt it for a second. He's waging a war. He's a good long way from being done with me."

Marco rested an arm across the back of the sofa. "Tell me everything you can remember from twelve years ago."

"I don't think I can," she muttered through clenched teeth. She didn't want to relive the horror. Not for him. Telling him would be too personal. What would he think of her? That somehow she'd caused what happened. One of her mother's best friends had asked that question, and had insisted that Lily had somehow given Sawyer the wrong message.

"You remember, you just don't want to." Marco touched her

shoulder.

His touch was at once reassuring and heady. His fingers massaged her though her to thin t-shirt. "No playing detective with me. I know how you people work."

For a moment, he looked like he was trying to control his impatience. Lily didn't care. This was her life, not some freak show.

"Lily," he said in a caressing tone, as though inviting her to confide in him.

His gentle tone rolled over her like smoke and silk. She tilted her head up at him. "Now you're flirting with me."

He looked startled, then grinned. "Whatever works best with you, lady?"

She dug her nails deep into her palms. "Don't treat me like I'm a fragile piece of porcelain. I don't want to talk about Joe Sawyer or what he did to me twelve years ago. I want to talk about my parents and what he did to them and to Natalie. And what about the heart and the homeless man without one. Sawyer probably killed him, too." Sawyer was escalating the terror and Lily wondered what had happened to upset the balance.

Marco gently coaxed her. "What happened to you twelve years ago is the starting point of what's going on now. I have to understand. I have to know if I'm going to find a solution."

"Then read the damn case file," Lily almost screamed.

"The real you isn't in the case file. Victim Lily is chronicled in the case file. You're not a victim anymore."

"Yes, I am. Joe Sawyer is doing all these things to me to keep me a victim." Tears prickled the edges of her eyes. "I can't leave my house because of him. I can't have a life because of him."

"Get off the pity train, honey." Marco's voice was harsh. "You survived. You got away. Do you think you were the only one? You have no idea if he abducted and killed any other women, but I can almost guarantee you, you weren't the only one. The difference is that you fought back and now is time to do so again. Tell me what happened." He pounded a finger on the back of the sofa.

Lily jumped to her feet. She didn't have to tell him anything. This was her house. She massaged her temples, a headache starting just behind her eyes.

Marco stopped her with a hand on her arm. "Don't run away from me."

Lily whirled. "You're not my keeper."

"I have a big, mean boss telling me I am. From this moment on, we play by my rules. No more poor, poor pitiful Lily running around like you're queen of your little empire. You're all big and bad on the surface, sister, but Joe Sawyer is still keeping you hostage."

Tears stung the corners her eyes, yet she refused to show weakness. She wouldn't give him the satisfaction of seeing her break down. She wanted to retreat to her bedroom where she could lock the door and Marco couldn't follow. "Who do you think you're talking to?"

"You. The real you. The you that's hidden deep inside."

"Who are you? You have a stupid dog that's drooling all over my leather furniture. You have a stupid motorcycle that makes way too much noise. I don't need you. I can take care of myself. I'm safe in my house and you don't need to be here. Understand me."

His mouth quirked into a thin smile. "Tell me another lie. You're not any safer now than you were twelve years ago. Now tell me what happened."

Lily rubbed the bridge of her nose hoping to keep the memories at bay. "If I tell you, it will be like I'm back there again." Just the faintest touch of the memories sent panic spiraling through her. Her chest tightened and she forced air into her lungs.

He touched her cheek. "I swear to God, I will never let that man hurt you. Not now. Not ever."

She stared at him, believing him. For the first time in a long time, Lily felt someone could help her.

Marco sensed the change in her. He led her back to the sofa worrying that he'd browbeaten her into compliance. He didn't like getting rough. He wasn't Mr. Confrontation. He was Mr. Buddy. Tell me your troubles and I'll make everything better. He pushed and pushed and when he finally had her up against the wall, he pushed one more time. For a few seconds he was ashamed of himself. He should have been easier with her. She was at an emotional breaking point and he was twisting her like a pretzel.

Either she told him everything now and moved on in her life, or he might as well pack his bags and let Sawyer do his worst. "First of all," he said, "my dog and my motorcycle are not stupid."

"I'm sorry." She looked contrite. "I was wrong."

"Say what you will about the hound, but Harley has championship lines, just like my motorcycle."

She laughed. Now that he'd made her laugh and things were back on an even keel, he was okay.

He sat her down on the sofa and seated himself next to her.

She took a deep breath, folded her hands in her lap and said in a quiet, tired voice, "A few weeks before I was abducted, I started feeling like someone was watching me. My dorm mate had moved out, and I had my room to myself. I thought I was just tired because of finals and imagining things, but then I noticed that my books would be arranged in a different order, and my clothes would be folded differently. One afternoon, I'd hurried back to the dorm on break from one of my classes because I didn't have my notebook. I thought I'd put it in my backpack, but the notebook wasn't there when I got to class. While I was searching my room, I received this phone call. One of the girls came and told me my mom had been in an auto accident and my dad was on the phone. When I got to the payphone, there was no one on the other end. I didn't know what to think. I called my dad back, but there was no answer. So I got my purse and car keys and headed to the parking lot."

Marco almost held his breath. From the look of pure terror on her face, he'd been afraid she would retreat from him and her fears. But she hadn't and he mentally applauded her for her courage.

"I don't remember much," she said, "just that one moment I was approaching my car and the next I was waking up in this old shack. I had no idea where I was, or what time it was." She paused taking deep breaths. "The room appeared to be small and the only light was from two candles. I was handcuffed to the bedposts. When I turned my head he was sitting on a chair next to me, wearing a ski mask. The only thing I could see was his blue eyes and his mouth. I kept thinking as long as he kept the mask on and I couldn't identify him, he wouldn't kill me." She paused, her eyes taking on a distant cast. Her hands had grown still, but her feet tapped nervously against the floor.

"Why do you think he chose you?" Marco asked.

"I don't know. I used to wonder that myself, but eventually, I figured he abducted me because I'm little and I don't appear to be very strong. I looked like a little kid."

He had a newsflash for her; as far as he was concerned she was all woman. From the tips of her curly hair, to her perky small breasts to her long supple legs. Too much woman for his well-being. He wiped his damp palm on the leg of his pants as he made a mental note to check with missing persons for other women who had been small, petite women around Lily's age who had gone missing from the University. His gut told him she couldn't have been the only one.

Lily glanced up at him. "I know you haven't seen it, but people tell me I have this vulnerable air about me."

Marco laughed. "Yeah, I spotted that right away."

She smiled. She took a sip of tea and that seemed to calm her a little more. "He fed me. We would have these formal dinners with highbrow conversation. He talked about art and music, like we were on a date. He made me wear these stupid fluffy dresses with high heels and pearl necklaces like June Cleaver used to wear. God, he was a stickler on table manners. I tried to hide a fork from him thinking maybe I could use it as a weapon, but he counted each piece when he arrived and when he left. That was the first time he hit me. He took that fork away and hit me. Just kept on hitting me like he couldn't stop. That's when he took the mask off and I knew I was going to die."

Her breath came in shallow, panicked groans. "I think he was mad because I wasn't what he wanted me to be. At times, I felt like we were playing house."

"What do you think he wanted from you?" Marco asked.

"I think he wanted some sort of perfect family thing. At times, I thought he was auditioning me for a part on a TV series. I asked him what he wanted me to call him and he told me the Duke of Windows. Now isn't that stupid. One time I called him Duke Windex and I thought he was going to cut my heart out. He beat me up again, pretty badly. I lost a molar. After that he started beating me every time he came. Then he'd leave and I'd lie on the bed trying not to move because I hurt so bad."

"You fought back, even when you were afraid."

She sighed. "It's funny, but when you figure out you have nothing else to lose, you say, what the hell. What was the worst he could do? Kill me. I was already prepared to die."

"'What the hell' is good. 'What the hell' is probably why you got away."

"To be honest, the man abducted me right in the middle of my feminist political theory class. I was pretty angry back then. I had just entered my *hate man* mode. Kept on saying to myself, what would Gloria Steinem do? What would Sojourner Truth do?"

She chuckled and Marco allowed his own quiet laugh to escape. "Girls can kick some pretty good ass, too. You haven't met my sister yet."

"I've heard about your sister. She's been dodging my calls. I'm thinking about a book on Billy Oakes."

Marco grinned. "If you're nice to me and play by my rules, I might slide you a favor."

"So now we're bargaining."

"Whatever it takes to get you to reveal your secrets, Lily Alexander."

She jumped up from the sofa and paced the room. Harley watched her, an alert look in her big eyes, her ears perked up with curiosity. Lily stopped to pat Harley's huge head, then she resumed her pacing. "I didn't know what to do. When he was gone, I'd drag the bed to the nearest window and look out, but all I saw was desert. I had no idea where I was, or which direction to go should I get away. I never ever heard or saw a plane. But at night, I heard coyotes and occasionally cars and knew I was near a highway."

"How did he get to the shack?"

"If he drove a car, I never saw it. He always walked to the shack. One night he came, and I sensed things were different somehow. He was all excited and fidgety. Couldn't stand still. He told me I'd failed the test. I didn't know what he was talking about. But I knew he intended to end it all that night. He uncuffed me and told me to put on this white flouncy dress that was really different from the other dresses he'd made me wear. And gave me these stiletto heels to wear. He said he'd wait outside. I was sort of surprised, because he'd never waited outside before, but would watch me change. I peeked out the window and he was gone and I thought where would he go. So I opened the door and left. I ran away thinking I was free and that he'd finally made a mistake. That's when I realized he let me go. So I pulled off those damn shoes and I ran. Then it occurred to me that I had taken a self-defense class and the instructor had told us high-heels make a great weapon. So I went back and got the shoes, and hoped I was heading in the right direction. I crawled up this hill and saw head-lights and realized how close to the highway I was. I headed toward those headlights and all the while I sensed him following me. He'd let me go because this was the chase, part of his agenda. I just kept run-ning; my feet were hurting but I knew if I kept running I'd get away." She ended on a breathless sigh. She sat back down as though drained.

"How did you identify him?"

"A cop stopped on the highway and picked me up. Told me they'd been looking for me. He took me to the hospital and this other cop came to talk to me. His name was Quinn Munson and I'll never for-get him. He had this mole on his cheek and he was so nice, like talk-ing to my dad. He treated me like a daughter." Her voice trailed away as she relived her memories at the hospital under Quinn Munson's delicate questioning. "He had a box of tissues in his hand and before he ever asked me one questions he gave me the box and told me to have a good cry now that I was safe."

Even though Quinn Munson had died several years ago, Marco

remembered him clearly. He had been a big bear of a man who could crush full beer cans with one hand and bench press three hundred pounds. But when it came to a victim, he treated them like they were his lost little lambs. He had been a good man and for all outward appearances, he had an inner core of strength and gentleness. "I knew Quinn Munson, he was a brilliant cop." And a caring cop.

Lily nodded. "He helped me remember things I didn't even know I knew. When I told him about feeling watched, Detective Munson brought me the student photos that were taken for our IDs and that the school kept. And Joe Sawyer was right there. I didn't even realize he went to school with me. Later, I found out we took a chemistry class together, but I couldn't remember him. He also worked as a part-time janitor."

She bit at the inside of her lip before she continued. "I didn't think I'd ever survive. Detective Munson stayed with me through the whole trial when the defense attorney made it seem as though I'd done something to entice Joe into his mad behavior and that somehow the whole situation was my fault. Detective Munson insisted I'd done nothing, but I used to worry that maybe I had. After the trial, Detective Munson kept in touch checking to see how I was doing. He insisted I go to lunch with him every once in a while. I felt safe with him. I'm sorry I missed his funeral, but I was in Delaware. My mom and I were visiting family."

Marco frowned. "I thought you never left the house."

"When my mother was alive, I wasn't allowed to be agoraphobic. She'd force me to go places every once in a while. I was okay as long as she was with me, but after she was murdered, I couldn't leave again." She glanced around the living room.

Marco could understand what had happened to her, but in his mind the house had become her prison, not her refuge. "Have you ever sought help, or talked to somebody about your fears?"

"Do you mean like a therapist?"

"Yes, a therapist."

She bit her lip again. "Cher is about as close as I could find to a therapist. I don't need to go outside. I'm fine just the way I am. What's out there? What would I want outside that I can't bring here?"

Marco grinned. "You can't ride a motorcycle in the house."

"Why would I want to ride a motorcycle?"

"It's fun. It's like being free. It's as close to flying without wings as humans can get."

"Detective," Lily said, "you're never going to win me over on the glories of the great outdoors."

"You don't know what you're missing."

"I want to keep it that way."

Marco felt a moment of sadness. She was a brilliant, educated woman and she didn't understand. She was right where Sawyer wanted her: isolated and alone. All Sawyer had to do was pick his time. He was playing with her and when he came in for the kill, Lily would be glad to have the whole thing over. "Lady, you have way too much to live for."

"Do I look like I'm having a pity party here, Detective?"

Marco smiled. "There's nothing pitiful about you."

"Thank you. I needed to hear that. Sometimes I'm not sure."

He touched her cheek. "I'm not going to let him hurt you." He bent over her and kissed her.

CHAPTER SIX

Beatrix checked her watch. Lieutenant Dawson was late for her own meeting. She'd taken another one of those extended lunches with her husband. But Beatrix had to admit, if she had a husband as good-looking as Luc Broussard, she'd take long lunches, too. Hell, she might quit her job.

Jacob Greyhorse rustled papers on his desk. Wyatt Earp Whitaker leaned back, his eyes closed. Beatrix wondered what he was thinking. For a seat-of-the-pants detective, Whitaker was good. He'd cleared almost every case he'd taken on. And he'd solved some of the most bizarre mysteries that had ever stumped the Phoenix P.D. Beatrix was a little in awe of him, and just a tiny bit jealous. He made being a cop seem like a piece of cake.

A strange man sat at Marco's desk. He was a handsome man, tall with broad-shoulders that narrowed down to a slim, tapered waist. His skin was the color of warm, toasted almonds with a golden under-tone. She loved nothing better than almonds. His eyes were a dark hazel. He wore Hugo Boss. Beatrix loved a man who could wear Hugo Boss well. Elegant and tasteful with just a hint of the bad boy. She shivered trying to drag her mind away from him.

He kept looking around the room, his eyes traveling back and forth and resting more than once on Beatrix. He smiled at her. She smiled back and felt a warm fuzzy heat travel up her spine.

Dawson walked into the room and the room came to life with the snap of an electric charge. Greyhorse sat up straighter and eyed

Dawson. Whitaker straightened his tie.

Dawson scanned the room and then walked straight up to the strange man, her right hand out-stretched. They shook hands and she spoke quietly for a few seconds and then turned around and called everyone to attention. "Boys and girls, I have a surprise for you. Cold Case has finally arrived." She gave them all a smug, satisfied smile. "We now have our own personal, brand-new county attorney assigned to do nothing but handle our cases. May I introduce Mr. Leland Davenport?" She gestured at the stranger.

The man stood and the warm heat in the pit of Beatrix' stomach spiraled out until she felt every nerve end vibrate. Her pulses fluttered and her heart thumped. She almost sighed out loud. He was so handsome. If he looked at her just right, she'd spontaneously combust.

Beatrix shook her head. How could she be attracted to a stranger so quickly? In her love life, she'd been nothing but cautious since the breakup of her engagement. And here she was zinging over some man who hadn't even said word one to her. For all she knew he could be a jackass. Some of her worst presents had come wrapped in the best packaging.

Leland Davenport smiled and Beatrix's heart melted a little more. Her fingers tingled. Her throat felt tight.

"Ladies and gentlemen," Davenport said, "let me say how happy I am to be working with the best Cold Case Unit in the country. I look forward to a long and successful partnership."

Okay, he'd spoken and Beatrix was in love. His voice was velvety smooth and rich, reaching down to her Gucci loafers and she thought she'd dissolve into crème brûlée.

Concentrate, Beatrix, concentrate. Stop drooling.

"Over the next several days," Davenport said, "I will be familiarizing myself with each of you, how the unit runs, and what cases you're working on."

Again, his gaze rested on Beatrix and her heart pounded so loud she thought he'd hear. What the hell was wrong with her? She couldn't be attracted to him. Her family would have a fit all the way back to her most illustrious Mayflower ancestors.

Beatrix closed her eyes and tried to still the wild beating of her heart. The meeting adjourned and she felt the people around her moving away.

"Hunter," Dawson yelled. "In my office." She whirled toward her door, Leland Davenport following her.

Beatrix jumped to her feet and followed.

—◆—

Lee waited until the blonde woman closed the door. She was magnificent and he was puzzled. He'd never been attracted to a white woman before. She was an American male's wet dream with her blonde hair, creamy complexion and brilliant blue eyes and the only thing that saved her from being too wholesome was her full, pouty mouth. She had a mouth like a sister and he kept staring at it. He'd seen her before in her guise as the media liaison between the department and the press, but she was so much better looking in the flesh. So much better looking.

"Lee," Cher said, "this is Beatrix Hunter. She's helping Marco Jackson with the Alexander investigation."

He stuck out his hand and grasped hers. She had as strong grip which surprised him. "It's a pleasure to finally meet you. Your reputation precedes you." He held on tight and for a second she looked startled and then gently pulled her fingers away from his.

"What reputation?" She finally managed to speak. "I've only been with Cold Case for a few days."

"Your media savvy is so prestigious that several of your press conferences are required viewing at the county attorney's office. You are considered the master of the deniable and the plausible." Because of past indiscreet comments made by men who should have known better, every new hire at the county attorney's office was now trained to talk to the media.

Hunter blushed. "Thank you."

He was charmed. A woman who blushed! Where had she been hiding?

Dawson cleared her throat. "Excuse me, the love fest is over."

Lee felt a touch of heat on his own face. He wanted to know this woman better and was shocked. He came from a long line of civil rights workers and upwardly mobile people who married light, not white. Wait! How did he go from attraction to marriage in two steps? He stepped back from her feeling confused.

He gestured toward a chair and Beatrix sat down. He sat and smiled at her. "I have some questions about the Alexander investigation."

"I've only been on the case since this morning and I don't know if I have any answers."

"I understand you're checking into this man named Joe Sawyer."

"Marco Jackson is the lead detective and I'm his legs. So far, this afternoon, I'm talking to his parole officer and then his boss. Apparently there was in incident this morning. Miss Alexander's secretary was attacked."

He glanced down at her legs, but she was wearing pants and he felt a moment's disappointment. "What is Detective Jackson doing?"

Hunter glanced at Dawson. Dawson nodded. "He's taking care...I mean he's...." She glanced at Dawson again.

Dawson shook her head. "He's handling Miss Alexander's part of the investigation."

Lee was confused. "That's a pretty ambiguous statement. I don't think that bodes well for our future relationship."

"Lily Alexander is my best friend," Dawson said, "and Marco Jackson has her under twenty-four/seven protection."

"I see." Lee didn't quite understand, but he had a feeling if he just left things alone, he'd find out.

What he didn't know about Dawson could come back and smack him on the behind. She was an enigma and he'd already been warned to be careful around her. She took no prisoners. He glanced at her and knew he couldn't push her around. He probably couldn't push Hunter around either, but if he had his choice, he'd go for Hunter. If the attraction was as strong for her as it was for him, he'd eventually find out what he needed to know.

※

Marco pushed himself away from Lily. What the hell had he been thinking? But she had looked so forlorn; he'd felt the need to comfort her in some way. "I'm sorry, that was wrong of me." All he needed now was to have Cher find out he'd been taking liberties with Lily.

Lily touched her lips. "Why did you kiss me?"

He had a dozen reasons why he'd kissed her. Foremost, because she was beautiful. Because he was lonely. Because she liked X-Men comic books. "I don't know."

"You can't go around kissing me. That's unprofessional behavior."

"I know. You're right." But Marco was at a loss on how to explain his impulsive action. "I wanted to. You looked like you needed a kiss."

Her eyes narrowed. "How you do you know what I need? You don't know me."

"I want to know you better." Jesus that sounded so lame. He hadn't been this tongue-tied since freshman year in high school. Women weren't a mystery to him. He saw one, took her home, and then said good-bye. That's the way he liked his relationships–uninvolved.

"I have to go," she said as she turned toward the door.

Marco didn't think he knew who he was anymore, much less her. He wanted to protect her. He wanted to love her. He watched her leave. She'd been carrying a big load on her shoulders for a long time and he wanted to take the burden.

He felt Harley gently lick his hand and he caressed the Great Dane's head. He should not have been hitting on Lily. She was a crime victim and he was a cop. How could he possibly be thinking about more than a kiss when he was solving her problems?

Yet he was living in her house and had no way to keep his distance. He could keep a professional distance, but every emotion in him demanded that he do more than protect.

His cell phone rang and he walked toward the window as he pulled it out of his pocket. "Jackson."

"Hey there soon-to-be birthday boy," his sister said. "What's happening?"

"I'm still on the case."

"I know that. Tell me it has blood, guts, gore and dismembered body parts."

"You are sick, Elena."

She laughed. "I can't wait for Sunday so I can hear all the details. Mom insisted I call again to remind you about Sunday. If I don't call, she'll nag me until I do. I told her I talked to you a couple days ago, but you know how Mom can be. Besides, I have news for you."

So much had happened he'd forgotten his birthday. "I don't think I'm going to make dinner." He could call Hunter to baby-sit Lily, but how could he leave her alone while he celebrated?

Elena chuckled. "Yes, you are if you don't want mother to track you down and kill you personally. You know how she feels about family celebrations. The only excuse to get out of it is if you're six feet under. Reardon is flying back from Boston to be here. Even he doesn't have the courage to defy our mother. His mother, yes, but never ours. Besides you have to get my news."

Marco felt sorry for Elena, but he understood her decision to leave the department, especially after she'd won a bitterly contested sexual harassment case against a fellow cop. She'd broken down the blue wall of silence that said you kept your problems inside the 'family.' If a cop had a problem, they handled it themselves. Elena had taken her problem to court and won.

As much as Marco respected her decision to go public, if she'd come to him, Marco would have taken the guy into a dark alley and castrated him. Then she could have stayed with the force and continued to do what she loved. Instead, she'd hung up her badge because she had too much to live for to take the risk that some cop, angry over her lawsuit win, would delay a backup call when she needed it most. Hell, even Marco had wanted her to quit. She had a good life—a man who loved her and a beautiful baby. Marco didn't want her to risk her future because some cop took exception to her action.

"What's your news?" he asked.

"You are now speaking to Phoenix's newest private investigator."

"Excuse me," Marco said, not certain he'd heard correctly.

"Yes," she said. "I needed a little something to get me out of the house every once in a while."

"Sounds good to me, but why a P.I.?" he asked even as he realized she'd be a great one.

"It's sort of like being a cop without all the rules. I work my own hours and choose my own cases."

"How does Reardon feel about this?"

"Since he put out his shingle, he's had a lot of cases that needed a P.I. to ferret out information. I'll be working with him."

"What about the baby?" Marco asked. "He isn't exactly something you take around with you while you're searching for answers."

"Sure I can. News flash, Marco, but babies are portable."

"But they cry." As much as Marco loved Daniel, he was still a baby.

"That's what our mom is for. You know we haven't had a baby in the family for a while, and mom is really grooving on Daniel. I'm lucky if I get to change a diaper when she's around. Not that I'm complaining, but let's face it, if I didn't have a snack bar attached to my chest, I wouldn't get a chance to hold my kid."

Snack bar! Breast-feeding. Women's issues. "I don't want to know, Elena."

She laughed long and loud. "You are so easy, Marco. Roberto is really happy I have you to tease. Otherwise, he'd be the target of all my sick, twisted commentaries. And if you refuse to come on Sunday, I will hunt you down and I will force you to look at my C-section scar."

Marco rubbed his forehead. "I don't want that. I don't want to see your scars, or know about your snack bar. I'll try to make alternative arrangements, but you'll have to tell Dawson why I'm at my birthday party and not on duty."

"I don't know how she intends to come to the party and expect you not to."

"Dawson's coming to my party?" He felt a moment of panic. He couldn't have his boss at his birthday party. What the hell had Elena been thinking to invite Dawson?

"Of course. Why shouldn't she?"

He had a thousand reasons why not. He didn't like bringing his work home. He didn't like the feeling that Dawson was keeping tabs on him. "Can you un-invite her?"

"Even if I wanted to, I would be too afraid."

He understood. No one crossed Dawson. Not even the newer, gentler Dawson who was still a bulldozer in her off moments. "Okay. I guess she can come." What was he going to do with Lily? Could he get her to come to his party? He doubted it. His reading on agoraphobia had been educational. What he'd learned had made his blood run cold. Not the concept of the problem, but the fact the Joe Sawyer could kill her any time he wanted. The man was toying with her. All he had to do was pick his day and she wouldn't be able to run away.

"Spoken like a true Jackson," Elena said.

Deep down he didn't want to leave Lily alone. In these past few days, he'd grown attached to her and her eccentric ways. "Though it wouldn't be much of a party if the birthday boy couldn't attend."

"Stop worrying. I have a plan."

Marco groaned. "Do I wanna know your plan?" When they had been kids, her plans had frequently gotten them into a lot of trouble with their mother.

"See you Sunday, bro." Elena disconnected.

Marco disconnected and then dialed the department to talk to the tech guys. He had an idea on how to set Lily's mind at rest as far as Natalie was concerned, but he didn't know if his idea was workable. After ten minutes with the tech department, he disconnected and headed toward the back of the house to tell Lily what he'd found out.

As he entered the hall, she opened the door to her office and smiled at him. "Guess what?" she said, "I just got off the phone with Cher Dawson. Your birthday party has been relocated to here."

Marco skidded to a stop. "What did you say?"

Lily looked delighted. "I understand you were talking to your sister earlier and told her you wouldn't be able to attend your own birthday party. Well, she called Cher Dawson and Cher Dawson told me the party would be here instead of your sister's house."

Fabulous, he thought as he glanced at his watch. Just what he needed; both his family and Dawson in the same room as Lily. "I only talked to Elena ten minutes ago. All this happened in ten minutes?"

Lily grinned. "Now you know, the girl grapevine has been hard at work on your behalf. This is the part where you say thank you?"

Marco's head reeled. How could he resist that sweet earnest smile? "Thank you." I think. He tried to imagine the Jackson clan in this huge house. The men would all congregate in the media room to watch all the sports channels known to human kind. And the women would sit in the living room and dissect their problems trying to figure out how to get Marco, Angelo and Giancarlo — the last of the single Jacksons — married off. "I appreciate your interference."

"Not mine. Cher Dawson had the idea to move the party here. I only gave my okay."

Could he just cancel the whole thing? If he called his mom, she would understand. No, scratch that. His mom would want to know why, and he didn't have an answer. "Now that the party location has been settled, I have news, too." Marco entered Lily's office and she followed him, her face alight with curiosity.

"What kind of news?" she asked as she sat down in the large recliner in front of her aquarium. Harley lay down in front of her and rested her head on Lily's feet.

"I've been trying to figure out," Marco said, "how to communicate with Natalie. Since her jaw is wired shut, she can't talk and with broken fingers, except for one index finger, she can't write. I spoke to the tech people at the department and they came up with the idea of putting a computer in her room along with a security camera so that you can see her to make certain she's all right. With the one unbroken finger she can type and the two of you can communicate."

Lily held up a hand. "I've got that covered. I called Home Bound, Inc. and they're already on their way to her hospital room to install a computer and a camera."

He'd been so proud of his idea and she'd already figured it all out for herself. "Wait a second. I don't want anybody going in Natalie's room I don't know about. She's under twenty-four hour guard."

Lily suddenly looked worried. "Do you think Sawyer will try to do something else to her?"

"Hard to say. The point of the whole attack was to frighten you. But when I was standing in the same room as this guy, all I could think of was that I would feel more warmth sitting on top of a glacier. Sawyer was nice and friendly, couldn't have been more helpful. But I got a bad vibe off him the minute I laid eyes on him. The point is, I don't know what he'll do."

"Thank you," she said.

"For what?"

"For everything. You're taking care of me and you're taking care of Natalie."

"No problem. I have to make a couple phone calls so that my people are expecting your people." *Don't look at me like I'm your hero.* Marco had made a vow he would remain distant, but how could he when she turned liquid chocolate eyes on him and smiled. He was uncomfortable. He was becoming emotionally involved with Lily and this worried him.

He needed to get away from her right away and find his bearings.

Lily watched him leave the room. She could still feel the imprint of his lips on hers. Every part of her wanted to do more than kiss. She yearned for him to touch her, wanted to feel his body next to hers. She shouldn't want more, not with Joe Sawyer gunning for her. Yet she felt a moment of hope that he could overlook the limitations of her situation and think about building something with her. No, probably not. What could she offer him?

She went to her desk and saw a piece of paper with doodling on it and the initials M.J. in a corner. Very accomplished drawing. She studied the paper and realized that Marco was a very good artist. How fun, she thought.

She turned the paper over and found a doodle of herself. She smiled. She was drawn as a super hero with one foot stamping on the neck of a snake. She peered closer and saw that the snake had Joe Sawyer's face on it. Beneath the drawing was a series of names. Super Lily with the super marked out. Lily Max with max marked out. Mighty Lily with Mighty inked out. And finally Tiger Lily with several circles around it and a tiny tiger face across her rather large and intimidating breasts. If she really had breasts that large, she'd fall over.

Marco thought she was Tiger Lily and she was oddly comforted by that. She wanted to feel strong. She thought her life was out of control, spinning crazily toward some horrifying rendezvous with fate. And here Marco thought she was something much more capable.

He was different from any man she'd ever met. He had a sweetness, a gentleness to him that attracted her. He wasn't at all like the cops she'd met while writing her books.

Marco reminded her of Quinn Munson. Despite the fact that he had been big and burly with a prizefighter face, he'd had a whole different personality inside. Marco had that same quality. Despite his broad shoulders, big hands and muscular body, he had a different personality inside, too. He was sensitive and thoughtful. And he had drawing talent.

The little ink drawing of her super hero persona almost jumped off the page. Marco understood composition and anatomy. Though she to admit, the breasts were a little bigger than reality. But there were no flat-chested comic book babes and Marco had the kind of talent the comic book companies looked for. If he hadn't been such a top cop, would he have chosen a different path for himself? Like a comic book artist?

Something nudged her arm. Harley looked up at her with a hopeful expression in her sad eyes. "I don't want to be your friend," Lily told the dog. "My cats don't like you. You're big and you drool." The dog licked her hand. "Stop that."

She had never much wanted a dog, but damn, here she was bonded with the man's hound. Lily hugged the dog and Harley licked her cheek. Lily rested the side of her face against the dog's neck and listened to the calm even breathing. Everything about Harley was calm and serene, as though nothing would ever rock her world. She had everything she wanted, a roof over her head, three meals a day and an owner who adored her. Lily was almost jealous.

Harley yawned and Lily was overcome with vaporous bad breath. She opened a drawer, pulled out a box of mints and tossed one into the dog's mouth. Harley chewed experimentally and sniffed the box. Lily was delighted to discover her breath was much improved, and tossed her another mint.

She picked up Marco's doodling and tracked him to the kitchen.

He was making a fresh pot of coffee and stood with his back to the door.

"What is this?" Lily held out the doodle.

He shrugged. "Nothing. I tend to doodle when I'm thinking. Helps me organize my thoughts."

She pointed at the Tiger Lily drawing. "I seem to be occupying your thoughts. I'm not sure I like that. What do you have to say about that?"

"Give me a sec while I think about an answer that will allow me to retain my masculinity."

She broke into laughter. "This is a great drawing. You could illustrate comic books."

He looked sheepish.

She stared at him. "You've thought about that, haven't you?"

"When we're kids, we all have fantasies and illustrating comic books was my fantasy job. What was your fantasy job?"

Lily bit her lips. She'd never told anyone her fantasy, not even her parents. "I wanted to be an astronaut. Go up in the shuttle, and do cool things floating around in space." Her mother had once told her that anything was possible, but Lily knew that her fantasy would never happen.

His eyebrows rose in surprise "That's different."

"I wasn't always agoraphobic. I played outside and rode my bike just like other kids." Even though the feelings had always been there, she'd managed to control them. But then Joe Sawyer had come into her life and changed everything.

"You don't think being a writer is a fantasy job?" He poured water into the coffee maker and turned it on. He opened a cabinet and reached for a mug.

"As far as jobs go, writing is probably one of the best you can have.

But I sort of stumbled into writing. I could write at home and after Sawyer, I thought the more I knew about the criminal mind, the better off I'd be. Writing true crime books is my way of dealing with what happened to me. Every time I write a book and expose the bad guy, it's like a victory for me. Another step forward in my life that distances me a little bit more from what Joe Sawyer did. There has to be a bigger reason why you draw than to just organize your thoughts."

He glanced at his feet. "I actually write stories to go with my drawings."

"Have you ever tried to get them published?"

He shrugged. "They're not that good."

"I don't believe you." She waved the doodle of Tiger Lily in front of his nose. "This is good stuff. Tiger Lily would make a terrific comic book heroine, even with those too big hooters. If you want I'll call my agent and see if he has any contacts in the comic book industry."

"No." Marco grabbed the paper away. "I don't want you doing that. My doodles are just a hobby. I like just having this as a hobby. I really like being a cop."

"But ...."

"I do more good as a cop than I ever would as a comic book artist. I don't need you calling your agent."

"Far be it from me to help you. Can I keep this?"

"Sure, be my guest."

So much for trying to be friends. This was going to be harder than she thought. "Thanks." She stamped out of the kitchen and headed toward her office. She hadn't promised not to help him in some way. She grabbed the phone and called Home Bound, Inc. to get the number of the rare comic book dealer in Memphis who hadn't left his house since 1987. Although she had never chatted with him online she knew he was in Home Bound Inc.'s business registry. Marco was in for a big surprise.

—⟋⟍⟋—

Walter Innis' office in the Capitol building was small and dark without any windows to give it some semblance of space. The desk overflowed with case files, and Walter Innis looked as though he wasn't making much headway with his violent crime task force.

Innis was an average looking man with brown hair receding from his forehead and alert blue eyes that saw everything. His nose had been broken one too many times and was slightly canted to the side. He gestured Marco to a chair. "What can I do for you, Detective Jackson?"

Marco had thought about the different ways he could enlist this man's help, and finally decided on a direct path. "Two years ago you were the lead investigator on the Alexander murder-suicide. Reading between the lines of the case files, I don't think you were satisfied with the final conclusion." Marco really wasn't certain that's what he intuited from the file, but Innis wasn't a stupid man.

Innis settled back in his chair, his face thoughtful. "What's Cold Case's interest? That investigation has been closed a long time."

"There's been some recent activity."

"Really." Innis sat up straight, looking interested. "What kind of activity?"

"Lily Alexander was sent a human heart the other day and her assistant was assaulted. Miss Alexander has been receiving threatening phone calls. She is quite adamant that her parents were murdered. I wanted your thoughts on the matter."

Innis sighed. He swiveled slightly in his chair. "I know Miss Alexander was not satisfied with the final conclusion. I wish I could have found something, anything to support her claims, but I couldn't."

This man was an important man and Marco didn't want to antagonize him by implying that the case wasn't as it seemed. "But you weren't satisfied either."

"Frankly, Detective, if I could have had more time on that case I would have been happy to use it, but the fact remains the most logical conclusion was murder-suicide. Her father was terminally ill."

"But according to the medical report from his doctor, Mr. Alexander still had a couple years left. He had bad days, but he wasn't bedridden."

Innis shook his head. "Suicide isn't uncommon in cancer patients."

Marco shrugged. "I'm not disagreeing with you. I don't know if I'd want to go through chemo. But murder-suicide. That's pretty drastic. Everyone who knew Regina and Lowell Alexander insisted they were a happy loving couple. Their social life was active despite his illness and they were planning a cruise to the Mediterranean. They'd recently contracted for some work to be done on the house, and Lowell had just signed on to an experimental program at the hospital which was showing a lot of promise. These are not the actions of a suicidal man."

Innis shook his head. "Playing devil's advocate, Detective, do you really know what goes on inside the mind of a man who's terminally ill?"

"No, sir, I can't say that I do. I'm simply stating the fact that Mr. Alexander was intending to keep his appointments, go on vacation and add an enclosed swimming pool to his house. What could have happened to change his attitude?"

"A dozen things you or I can't comprehend."

"But still, if Lowell Alexander were planning suicide, don't you think he'd cancel everything. If he's not going to benefit from that swimming pool, then why bother making the arrangements? And making a hefty down payment. The man was still working. Let's face it, if you knew you were terminal, would you still want to be a cop, or take yourself down to Mexico and wallow in Margaritas and senoritas."

A faint smile appeared on Innis face. "I'm a skiing man. Have a cabin in Colorado. That's where I would want to check out."

"One other thing that bothers me, the Alexanders hadn't updated their wills. In fact, they hadn't even started to get their ducks in a row. Most men who suicide tend to make certain their affairs are in order. He wouldn't have wanted his daughter to have to sort through all the leftover debris without some safety net."

Innis nodded. "You've raised the same questions I had. I went over this in my head a few dozen times myself, but kept coming back to the logical conclusion. I looked at the crime scene a dozen times trying to see if I'd missed something, but there was nothing there to support that they were both murdered by someone else. I was backed up, carrying several cases, including a child homicide, and I was under a lot of pressure to wrap up the investigation. I just didn't have the time to devote to developing other leads. Sorry, Detective Jackson, I know you were hoping for some insight. I just don't have it."

"No need to apologize," Marco said. "I remember the pressure to find the murderer, or move on." And he hadn't been the least bit unhappy to leave all that tension behind when he'd been transferred to Cold Case. At first, Marco thought he'd miss homicide, but he hadn't. And now he knew he wouldn't go back without a fight.

"I'll be honest with you, Jackson. The whole set up bothered me. I've been a cop way too long to know when something doesn't feel right, but I couldn't come up with anything concrete to support my gut feeling that Miss Alexander was correct in that both her parents were murdered."

"What about Joe Sawyer?"

Innis frowned, shaking his head. "That man is a popsicle. There's nothing going on inside him. I doubt he registers a pulse."

"So you're saying you didn't much like him."

"Hell, no. I'd rather get in bed with a sidewinder than split a soda with Sawyer. But if you're leading up to the question of where Sawyer was at the time of the Alexander deaths, I checked his alibi three ways from Sunday and couldn't find a hole in it. He's an upstanding deacon in his church and according to his church members; he was feeding the homeless, or clothing the poor, or taking care of the huddled masses. Whatever he was doing, his alibi was tight. I couldn't shake it and I couldn't prove otherwise. What's your course of action?"

Marco thought for a long moment. "I am going to wear Sawyer down until he makes a mistake. I have Lily Alexander under twenty-four/seven protection. But the fact is, I don't have a time frame. I can work this case for the next three days, or the next three months. My gut tells me Sawyer is the one. I just need to catch him doing something and then he's mine."

"I like Lily Alexander. She's one of the good guys. If there's anything my office can do, or anything I can do, just let me know. I have a lot on my plate right now, but I can spare some time to help."

Marco stood and extended his hand. "I just might take you up on that offer."

"Don't quote me," Innis replied, "because I will deny this until my dying breath, but as far as I'm concerned Sawyer fucked with Lily twelve years ago and he's doing it now. He killed her parents and he's behind what's happening now. He's not going to stop until he kills her.

She got away from him and that isn't sitting right with his twisted ego."

Marco thanked Innis and left, walking out into the hot summer sun. Innis felt that Joe Sawyer was one slick, smart bastard who had managed to slide around his suspicions and that wouldn't have been easy. But Marco was a different story. He had nothing better to do than dedicate all his efforts toward insuring that Sawyer got what he deserved ... a needle in the arm and a pauper's grave.

CHAPTER SEVEN

The Kentucky Fried Chicken was filled almost to capacity. Students, with off-campus privileges from a local high school, stood in long lines at the counter. The servers scurried back and forth rushing to keep up with the flow of orders.

Marco loved KFC. McDonald's was number one on his list of great places to eat. KFC was second.

Beatrix sat across from him in a booth. "Marco Jackson, you're related to one of the city's finest restaurateurs, and you want to eat at Kentucky Fried Chicken?" She pushed the pile of books to the back of the table.

Marco shrugged. "I like KFC. What's wrong with that?" He liked eating at Reardon's restaurant, but it required a suit and tie. He wasn't dressed for fancy meals. Hell, he didn't feel like he was properly dressed to even drive Lily's Volvo. But she had insisted he take it rather than letting it sit idle in the garage.

Beatrix pointed to his four pieces of fried chicken. "Heart attack. High blood pressure. Cellulite. Zits." She pointed at each piece.

Why did some people feel the need to point out the dire consequences of grease, spicy coating and fat? He stared at his food. "I myself would consider it winning the game if I checked out with a piece of fried chicken in my mouth, rather than in a hospital with tubes sticking out all over me and hooked up to a thousand machines."

Beatrix frowned. "I can see your point, but I don't happen to agree with it." She took a bite of her salad.

Marco grinned at her. "You just want to look pretty when you die."

"I'm not amused." She sipped her iced tea, her slender fingers tapping against the plastic.

Marco held up his fork. "Cole slaw." He almost smacked his lips at the dripping sauce, already feeling the tart taste against his tongue.

She eyed the slaw with disdain. "Thank you, no. Who's with Miss Alexander?"

"She's bonding with my sister and mom." He tried not to worry about the plans the three of them were probably hatching for his birthday. He didn't understand why he had to celebrate growing another year older, sort of like celebrating another year closer to the big end. "Tell me what you've found out regarding Sawyer."

She shuddered. "I've been checking into his paper trail. There's really been no unusual credit card activity; he maintains a stable bank account, no odd purchases. He goes to the dentist every six months and has filed his taxes on time. He seems like a model citizen. Sort of."

"Sort of in what way?"

Beatrix frowned. "He's making all the right moves, but there's something calculated about it. Like he's trying not to draw attention to himself. Except I did find out that he's trying to get his voting rights re-instated."

Marco stared at her in surprise. "How do you know that?"

"Because I have a friend from college who works in the voter registration office."

"So why does this raise your suspicions?"

"Because everything he's trying to do, and is doing, is designed to prove how upstanding he is. And one of the things about predators like Sawyer, they don't suddenly recover. One of the pieces of information I've found regarding predators who've been prosecuted is that they just become better at being hunters."

"You've been reading those criminal justice books again, haven't you?" Marco said.

She patted the stack of books next to her. "Let's just say, I'm revisiting old friends."

"Hunter, by the time I'm done with you, you're going to be one damn good detective."

She smiled and blushed slightly. "That's what I want."

"Can I ask you a personal question, Hunter? Why, of all the things you could have done with your life, did you join the police department?" She just didn't seem like cop material. She was too refined, too ladylike and too sophisticated to be a cop. Not that she couldn't be, she just didn't feel right.

She smiled. "Because it upsets my mother no end. When I graduated from college at the top of my class, the only thing my mother said to me was 'what are you going to do with an education when all you need to know is how to find the right kind of husband, get married and produce refined, well-bred children.' And I thought to myself, that can't be my only purpose on this earth."

"That's a pretty tall order." Marco wiped his fingers on a napkin. The napkin fell apart. So much for eating neat.

"Confidentially," Beatrix said, "and pushing my ego aside, I thought I had more to offer. Not that marriage and children aren't important, but I wanted more. Your own sister wanted more. Any man can have his career and his family. How come women are supposed to choose between them?"

"My sister did choose. She chose marriage and family."

"But she's applied for her private investigator's license and intends to open her own agency. I think she's going to have more fun being a

PI than she ever had being a police officer."

"How come everyone finds out before me?"

Beatrix laughed. "Your sister and I have lunch together a couple times a month."

He wondered what they talked about. "My sister is having way too much life for a married woman."

"Spoken like a true man." Beatrix frowned at him. "I'm jealous. Elena has everything, a great husband, a beautiful baby, and a new career she's going to be incredibly successful at. And she has really great hips."

"Excuse me." Marco stared at her. What did great hips have to do with success? Sometimes women totally confused him.

"We took a sauna together. Her C-section scar is this big." She held up her fingers about two inches apart. "I don't know how the doctor removed a baby through it."

Not C-section talk again. Marco held up his hands. "Stop with the chick talk. Dammit, I'm a man and I don't want to know." Why did every woman he knows confide in him?

Beatrix laughed. "Elena told me you have a thing about the realm of women. What are you going to do when you get married? Keep your wife wrapped in cotton?"

"Cotton's good." Was something wrong with him because he wanted to take care of a woman? A woman like Lily. He would enjoy taking care of her.

Hunter shook her head. "Now that we've established that you're still a male chauvinist, shall we move on to the case?" She flipped open a leather bound Day Runner.

Back to Joe Sawyer. Marco had a bad taste in his mouth. He didn't like Joe Sawyer. "I know Sawyer murdered Lily's parents. I know he's stalking her. I don't know how, but I'm going to get him."

Hunter gave him an odd look. "Is a gut feeling considered proof of guilt?"

"Not proof of guilt, but a reason to look deeper."

"Then you'll be pleased to know I have an appointment with his parole officer at 2:30. I'll let you know what he says, but first, you may as well know Sawyer is man a lot of people respect. I talked to some members of his congregation this morning and they all think he walks on water."

"They don't know him like we do." Marco sipped his chocolate shake. "Doesn't he have a ministry downtown? If I remember correctly, some hole-in-the-wall church that ministers to the homeless and needy."

The homeless!

For a second Marco's mind turned around that fact. "After you meet with his parole officer, go down to the coroner's office and get a photo of that homeless John Doe they brought in a couple days ago without his heart. Head back to Sawyer's church and see if someone can identify him. And if someone does identify him, see if you can find out if he was close to anyone there, namely one Joe Sawyer."

Hunter wrote something in her notebook, nodding. "What else?"

"Find me a smoking gun."

She slanted a glance up at him. "You don't ask for much."

Marco sighed. "You're a real detective now, Hunter. Asking questions is what you do." She'd make a good detective once she decided that she was. No one quite understood why a woman with a hefty trust fund wanted to work for a living. Especially at a job as thankless as being a cop.

"Okay, smoking gun." She wrote in her book. "How are things with you and Lily Alexander?"

"That's kind of a personal question, don't you think?" Marco wanted to snatch the words back as soon as they came out. They made him sound personally involved.

A speculative gleam shone in her eyes. "But inquiring minds want to know. How come you managed to obtain such a cushy stake-out job?"

"You think I want to stay in that house, being a nursemaid to some neurotic writer?" *Hell yes.*

"Let me put my spin on this. You get to spend your days in one of the most luxurious houses in Phoenix with one of the most famous people this fair city has to offer who also is quite beautiful."

"I hadn't noticed." Hopefully he sounded convincing.

She gave him a look that told him she didn't believe one word of that comment. "That the house is nice, that she's famous, or that she's beautiful?"

Hunter was certainly a lot smarter than she looked. His best tactic was plausible deniability. "You have been hanging with my sister way too long." Marco shuddered to think what they talked about. "I don't want you seeing my sister anymore. You're getting ideas just like hers."

Hunter burst out laughing. "A woman with an idea, isn't that a lethal combination. Everybody down at the station is jealous of Ms. Alexander. Especially Whitaker. The Lieutenant brought in an article from Architectural Digest and he saw her media room, and he wants that room. Plus, she has her own state-of-the-art gym which Greyhorse is salivating over. And frankly, I saw her kitchen. I want that kitchen. If I had a kitchen like that, I might learn to cook."

They had no idea what a price Lily paid for all that great stuff. She couldn't leave even if she wanted to. "It's still a prison."

"But with velvet bars. I did some reading on agoraphobia and the doctor who wrote the article said some agoraphobics don't want to leave."

Anger surged through Marco. Beatrix didn't understand. She made Lily sound like a grade A kook. Which she wasn't. She just had a big, ugly problem. "The woman has been through hell. If she wants to sit in her house for the rest of her life, then she has every damn right to."

Hunter opened her mouth, closed it, and smiled. "I can see the lady has quite a knight in shining armor in you, Jackson. No matter how you try to deny it, I always thought you had a lot more chivalry in you than you like to show."

He relaxed; he should have known Hunter didn't mean to be unfeeling. She was one of the nicest people he'd ever run into. He held his finger to his lips. "Don't tell anybody."

"Your secret is safe." Hunter glanced at her watch. "If I'm going to make my meeting with Sawyer's parole officer and still get to the church before dinner time, I'd better get going. Don't you have a fair damsel to protect?"

"Yeah, I guess I do."

After Hunter left, Marco sat in the booth to finish his chicken. He liked being needed by Lily. She seemed so fragile and delicate on the surface, what man wouldn't want to protect her, but he knew deep down inside she was a survivor. She walked through hell and came out with most of her soul intact. She had a core of steel that had helped her weather any storm.

Over the years he'd seen his share of victims who were broken by what happened to them. After Sawyer, who could expect her to still be whole, but she did carve out some kind of life for herself. And he had to admit he liked being her protector, even though he had the feeling she was going to drive him crazy over the next few days.

Beatrix sat in Gregory Hammond's office. He was a middle-aged man with a receding hairline and a look of perpetual anxiety on his round face. He searched through the towering pile of manila file folders on his desk, muttering, "Sawyer. Sawyer. I'm sure it's here somewhere." He swiveled in his chair and opened a drawer of his file cabinet and ran his fingers over the tabs, his lips moving as he read the labels.

Finally, he pulled a folder out of a drawer and smiled. "Here it is."

Beatrix breathed a sigh of relief. She'd started worrying she'd be stuck with him all afternoon. "What can you tell me about Joseph Sawyer?" She gave him her pleasant, never-fail smile, the kind she used when she was inviting confidences.

He blushed and flipped open the file, read for a few seconds and then smiled. "He's the kind of con who makes my job easy. He's on time for his appointments, he passes his drug screens, he's polite and well-mannered. Has a job and is paying taxes. He's a poster boy excon. Don't have too many like Sawyer."

"How do you mean?" Beatrix asked, tapping her forefinger on the battered armrest.

Hammond frowned. "You know, within a year most of the cons have re-offended and are sent back to prison. Sawyer doesn't even have a ticket for jaywalking."

"That doesn't necessarily mean he's rehabilitated. In my opinion criminals who do jail time simply come out of jail bigger, badder, and smarter. Prison isn't hard time, it's more like Crime University."

"Detective." Hammond sneered at her. "I've been doing this job for twenty years. I've seen every criminal there is from the petty misdemeanor to the hard-case. All of the visible signs tell me that Joe Sawyer is reformed. He's changed his ways. He goes to church, is an ordained minister and doesn't give me grief. I have no reason to harass him. Why are you looking at him again?"

Hunter's eyebrows rose. Interesting, she thought. "What do you mean–again?"

Hammond shrugged. "A couple years back, some detective came in to ask me questions about Sawyer in connection with a double murder. He didn't give me any details. And I gave him the same speech I'm giving you. The man has a job, a wife, and found God. He doesn't cause me to lose any sleep."

Beatrix wondered how much she should tell this man. In the end she figured honesty was the best way to deal with him. "We believe he's stalking a woman, and that he's connected to the brutal assault of her assistant."

"And you have proof?"

Beatrix almost sighed. "Nothing concrete." How could she tell this man, who wanted to believe in Sawyer's redemption, that she had nothing to go on but the gut feeling and sweaty palms of another detective.

Hammond's eyes narrowed and he fingered the edge of a file. "So you want me to take your hunch in a handbag and rip this man's life apart?"

Beatrix understood that the parole office was under-staffed and over-worked, but they owed the public safe streets. "It's not as if you don't have the authority."

Hammond shook his head. "I am not going to bring him in, do a strip-search, tear his house apart, go to his job and remind everyone he's a convict. To all appearances, Joe Sawyer is doing his best to fit into society and keep a low profile. Unless you have some hard evidence that I can act on, I'm not disrupting this man's life."

Beatrix leaned forward. "I don't understand why you're making my job harder."

Hammond patted the pile of folders on his desk. "If you had asked me to do this with anyone else, I'd do so in a second, but Joe Sawyer simply hasn't given me any reason. He counsels ex-felons. He's paid his dues. I can't help you."

"Twelve years ago, he kidnapped a young girl and held her for five days in the desert. He tortured her."

Hammond shook his head. "I say again, Detective, Sawyer has done his time. In the eyes of society, he's reformed."

Beatrix cast about for an argument that might sway him. "What about Lily Alexander? She's still doing time. Where's the fairness in that? That man brutalized her and we believe he's still doing so. Excuse me, if we inconvenience your model ex-felon a little bit."

He pointed at the stack of files that littered his desk. "Do you see these files? In that pile, I have three arsonists, seven child molesters, two wife beaters, a handful of murderers, robbers, and any other criminal you could care to name. I even have some guy who likes to make time with the local pooches."

The mental image in her mind made her shudder. "I don't want to meet this guy." She didn't want to meet any of them. But being a cop meant she would eventually be exposed to all kinds of criminals. Maybe she should go back to being Officer Friendly. At least she didn't have to face the harsh realities of her job. Her mind rebelled. No. No matter how hard her job was, she would never go back to being Officer Friendly ever again.

"Don't worry, you're safe from him, unless you sprout a tail and two hind legs, he doesn't want to meet you either. I have to run rough shod over these guys. I don't have time to roust out Joe Sawyer, who's playing by the rules."

Be at one, girlfriend. Be at one. She forced herself to calm down before she said and did something stupid. "I understand you are

115

incredibly over-worked, but I'm in the middle of an investigation. I wish you'd be more cooperative because you make me feel guilty about going to the county attorney and filing a complaint. Tomorrow morning, you can have this same conversation with him." She stood up and gathered up her stuff.

"You do what you have to do, Detective." He opened a file and bent over it, dismissing her.

Beatrix felt as though she were five years old and having her hand smacked. "Good day, Mr. Hammond. I'll talk to you tomorrow." She stalked out of the office, and down the hallway to the bank of elevators. The doors of one obligingly opened and disgorged two women and a scruffy looking youth who shuffled down the hall after tossing a leer at Beatrix. She frowned at him, then stepped into the elevator.

My God, I'm a hard-ass. I'm a true hard-ass. Pride swelled in her. She couldn't wait to tell Marco that she'd acted like a real detective. For the first time, she knew she was going to love working in Cold Case.

In her car, she flipped open her cell phone and called Leland Davenport. Her heart went into overdrive at the sound of his husky voice when he answered the phone. "I need your help." She explained Hammond's lack of cooperation to him.

There was a long silence. "That's highly unorthodox, Detective."

"Yes, I know." She felt vindicated dropping Davenport's name.

"You thought you could drop my name out of the blue to get what you wanted." He sounded annoyed.

"The governor is my godfather. I thought I'd work my way up slowly." Beatrix tightened the grip on her cell phone, trying not to snap at him. "Why are you giving me a hard time?" She'd had enough 'hard time' from Hammond to last a lifetime. "I thought we were on the same side."

"Detective Hunter, you may handle your job in a free-fall manner, but I like rules. You should have come to me first."

He made her sound like a shoot-from-the-hip cop. She was no such thing, and she started to object, but decided tactfulness with Lee Davenport would work more to her advantage. "I'm sorry. I had no time. The parole officer should be cooperating with the police department, not the parolee. Had I known it would turn into an issue, I would have happily come to your first." That ought to satisfy him.

His tone was resigned. "Meet me at nine tomorrow morning at the Starbucks across the street from the courthouse and we'll talk."

The thought of seeing him again made her breathless. "You were giving me a hard time on purpose, weren't you?" She didn't know whether to be angry or amused.

"I rather did enjoy doing that." He chuckled.

Beatrix leaned her head against the headrest. "I'll see you in the morning." Again that breathless little thrill slipped through her.

"I'm looking forward to it. Until then...." He disconnected.

Beatrix stared at her phone. What was it with these people? Everyone tested her, pushing her to see how she would react. First Cher. Then Marco, and now Leland Davenport. Why couldn't they just trust her? Did she have to shoot someone, to get some respect on this job?

Lily watched Marco kiss the baby on the cheek, kiss his mother on the cheek and then ruffle Elena's hair as though she were only five years old. Watching him interact with his family reminded her of how much she missed her parents. With them gone, she often felt rudderless. Her mother had been such a powerful force in her life, making her leave the house, do the research on her books, even accept a couple dates here and there. Nothing major, nothing with a man she might want to form a relationship with. Most men had little patience with her problems.

But Marco did. And she studied him as he opened the front door and helped his sister stow all her baby stuff in her minivan. He never chided Lily about her inability to go outside. One man she had dated a few times had thought that by leaving her in the restaurant to force her to cope would make her grow up. Instead, she ended up in the hospital under heavy sedation after a severe panic attack. She'd never spoken to him again.

Another thought occurred to her. She had really missed him while he was gone. During the afternoon, no matter how much she enjoyed visiting with Elena North and Connie Jackson, she caught herself looking at her watch, almost counting the seconds before he would return. What a novel feeling. As radical as it was disconcerting.

Connie smiled at Lily. "We'll see you on Sunday. I realize we've sort of taken over your day."

"Not a problem," Lily responded. "I'm pleased to have the party. My house hasn't seen much activity lately." At least not the happy kind. Maybe the party would take her mind off her own problems.

She liked Connie. The woman was a dynamo and she could understand why Marco was in awe of his own mother.

Marco kissed his mother on the cheek and helped her into the car. He slammed the door and stood on the path watching Elena navigate around the curved driveway and out onto the street.

Then he turned and glanced up at Lily. "You seem to have hit it off with my sister and mom."

"We had fun." Lily stood back from the door, watching as he

stepped into the shadowed foyer and loosened his tie.

He stuffed his tie in his pocket. His lean fingers almost tore at the buttons of his shirt. His honey gold skin stood out against the stark whiteness of the white fabric. She had to stop herself from sighing with delight.

"What have you found out so far?" Lily asked as she led the way down the hall and into the kitchen.

"Do you really want to hear all the boring details?" Marco perched on a stool and bit into an apple.

"Yes, every single one of them. I live for detail." Writing was detail work, following trails of evidence and verifying every bit of information. In some ways, Lily loved the details best.

He swallowed his food. "I talked to Detective Innis to get his perspective on your parents' deaths."

"What did he say?" Lily opened the refrigerator. Marco looked uncomfortable. Innis had never been particularly forthcoming with her. Not that he'd ignored her, but he hadn't really listened to her either. He'd shown her every courtesy, but in such a detached manner that Lily had sensed a certain indifference with regard to his handling of her parents' death.

"He wasn't exactly satisfied with his conclusions."

She slammed the door. "What the hell do you mean by that?"

She set a head of lettuce on the counter and reached for a salad bowl. Innis had never once hinted to her that he wasn't happy with the investigation.

Marco eyed the salad dubiously. "Is that all we're having for dinner?"

"I made ribs. I just have to heat them and you'll get your fat quota for the whole year."

"Did my mom help you?"

"Yes, she gave me your great-great-grandmother's secret recipe."

Marco smacked his lips. "Okay, for that I'll suffer through the rabbit food."

This felt so domestic and comfortable. "You didn't answer my question." She pulled lettuce leaves apart and dropped them in the salad bowl.

"I was hoping to avoid an answer." He took another bite of the apple.

As she tore the lettuce leaves into bite-size bits, she glared at him. "Don't try to distract me. I know all your tricks. What did Innis say?"

Marco finished the apple and tossed the core into the garbage disposal. "He said no matter how he looked at the case and the facts, he didn't believe your father murdered your mom and committed suicide, but he didn't have any evidence to suggest otherwise, nor the time to find it."

"I see. So that means my parents were pushed out of the way for the sake of convenience." She knew she shouldn't be so unsympathetic, and she knew the pressure homicide cops were under to solve the crimes they could solve to make their numbers look good to the media.

He shook his head. "You're taking this the wrong way."

She sliced a tomato, hacking away at the red globe, venting frustration. "How am I taking this the wrong way?"

He took a deep breath. "You're not going to let me sugar-coat this for you."

"I want it between the eyes with both barrels." She worked best with the truth.

Marco sighed. "You've worked with enough cops, and know as well as I do that homicide cops are overworked. There's always pressure to get in and get out as soon as possible. If a case is a sinker, we move on to the one that can be won."

At least he looked a bit ashamed having to admit the truth to her. "So my parent's murder was a sinker." Her voice was flat and emotionless. She knew Innis had tried, but from her perspective not hard enough. Pain knifed through her to think her parents had been shuffled to the side for the sake of something that could be solved more easily.

"Frankly, Lily, after examining the official paperwork, it was. Half of homicide work is on hunches. All too often the hunches go nowhere. I didn't feel right about your parents' murder, and the fact is, if my photo and a human heart hadn't ended up on your doorstep, I wouldn't be here either, no matter what my sweaty palms are telling me."

A shiver went up her spine. No matter how this turned out Marco was on her side. He had no idea how important that was to her. "Thank you." At least, he intended to try.

"For what?"

"For calling my parents' death a murder." She couldn't look at him. The light that shone in his eyes was too overpowering. He was becoming very important in her life, consuming her thoughts and sending her emotions into overdrive. She should make more of an effort to distance herself from him, not let her emotions rule. Eventually, he would leave and she would stay behind unable to go away with him. She couldn't face the pain.

She turned away and opened the refrigerator again and pulled out the tray of ribs. She opened the oven and popped the tray inside to heat while she set the table. If she kept busy she wouldn't have to look at him with his deep soulful eyes brimming with sympathy for her.

"You've worked your way around murders before," Marco said, "at least through the back end as a writer. You're pretty savvy about the criminal mind. Tell me what you think Joe Sawyer saw in you."

She could talk about this. Talking about Sawyer meant she didn't have to bare too much of her soul. "With only one known victim, me, I can't come up with a victim profile where anything in particular stands out."

"You're the only victim that we know of."

"That's true. But maybe he's simply obsessed with me."

"Maybe." Marco frowned.

"I have a contact in missing persons."

"You get around, don't you?"

Lily smiled. "I have a pretty good rep with a lot of police departments, district attorneys, the FBI, and I have a confidential source inside the CIA. Just in case I want to do something international." She worked hard to maintain those contacts. And she could see he was impressed. She liked being able to do that. Somehow she figured impressing Detective Marco Jackson took a lot of hard work. She liked that she could do that.

"My, my, for someone who doesn't leave her house, you do get around."

"I do my best." She took a bottle of wine from the wine cooler and opened it to breathe for a few minutes. She enjoyed having someone to cook for, to do things for. The heating ribs began to cast a spicy aroma over the kitchen and she felt a growl of hunger deep in her stomach.

The phone rang and Lily answered. For a long moment, she frowned hearing nothing and then she heard a loud thump and a blood-curdling scream. "Please don't hurt me," came Natalie's voice. A few more thumps and a slapping sound. Yet it couldn't be Natalie, she was safe in the hospital with her armed guard. Had Sawyer somehow gotten to Natalie anyway? No. Something was odd about the voice. It had a tinny quality. Then she realized she was listening to a recording. She almost dropped the phone, but had the presence of mind to hand it to Marco.

Marco put the receiver to his ear and listened, his face grim and tense. He glanced at the caller ID box. "Who's number?" He pointed at the digits outlined on the display.

Lily clutched at her throat with cold hands. Black dots danced in front of her eyes. Her whole body felt tight. She couldn't breathe, couldn't move, almost couldn't speak. "That's Natalie's apartment."

CHAPTER EIGHT

Leland hung up the phone and stared at it. Beatrix was right. He had been giving her a hard time. Why, he didn't know. The fact that she was smart, sophisticated and beautiful probably had something to do with why he felt the way he did.

He didn't really mean to be a hard-ass, but this was his first job working in a criminal capacity, and every minute since he'd accepted the job, he was feeling his way through hoping he was doing the right thing. But truth be told, he felt like a baby fish swimming up stream.

As low man on the totem pole, he had not been in a position to reject the offer. Despite the fact that Cold Case was doing a good job, the county attorney's office had the attitude that Cher Dawson's success was just a fluke, a temporary thing that would eventually fade away.

Had he made the right decision to leave his job as a clerk with the Supreme Court? Why had he come back to Phoenix? He could have gone anywhere from a Wall Street firm to the upper political echelons in Washington D.C. But deep down inside, those jobs had not appealed to him. He had wanted to return home because he wanted to break through the big glass ceiling of Phoenix's conservative, cowboy mentality.

He picked up the phone and his secretary answered. "Get me Gregory Hammond at the parole office."

While he waited, he studied his office. It was small, plain, functional, and lacked a window. Some day, he'd have a corner office and a view of the city. Don't let anyone say that Lee Davenport didn't have ambition.

When Gregory Hammond answered, he sounded flustered. "What can I do for you, Mr. Davenport?"

"Tomorrow morning at 9:30," Lee said, taking pleasure in the other man's discomfort. "Detective Hunter and I will be paying you a visit. When I get there, I want every report, every notation, every scrap of paper you have regarding Joseph P. Sawyer."

Hammond stammered. "But ...."

"No buts, Mr. Hammond. This is official business. And officially if the information I've requested isn't on your desk, the only butt you'll be worried about is your own. Have I made myself perfectly clear?"

"Yes, sir."

"Good. Have a nice evening." Lee hung up the phone feeling cocky. He'd exercised his power and felt righteous. He was on a crusade.

He would have a good time cleaning up this cowboy town. Today, the county attorney's office. In a couple of years, the mayor's office, and a few years after that, he could see himself in the governor's mansion. And who knew where he would go from there.

Marco put his cell phone down on the counter. What the hell was happening with Lily? Her face had gone ashen. She gripped her throat with one hand and her chest with the other. Each breath she drew seemed to take huge amounts of energy. She was having an anxiety attack. He remembered her breathing into a paper bag the day she'd received the human heart.

He opened drawers in the kitchen and finally found a pile of brown paper lunch bags. He grabbed one, opened it and covered Lily's mouth. She grabbed the bag and started breathing into it. He held the bag to her lips, her hands wrapped around his. Her fingers were as cold as ice.

Her eyes were wide with panic and she looked so fragile he wanted to hold her.

"It's okay," he murmured soothingly. "It's okay. Do you have something you can take? Where is it?"

"No ... meds." She breathed into the bag.

He helped her sit down. "A glass of water. Some whiskey. What can I do for you?"

She stared up at him. "Hold...me."

"I can do that." He slipped his arms around her. Her whole body was cold and she trembled. "Do you want me to call an ambulance? A doctor?"

"I'll...be...fine." She breathed and after a few minutes seemed calmer.

He reached for his cell phone with one hand and quick-dialed Hunter. When Hunter answered, Marco outlined what had just happened and told her to get to Natalie's apartment ASAP. He disconnected.

"Let's get you to bed." He eased her off the stool and out of the kitchen. She leaned heavily against him all the way down the hall to her bedroom.

When he opened the door and eased her inside, he discovered a new aspect of her personality. The room looked like the African plains except for the huge bed covered in a canopy of mosquito netting in the center of the room. One wall was painted with a huge mural of the Serengeti plains. The chairs were upholstered in leopard print and white and a black zebra-striped rug was positioned in front of them. Spears and masks were mounted on wall. Plants decorated every surface adding to the jungle setting.

He eased her onto the bed. She lay back against rust red pillows and closed her eyes. He tried to back away, but she wouldn't let go of his hand, so he lay on the bed with her, easing his arms around her trying to still the bone-shattering trembling.

Though her skin was still cool, she was soft and curvy in all the right places. Heat gathered at his core, and an arousal started, and he felt guilty.

He curled her into the curve of his arm. She gripped his hand tightly as though she'd never let go. She was strong.

He had to stop himself from getting turned on. He started running through a montage of random thoughts. Baseball. Basketball. Football.

Lily's breathing seemed to calm. She still held the bag tight to her lips. When her breathing finally evened out, she closed her eyes and started to drift into sleep. Marco tried to ease away, but she wouldn't let go of his hands. She snuggled closer to him, the chill leaving her body. Marco held her. She smelled like baby powder, fresh and clean. His eyes started to close.

His cell phone rang. Marco came wide-awake and stared around him. Lily murmured, but didn't wake up. He eased away from her and answered his phone as he walked across the room and out into the hall.

"Jackson," he said.

"Hunter, here. I'm at Natalie Gould's apartment."

"What's going on?"

"We found a tape recorder next to the phone. Apparently, Miss

127

Gould's attacker recorded everything. The crime scene people are here, but whoever broke in is pretty slick and didn't leave anything behind for us to find. I've got a couple of uniformed officers canvassing the apartment building, but I'm not holding out any hope."

Marco had dealt with some really sick stuff in his day, and Sawyer was up there with the major league freaks. "Did you talk to Sawyer's parole officer?"

"Yes, and what a cooperative man he was." Hunter's voice was heavy with sarcasm.

Marco glanced in the bedroom. Lily clutched a pillow to her chest. She looked five years old. He backed away and headed toward the kitchen.

"Did you take the guy to the mat?" he asked.

"No, I'm letting our brand new county attorney have the pleasure. According to the parole officer, Sawyer is a model everything. Every criminal who gets out of jail should be so reformed; so rehabilitated. Sawyer has everything but a halo."

"Call me a cynic, but anyone who's that good is covering something up. Trust me. I ought to know. That's how I got through my childhood."

Hunter chuckled. "Elena told me you were one of those. She said they had this name for you."

Marco groaned. "Please, just leave it unsaid. My siblings were jealous because they weren't smart enough to avoid trouble."

"If you say so, Squeaky."

Marco closed his eyes trying not to growl. He was going to punish his sister. She would inform no more.

"Do you want me to bring Sawyer in for questioning?" Hunter asked.

"We don't have anything concrete at the moment. If he lawyers up, we could lose him in the shuffle."

"But—"

He thought about his meeting with Sawyer the other day. "This guy has learned all the legal tricks and is playing them with ease. I'm not losing him because I don't have enough evidence yet to play with. Let him think he's pulled one over on us. Let him get comfortable."

"But," Hunter objected again, "is that the right course of action?"

"Hunter, a good detective never does what the suspect expects. Sawyer is sitting in his house right this minute waiting for you to show up. He has his lawyer's number on speed dial. Let him think we're stupid. He's counting on that fact. When he finally gets comfortable, he'll get arrogant. The more arrogant he is, the more likely he'll make a mistake. And then we'll have him."

"So we're playing chess, are we?"

"This is the ultimate cat and mouse game. Sawyer's a pussy cat, I'm King of the Beasts." Marco mentally rubbed his palms together. This was the kind of investigation he thoroughly enjoyed. In homicide, most of the cases were slam-dunk. The investigator went right to the family, rattled the tree and a nut fell out. This was a different animal all together. Sawyer required another playbook.

"Correct me if I'm wrong, but I just got a sense that you're enjoying this case."

"Hunter, it's all about the thrill of the hunt. This goes back to cave man days, me and the saber-toothed tiger, one on one, with nothing but what God gave us."

Hunter sighed. "This is way too much testosterone for me."

"Tell me you don't feel that little tingle, that rush telling you you're on the right scent."

"I never thought about cop work that way."

"You've been stuck in media way too long."

"Not by choice."

"You have two options here. You can either stay on the porch like a good little puppy, or you can take your place in the pack. And if you're going to be part of the pack, then you'll have to be a hunter. No pun intended. And if you hunt, then you have to know how to kill. Are you ready to make a kill?"

A long silence, and then Hunter said in a somber tone. "Do you trust me to make the kill?"

"I do."

"Then I hope he stops at the water hole soon."

"That's what I'm talking about, Hunter. Beneath that Grace Kelly demeanor, those polished debutante manners and your designer suits, you have a taste for blood." He disconnected. For second he stood in the hall contemplating his next move. His stomach rumbled and he remembered the ribs still heating in the kitchen. He opened the oven. The ribs were still drenched in sauce and would keep for another time. He turned the oven off and put the ribs back in the refrigerator. The salad had wilted and he tossed it. Then he headed back to Lily's bedroom.

She lay on the bed curled into a fetal position. Marco debated the wisdom of crawling back into the bed with her, but he couldn't stop himself. As he settled his body against her, she snuggled against him. He smoothed her hair.

Joe Sawyer was a sadistic, evil bastard. Marco wasn't going to let him hurt Lily. He didn't care what he had to do, or what price he had to pay, he would keep her safe.

Lily felt warm and comfortable. She floated through the gentle, billowing clouds of sleep. As she snuggled deeper, a hand crept around her waist and she came to full wakefulness in a second. A hand at her waist!

She felt someone shift and she twisted her head to find Marco in bed with her. For a moment she was startled.

He lay on his side, his eyes closed. He looked so at peace. Afraid to move, she studied him. In his sleep, he had a little boy quality about him that she found endearing. He had the longest eyelashes. She had to buy stock in Maybelline to get eyelashes like that. His lips were pouty, sensual, and almost feminine, yet they didn't detract from his masculinity. She wanted to kiss his lips, to taste the sweet nectar of his promise.

She edged closer to him, touching him lightly, feeling the power that seemed to hover just beneath his skin. She eased up on her elbow.

The memory of his last kiss surfaced and she paused to relive the moment. She closed her eyes and again felt the pressure of lips against her. A tingle started deep down inside her that spiraled outward until her fingers trembled.

She eased closer to him breathing in his scent. He smelled of Spring Breeze fabric softener and spicy aftershave. She ran her fingers lightly across his cheek and she could just feel the stubble of his beard.

Marco's eyes fluttered open. "Hi."

"Hi yourself."

"What are you doing?"

Lily could feel the heat of embarrassment on her cheeks. "Would you believe thinking about my mystery novel?"

"Nope."

"I'm thinking that you have really long eyelashes."

His eyebrows arched and he scooted closer to her. "And what was your conclusion?" He fluttered his lashes at her.

"That life is so unfair."

"You garnered all that from staring at my eyelashes?"

His leg crept in between hers. A man hadn't made a pass at her in a long, long time, but she knew exactly what Marco was doing. And the gesture was really nice. "Yes."

"And to think I wasted all that time in Psych 101, when all I had to do was study my eyelashes."

She laughed. More like giggled. Marco had a marvelous talent for bringing out the little girl in her. "Women spend a fortune in cash and pain for the eyelashes you were born with."

"I'll donate them to some deserving female on my deathbed."

"You are really silly sometimes."

"But in a good way," he teased.

"Have you ever been in love?" She couldn't believe she could be so bold as to ask such an intimate question at such a critical moment. His mouth was so close to hers, his hot breath fanned her cheeks. One small move forward and her lips would connect with his.

"No." His voice trembled.

"Me either."

"Why is that?"

Somehow, she paused worried she would come off sounding like a whining two-year-old who couldn't get her own way. "My life is complicated." *Now that was an understatement.*

"Okay I lied," he said. "I was in love once."

"With who."

"Emma Glass."

"Oh."

"She was my second grade teacher. Had a thing for older women when I was seven. I was in love with the girl who sat in the front row, too, but that was just puppy love. She was two weeks older then me.

I'm a man now and love takes on a whole new meaning. And when the right woman....." He ran his fingers along the curve of her hip.

Lily could feel her nipples grow taut as his hand slid up her arm. What the hell was she doing? This was all wrong. "The right woman?"

His fingers slid under her shirt. "When the right woman comes along, a man forgets about any woman in the past and begins to think in terms of forever."

"Do you think you'll ever find such a woman? As a grown-up?" *Any woman loved by him would be nurtured and loved for the rest of her days.* She held her breath while waiting on his answer.

"Perhaps." His fingers slipped over her belly, fanning outward.

Lily bit the inside of her bottom lip. Marco kissed her, his lips claiming her with raw intensity. His tongue probed between her lips. She leaned back against the pillows. Slowly, he unbuttoned the front of her shirt revealing her small breasts. "I want you."

"I know." She stared at his hands, soft and tender on her skin. His callused thumbs circled her nipples. He took one nipple in his mouth, tugging at it with his teeth. Lily groaned. Heat spiraled outward. His tongue flicked a nipple and he licked the underside of her breast. Hunger tightened in her stomach. She was lost.

"Are you sure you want to do this?" he asked.

Lily arched her back. Her mouth opened and his tongue moved over her lips. "Love me." Her skin burned, the sweetness of arousal grew until she thought she would burst.

Emotions played across his face as he slid her shirt off her shoulders and then down to the waistband of her skirt. He undid the zipper and pushed it down. She raised her hips to help him, aware of his fingers as they moved down the length of her leg brushing against her skin leaving hot trails behind. Free of her skirt, he shoved it off the bed. He leaned back to look at her. She resisted the impulse to cover her body.

He undid the button on his pants and in seconds he'd slipped out of them. He was ready for her.

She took in his wondrous body. Every muscle on his chest was defined and sculpted. A thin trail of black hair dusted his honey-colored skin. His small flat nipples were the color of milk chocolate. The sight of him excited her beyond reason.

She touched his chest, feeling his heartbeat. His nipple hardened beneath her searching fingers. She slid her hands across his tight stomach, feeling every corded muscle beneath the smoothness of his skin.

He grabbed her wrist as her hand moved lower. "Don't." His voice was choked.

"Why?" She felt powerful and ready to show him how ready she was to be loved by him.

"Are you sure?"

"One would think you haven't had a woman in a long time." She was amazed at that thought.

He swallowed hard. "Not a special one."

"Why?"

"Casual encounters hold no allure for me." His eyes were intent on her face.

"You mean this isn't casual." A nervous tremor vibrated though her. How could he consider her anything but a casual moment in his life?

"Nothing about you is casual." He nudged her legs apart and lowered himself to lay between them, his sex hard against her thigh. He nibbled at the hard nubs of her nipples.

She writhed, whispering his name. Her gasping cry sounded needy and incomplete.

"You're so beautiful," he murmured against her ear.

Each stroke of his fingers electrified every nerve in her body. He kissed her in the valley between her breasts.

"I want to look at you." He rolled on his back and pulled her over him, her legs straddling his hips, his arousal tight against her inner thigh.

He caressed her breasts, his thumbs moved over the soft skin. "Do you trust me?"

She nodded too overwhelmed to speak. The muted glow of the night lights highlighted his skin, his face. Carefully he lifted her, shifting her body to allow him to penetrate her. She settled on him again, her knees against his waist. He was so big he filled her. She couldn't comprehend where she ended and he began.

He stroked her, gently touching the entrance to her body, to caress the sensitive core.

Lily shuddered in passion. Waves of desire crashed through her. Her skin was on fire. A spasm built inside her. She arched her back and began to rock back and forth. She spread her hands on his massive chest, balancing for a better position to increase the intensity of her pleasure.

He pulled her face down to kiss him. His breath ragged. "That's it, Lily. Love me." He moved his hips beneath hers.

The pressure built and built. Lily had never felt such exquisite pain and torment. Her body sought release, the friction sending her into a frenzy of wild, voluptuous pleasure. She cried out, whimpering his name over and over. Her moans tangled with his voice as he repeated her name over and over again.

His back arched, driving him deeper into her until finally the pressure exploded, rippling through her. They climaxed together.

Long after Marco fell asleep with one arm over his face and the other holding her tight to him, Lily lay on her side, cheek against his chest listening to his heart beat and feeling the rise and fall of his breathing. She ran her hand up and down his chest and he turned toward her, his arm tightening.

She didn't want to go to sleep; she wanted to lock this memory in her mind forever. She loved him. *Strange that is such a short time she could come to love him so much.* She would love him forever.

Lily woke a few hours later to the feel of a strong hand teasing her breasts.

"Lily," he said in a lazy tone. His hand slid lower, roaming down her stomach until his fingers moved against the nest of curls between her thighs.

She clamped her legs together capturing his hand.

He nibbled her ear. "You're a feisty woman. I think I have to love you into submission." His fingers wriggled against the sensitive skin.

She opened her arms to him and surrendered to his demands.

CHAPTER NINE

Marco woke with the sun streaming through the window. He was starving. He reached out, but Lily was gone.

A faint, tantalizing smell wafted into the bedroom and he smelled cinnamon and bacon. She was cooking breakfast, so last night was okay with her. *Damn, it had been okay with him.*

He lay on his back and stared at the ceiling. For a woman who didn't get out, she knew a hell of a lot about loving a man. Though she'd been tentative and nervous at first, she hadn't been afraid. He wanted her again and again. His body responded to the memories of the night, and he wished Lily were still with him.

He stomach growled again. Food or sex. Food won. He would need sustenance to love her the way she should be loved. Did he have time for a shower? No, he liked smelling of baby powder, smelling like Lily.

He sat up and pushed off the sheet. He searched for his pants and was surprised to find a stack of clean clothes on the chair next to the bed.

Lily opened the bedroom door and stuck her head inside. "Breakfast in ten minutes. You have plenty of time for a shower." She started to close the door.

"Wait a minute."

She blew him a kiss. "Can't wait. My bacon is burning." She shut the door.

Marco stood and stretched. Last night had shifted his universe.

Behind that feisty exterior Lily showed the world, she was one hell of a passionate woman. She'd been insatiable. Just the memory made him hot.

He headed to the bathroom and found that it was an extension of the bedroom with leopard print towels, tiger striped rugs and elephant prints on the wall. He started the shower and stepped in to let the water wash over him.

The depth of Lily's passion surprised him. Once she'd gotten over her initial shyness, she'd explored every inch of his body and when they had settled into a comfortable rhythm, he had been enchanted with her. The memory brought a smile.

Out of the shower, he dressed and headed toward the kitchen. He entered and stopped to stare. Harley stood on her hind legs, towering over Lily. She fed the dog a piece of bacon, then she settled back on all fours. Lily picked up another piece of bacon and Harley rolled over on her back, all four paws in the air. Lily bent over and patted her head and gave her the bacon. Her two cats wound around her legs and she tossed them little nibbles of bacon as well. They gobbled the meat down as greedily as Harley.

Marco chuckled. "You two seem to be getting along pretty well."

"She's not bad for a dog who thinks she's a Chihuahua." Lily picked up another bacon strip and held it. "Roll over." Harley obeyed, Lily dropped the bacon and Harley gobbled it down.

"You're not giving away my breakfast, are you?"

"I made you waffles. I made Harley bacon."

"I do tricks for bacon, too." He thought about his first one.

She grinned at him. "Had I only known that last night."

His heart did a funny little wobble at the sight of her elfin grin. She tossed another piece of bacon to Harley who snapped it out of the air and gulped it down. She offered another nibble to the cats. One sniffed and decided she was full. She jumped up on a chair and stared with bright green eyes at Marco.

Marco sat down at the table, studying the way Lily poured coffee into a cup and handed it to him. She seemed different somehow. Or maybe he was. She wasn't an investigation anymore, but something more personal. He had a stake in keeping her safe.

"We need to talk," he said as she set a plate of waffles in front of him. She placed butter and syrup on the table.

"About what?" She sat down across from him with her own plate of waffles. She dabbed butter on the waffles and sprinkled them with powdered sugar.

"You." He spread butter over his waffles glad his mother wasn't there to scold him over his eating habits, then lathered them with syrup. He stopped pouring, assessed the level of syrup and then added more.

Her face took on a wary look. "What about me?"

He'd been thinking about her safety all night long. "I want you to leave this house and go some place safe."

Her hand paused over her coffee cup. A look of panic filled her eyes. "I...I can't."

"Not can't. Won't."

She bit the inside of her lip. "What's the difference? I'm not leaving this house."

"You're not safe."

"You're here." She held herself rigid.

A pit had opened in his stomach. "I don't know if I'm enough to stop Sawyer. Cher would take you in a minute." He would never forgive himself if something happened to her.

"I can't live with Cher. She has a brand-new husband and a daughter."

"What about my mom? You like her. She likes you."

Lily shook her head. "What if Sawyer does to your mother what he did to Natalie?"

Marco almost smiled. "My mother would kick his ass. We don't call her the Italian lethal weapon for nothing. When she was done, we'd need DNA to identify the body."

She frowned. "Your mother was so nice when she was here."

"You've never been on the other end of her wooden spoon."

Lily look surprised. "Your mother spanked you?"

Even though he was an adult, the memory of being spanked was still fresh. "Just once. After that the threat was enough. I got the message. But we're not talking about my personal life; we're talking about you. This is too much house for one person to guard properly."

Stark fear radiated from her whole body. "I'm not hiring security guards. I won't have strangers in my house."

"I was a stranger once."

She smiled at him, her eyes soft and inviting. "You were never a stranger."

"Stop practicing your feminine wiles on me. This is a serious issue." He forked waffle into his mouth and chewed, realizing that these were better than his mother's, and Connie's waffles were the best.

"Do you think I don't know how serious this is? I've been living with the threat that Joe Sawyer intends to kill me for a long time now. I'm not leaving. I'm not hiring strangers. Whatever Sawyer has in mind for me, I'll face him here on my territory." Her voice held a bitter tone.

Marco understood her fear, but he couldn't let that stop him. "Do you know how to use that gun you own?"

"Point and click." She raised a finger and pointed it at the wall clock.

"Do you think you can look someone in the face, and squeeze the trigger knowing you're going to take their life?" Marco thought about the first time he'd killed a man and he still had nightmares. "Taking a life isn't easy, not even for a cop."

She closed her eyes and sighed. "I don't know."

Marco pushed his plate away, his appetite gone, his mind whirling with the problem of protecting her. "That's not the answer I wanted to hear."

She opened her eyes. "You tell me, Mr. Cop Man, can you kill someone?"

"I already have."

She turned away, a pensive expression in her eyes. "Tell me about it."

Marco refused to be sidetracked. "You're not taking this conversation down a different path. I want to know if *you* can kill someone. Or are you going to be one of those women who have their gun taken away and used on them?" He didn't add that too many female assault victims were killed with their own weapons because they hesitated. When a cop took his weapon out of his holster, he was primed to kill with it. Otherwise the weapon remained in the holster.

"Sawyer killed my parents. He's stolen a large part of my life away from me." She straightened her shoulders. "I could kill him. I have in my dreams. Over and over again. You don't know how many times I've wanted to leave this house, find him and make him suffer the way he has made me suffer. I still have nightmares about being trapped in that shed wondering when he was going to kill me. He dressed me up like his doll; he touched me; he told me he loved me and that I would be his forever. After he went to prison, I didn't leave this house again for a long time. I could kill him, just to get a good night's sleep again." The new resolve formed in her face. She gripped her fork and stared at it. "I'll kill him."

Silence fell between them. Marco could hear the ticking of the clock on the wall. "I won't make you leave, but I want you to hire someone."

She shook her head. "I won't involve anyone else in this madness. Only one person stands between me and Sawyer and that's you. I'm depending on you and I'm putting my money on you."

The weight of that responsibility landed squarely on Marco's shoulders, and he felt slightly dazed by her vehemence.

Lily licked her lips. She pushed away from the table and stood. "I need to clear my head. If you want me, I'll be in my exercise room."

Breakfast lay forgotten on the table. Marco slid back his chair. He carried his coffee into the office and pulled out his cell phone. He called Hunter and when she answered, he asked about Natalie's apartment.

"I had the crime scene team go over that apartment with a fine-toothed comb. This guy is a ghost. He didn't disturb one speck of dust, or leave behind anything. Except that he broke off the crime scene tape on the door. I even had them take the phone to the lab to see if they could find anything."

"He's smart." Actually Sawyer was frightening. The only way they would get his is if he made a mistake. "Lean on him. Lean on him hard." As Hunter talked, Marco doodled. He found himself re-drawing Tiger Lily and changing her costume to one even skimpier than before. He deepened the cleavage and added prominent nipples.

"Leland Davenport," Hunter said, "has been reviewing the situation and he's in our corner. In fact, we're going to have another talk with the parole officer. By the end of this day, I feel that I will be witnessing Sawyer's strip search."

Marco winced. "I remember those days."

"You've been strip-searched."

Marco flashed on the image of Lily sitting on him, her hands stroking him, bringing his body to full arousal. He chuckled and didn't answer.

"Marco Jackson," Hunter said, surprise in her voice. "Are you telling me that while I've been working my fingers to the bone, you've been having more than a professional relationship with the beautiful, intelligent, charming, and might I add, extremely wealthy, Lily Alexander?" Hunter burst out in a musical giggle. "I'll finally have something to bring to the lunch table next week."

"Hunter," Marco's voice was low and husky, "if you even begin to imply that my relationship with Miss Alexander is anything but appropriate, I'll smack the blonde out of your hair."

"You can't, it's natural."

"You're a natural blonde?"

She giggled again. "There are a few of us in the world. But don't worry; your secret is safe with me. I wouldn't do anything to harm Lily; I really like her. And so does Elena. And your mom."

Great! He was doomed. He might as well pop the question and marry Lily now. "Have you done the background check on Lily's parents?" Back to business, he thought, not liking where the conversation was heading. Next thing he'd be hearing about Hunter's sex life. Or what she knew about Elena's sex life.

"I've been talking to friends," Hunter said, "and a couple of distant cousins, and the most I've gotten out of anybody is that her parents were terrific people, well-liked in the community and that her father was the last person anyone would have thought would murder his own wife and then suicide. In fact two people who don't even know about Lily's problems with Sawyer swore that her parents' death had to be murder and that the police didn't do their job."

"Good job, Hunter."

"Thanks," she replied.

"I'll talk to you later." He disconnected and put his phone away.

Lily walked in. She held her portable phone to her ear, and wore a gray sweatshirt and matching baggy pants. "I need it here by Saturday," she said into the phone. "Charge my American Express." She disconnected and looked up, startled.

"Put what on your American Express?" Marco asked casually. Not that Lily's business was his business, but he was curious and suspicious. With his birthday party being moved to her house, he wondered if she were getting him a birthday present. He worried that Elena had explained about the family tradition of gag gifts. "Nothing." She connected the phone to the charger and a tiny red light went on.

"I thought you were working out."

"I'm on my way. I just had to do something first. Boy, a woman sleeps with a man and he thinks he runs her life."

Marco felt heat spread across his cheeks. He hadn't been thinking that.

Lily circled the desk. "What I should be doing is working on my book. I can't seem to get around a block."

Marco was amazed. "How can you have writer's block when you write true crime stories?" All she had to do was write what already had happened.

She bent over, opened a file drawer, and pulled a pile of papers encased in a red file folder. "My agent and my editor talked me into attempting a fictional mystery. It's not going well." She frowned as she opened the file and held up the top sheet.

Marco craned his neck to read over her shoulder. "I've taken a few writing courses. Maybe I can help."

She glanced at him. "What do you know about writing? The only thing I've seen is your doodles." She pointed at the scantily clad Tiger Lily posed on the open sketchpad.

"I've dabbled in writing." He'd taken courses in comic book development, creative writing and a few art classes to control his artistic muse. "A story is a story. You have the basic elements of structure, dialogue, conflict, mystery. What else can there be?"

She eyed him skeptically. "Are you one of those secret cop writers?"

"Like I said, I've dabbled, but haven't the time for anything bigger."

"Ideas don't make a novel. Writing makes a novel. Something of which I haven't been doing a lot of lately." She replaced the paper in the folder and closed it, her fingers tapping the desk.

"Why not let me read your story while you're on the treadmill?" He would have done his own exercising, but he'd already showered and he didn't want to change into his grubby clothes and then shower again. Besides one night with Lily was probably equal to the Boston marathon. She'd been insatiable and he still could feel the tickle of her fingers on his skin.

"Okay." She stood, pointing at the pile of paper. "This is it. All one hundred and four pages. Which at some time, in the near future, needs to stretch to four hundred pages."

He thought about telling her about his own modest effort at short story writing, but didn't. The two stories he'd had published had been in cop magazines, and he didn't know who that would impress except other cops. Certainly not Lily, who'd already published so many books.

She kissed him and wished him good reading and left the office for the exercise room. Marco picked up the manuscript and whistled for Harley. When the Great Dane had thumped through the house and out the door to the back yard, Marco found a lawn chair on the patio and started reading while Harley sniffed curiously at rocks and rolled in the sandy dirt.

The morning was still cool, but heat waves shimmered in the distance. In an hour, the temperature would be in the nineties. But for the moment, Marco enjoyed the pleasant feel of the desert.

A few storm clouds had gathered on the horizon. Summer was monsoon season and Marco liked seeing the desert come to life. A hawk flew in an ever decreasing spiral and then suddenly dived into the brush. When it reappeared, it clutched something in one claw and headed toward the mountains to the east.

Marco read, engrossed in Lily's story, and not until he turned over the last page did he come back to the present. The story was good, but he could see where Lily had boxed herself into a corner. He thought of different ways she could solve the problem, making a few notes on his sketchpad.

As always, his pencil started doodling again and a new Tiger Lily emerged on the page. This one with no clothes and only long, curly hair hiding her most important assets from view. He'd been turning a story over and over in his mind and he'd even sketched the first couple of frames, but hadn't gotten too far. Suddenly it gelled and he started reworking it. Tiger Lily to the rescue! Then he crossed that out and wrote The Adventures of Tiger Lily.

Harley growled low in her throat. She sniffed the ground and suddenly took off on a gallop toward the fence.

Marco looked up, the manuscript and the comic book story forgotten. The hair on the back of his neck stood. For a long time, he sat in the chair analyzing why he felt so odd, as though someone was watching him.

At the wall surrounding the house, she barked and whined. She reared back and braced her front paws against the stucco.

Marco placed the manuscript on the glass patio table, stood and discreetly looked around. He saw nothing but the sandy desert, two saguaro cacti, and lots of rocks and sand. Yet the feeling someone watched him wouldn't go away.

He whistled for Harley, but Harley wouldn't leave the wall. Marco walked down toward her. She whined at his approach. All the while he searched, trying to find anything out of place. Nothing.

He walked along the edge of the wall toward the wrought-iron entry gate. He peered out through the gate at the neighboring houses. The houses in this area were far apart with empty expanses of desert between them—a sharp contrast to his postage stamp back yard.

Too much isolation for Marco. He liked his own little house tucked away in its own little neighborhood with his neighbors only twenty feet away on either side. Not too close, but not too far away. He opened the wrought iron gate and ordered Harley to stay inside. He walked down the street. A woman at the house across from Lily's stood out on her driveway with two poodles dancing around her legs. She waved at him and he waved back.

As Marco headed back toward the house, he again felt as though someone watched him. He scanned the surrounding area trying to pinpoint where a watcher would be, but saw nothing that would seem an obvious place. If Sawyer was out there, he'd concealed himself well.

He needed surveillance on Sawyer, but didn't think the department would approve it. As much as Dawson was behind him on this investigation, she still had a budget. He whistled to Harley, who came lumbering across the patio. Marco retrieved the manuscript and slid the patio door open and walked inside the cool living room.

He pulled his cell phone out of his pocket and dialed his father.

His dad had been a Phoenix cop and had retired to a plush position as a pretend cop on a TV show filmed in Phoenix. The show was on hiatus for the summer and his father was always looking for something to do that would get him out of the house and away from Connie watchful eye.

"Hey, Dad," Marco said when his father answered.

"What's up?" his father asked.

"How would you like to organize some of your old gang to do some surveillance work for me?" Marco's father had found jobs with the TV show for a lot of his retired cop friends; Marco figured they might relish a chance to get their hands wet again.

His father whispered into the phone, which meant Mom was nearby. "Can I have donuts?"

Marco grinned. His mother had been on a health kick for forever, determined that his father would live to be three hundred years old whether it killed him or not. "As long as you promise that this conversation never happened."

Marco explained to his father what he wanted. The gloves were off with Sawyer, and with his father on the job, Marco would know that man's every move from now until the time he slapped the cuffs on him. The game was over; this was now war.

Lily sat at her desk. One cat was curled up on a corner of the desk, and the other watched the darting fish in the aquarium.

"What took you so long?" She asked when Marco entered. The whole time he'd been reading her manuscript, she'd kept peeking out the patio doors to watch him, wondering what he thought about her story.

"Keep in mind, you are a best-selling author and I've only had two dinky short stories published."

"You have! Why didn't you say so earlier? I'd love to read them."

"I sold them to two cop magazines, which means they don't count in the real world."

"That's more than what most writers ever do." Lily was surprised but quite pleased that they shared more than a love for comic books. They were writers.

Marco fidgeted nervously. "I'd prefer to do a graphic novel."

Lily liked the fact that he was sensitive about his accomplishment; it made him so much more human to her. "You mean like a comic book?"

"You don't need to flatter me. Doing my own graphic novels is a pipe dream. I'm a cop and I'm not serious about writing."

"I think you are." She was certain that somewhere inside of him beat the heart of a writer. She would just have to dig it out.

He shrugged. "Writing is what I intend to do when I retire from the force."

"Why wait so long? Do it now." She wagged a finger at him. "I can see I'm going to have to nag you."

"Let me start by returning the favor now. Do you want my honest opinion about your novel, or not?"

Lily held her breath waiting. She really wanted him to like her story. "Yes, I do."

Marco held the manuscript pages out to her. "You have the great beginnings of a story here. Interesting characters, fabulous voice." His full mouth pouted. "But you can't plot your way out of a paper bag."

That stung. She'd wanted honesty, but not so boldly put. "Okay, my feelings aren't hurt." A little bruised, maybe.

"Before I get into the plot, you're writing this story like it's one of your true crime books. You're telling the action, not involving me in it. You need dialogue and description and you have to iron out your viewpoint. You gave the cat a viewpoint and that's fine if you're going to write a cozy mystery. If you're going to do a hard-boiled P.I, no one is going to care what the cat thinks. Hell, the readers are probably waiting for the cat to buy it."

Lily sighed. "And I was hoping to make it on my name."

Marco laughed. "Listen, let's spend this afternoon just working out the plot."

"What would you do if this were your story?"

Marco shook his head. "This isn't my story. What do you want to do?"

Lily started telling him her ideas and he turned over the first page of the manuscript and wrote them all down. She watched his hands, the same hands that had roused her body to fever pitch during the night. His fingers were blunt, strong-looking fingers and she marveled at how lightly they had danced over her skin.

Harley entered the office and padded over to rest her head in Lily's lap. The dog's breath wafted over her. She opened the center drawer and pulled out her box of mints and dropped one on Harley's tongue.

Marco's eyebrow raised. "What are you doing?"

"Giving Harley a breath mint. She has terrible breath."

"She's a dog."

"Then she has terrible dog-breath." Lily patted her on the head, and the dog lumbered over to Marco and collapsed in a heap at his feet.

"I brush her teeth every week," Marco said. "The vet says she has show-quality teeth."

Lily shuddered. What did show-quality teeth mean? "Are you

telling me they're supposed to smell like that?"

"You just watch. My baby girl is going to be standing center ring in Westminster." Marco patted Harley's head and fondled her pointed ears.

"You show your dog?"

"I don't, but I have a handler who does. Harley has taken every ribbon for the last two years. She's number three in her breed nationwide."

"Really? How can you afford such an expensive dog?"

He batted those long eyelashes. "Mommy loves me best."

Amazed that he could still retain his masculinity, Lily tried not to laugh. "Your mother pays for this."

"My mother bought the dog. She thought if I had a dog, it would show I could commit to something. Besides, dogs are big chick magnets."

She took another look at Harley. What about a Great Dane was a chick magnet? "You are kidding me."

He gave her a solemn look. "Not at all. I take the dog to the park and I can leave with ten phone numbers. And I'm talking about phone numbers from little girls who come over to play with the dog. White haired grandmothers who want to play with my dog, and every age woman in between."

Lily stared at him. She needed to get out more for sure. Too bad she couldn't. "Do all single men know this?"

Marco shook his head. "The average single man is pretty stupid. They think women are attracted to Hugo Boss suits and Gucci shoes. But a dog proves that a man can love and cherish something other than himself. A happy hound means a man can make a commitment. That's the kind of man a woman wants to have children with and make a future with." He patted Harley's head. Harley slobbered all over his hand.

"How come you're not married?" *Thank God he wasn't or they wouldn't be having this conversation.*

"That's what my mother explained to me when she brought Harley home. Personally, I think she was hoping my paternal instincts would kick in; I'd find myself a wife and breed a pack of grandkids to make her happy. Connie is the most devious mother on record."

"Why haven't you?" The question had been on her mind all morning. Men like Marco Jackson were few and far between. How had he managed to elude marriage and family?

He pointed a finger at her. "Now, I'm going to give you a quick lesson on plot structure."

Lily glanced around the room. "Was that me, or are you avoiding the subject?"

He grinned. "Pacing is an integral part of plotting."

"Okay, hint taken. No more nookie talk." He was the most endearing man she had ever known. In some ways, he reminded her of her father. He had the same low-key type of charm that tended to embrace instead of smother, and just enough boyishness about him to be extremely appealing. But he was still all man.

The memory of his maleness again sent heat spiraling through her. For several seconds she held her breath, reliving the long hours of their lovemaking. He had done things to her body she didn't know could be done. After her one affair in college, she'd felt very liberated and sophisticated. And despite a broken heart, she'd made the decision to wait until someone worth the effort came into her life. Marco was worth the effort.

His voice trailed away. "You're not listening are you?"

"Sure I am. I'm listening with my ears, my mind is somewhere else."

"Where is your mind?"

"How did you get the sickle shaped scar on your back?"

"Revealing that information would break the 'sibling code of silence.'"

She crossed her arms. "Now I'm intrigued."

"If I tell you," he said, "then somehow, someway my mother will find out and that was one of the few things my brother Nick and I got away with."

"Do tell." She crossed her heart and lifted her other hand. "I swear, as long as there is breath in my body, I will never reveal your secret."

"I refuse to answer on the grounds that is may incriminate myself. I can do that, it's in the Constitution."

Lily laughed. "That sounds positively felonious."

"A misdemeanor at best. There's no true crime book in this. Just a kid prank."

"No dead bodies hidden in the bushes," she teased.

"You're not going to let this go, are you?"

"I can break you with a snap of my fingers, Jackson." She snapped her fingers.

"Dare you."

She sniffed the air. "I smell a challenge. But at the moment retreat is the better part of valor." Already her mind churned with ways of finding out his secret. She would sniff out the facts. If a direct approach didn't work, then an indirect approach was called for.

"In my neck of the woods," he said, "we call that wimping out."

"Be afraid." Lily winked at him. "Be very afraid."

Marco laughed, sending shivers of desire through her.

CHAPTER TEN

Marco opened the kitchen door and watched as a minivan backed up to the patio, braked and a driver in a gray uniform with a patch over one pocket got out.

"Morning," the driver said as he opened the back door and started lifting out bags of groceries. "Grocery delivery for Miss Alexander." He was young, maybe eighteen or nineteen with flaming red and black striped hair that was too orange to be natural, a stud in his tongue and innocent looking blue eyes that reminded Marco that good kids still existed in the world.

"What's going on?" Marco asked as the young man entered the kitchen holding plastic sacks in each hand.

"How the hell should I know?" He placed the sacks on the counter and headed back to the minivan for more. "I just deliver food."

"Now I can get started," Lily said as she entered the kitchen. "The food is here."

"The food for what?" Marco demanded not liking what he was seeing. If she were going to create a feast for him, he'd never live it down. His brothers would pounce on him and demand to know what was going on between him and Lily. Marco had never been too good at keeping things from them. They could worm things out of him he didn't know he knew.

"Your party tomorrow. Today we're cooking." She opened a tall cabinet containing brooms and hooks with different kitchen type items hanging on them and pulled out an apron.

"You don't have to host the party." Another birthday was no big deal. He'd have to listen to his mother hint about advancing age and a lack of grandbabies as though she didn't have enough of the ones she already had. Then his father would clap him on the shoulder and ask him how his love life was going. His brothers would tease him endlessly simply because they were his brothers, and Elena would act smug because she had found a path for the rest of her life.

"Of course, I do. I want to do this for you." She wrapped the apron around her slender waist and opened the first of the plastic sacks.

The grocery guy brought in more sacks and handed Lily a clipboard. "Please sign, Miss Alexander."

Lily scribbled her name and went back to unpacking the sacks.

The intercom beeped and Marco reached out to answer it. "Yes."

"Delivery for Miss Alexander," came the electronic voice.

"This is ...." Marco queried.

"Special delivery from Home Bound, Inc."

"Buzz him in," Lily ordered.

Considering that Marco was with her all day, he wondered when she had time to place these orders. He buzzed the gate open and a few minutes later the van backed up to the patio. The deliveryman opened the back doors of the van and started hauling boxes into the house.

Marco glanced at the boxes. Each one was tagged with Lily's name and a second label with Home Bound, Inc emblazoned on it.

Marco poked at the boxes. The intercom beeped again. Lily answered, asking for identification. When the delivery person answered, a sly grin came over Lily's face. She directed the newest visitor to the kitchen door. She darted a look at Marco.

Marco opened the door as a car, with *Metro Armored Transport* painted on the side, parked alongside the first minivan. A beefy security guard in a blue-gray uniform got out. He held a briefcase in his right hand that was attached to his wrist by handcuffs.

Marco stared at the handcuffs. "Lily."

The security guard entered the kitchen. "Special delivery for Lily Alexander, please."

"Get out of the kitchen, Marco," Lily ordered.

"What?"

"Leave." She looked excited, with her hands clasped to her chest. She couldn't stand still. "Go." She planted her hands on his chest and backed him out the door.

When Lily told him he could return, the security guard was gone and the briefcase lay in the center of the table.

"What kind of drama is this?" Marco demanded.

"It's here." She patted the briefcase.

"What's here?"

"You can't find out, yet. Not until tomorrow."

Marco stared at her. "You bought me a birthday present that came with an armed guard." Curiosity flared. What could she have bought?

She danced around the kitchen. "You're gonna love it," she sang. "You're gonna love it."

"Give me a hint." He hated the wheedling sound in his voice. Once, he'd found his presents hidden behind the upright piano his mother had forced him to take lessons on. She discovered him peeking at the gifts. She's scolded him, sent him to his room and when he returned the gifts had vanished. He'd searched for days, but didn't find them again until his birthday. Even then he'd hardly recognized them; his mother had completely re-wrapped everything.

"No hints," Lily said.

"Just a hint." His curiosity at the boiling point. "One little hint." Damn it, she'd reduced him to begging.

She tilted her head at him. "All right, one." She grinned. "You're gonna love it."

"That a taunt." Marco pounded on the table.

She rubbed the top of the suitcase. "I have things to take care of. Don't try and open this."

"That's a challenge I can't ignore."

"Tit for tat. Tell me about your scar."

"Tell me what's in the briefcase."

"I can be generous."

"That's not an answer."

She ran her hand along the top of the briefcase. "That's all you're going to get." In a cheesy accent, she said, "I know what your heart desires. I have ways of making you talk."

He grabbed her and kissed her. "Yes, you do."

She laughed and danced away from him. "I have to make a phone call. Be back in a minute."

Marco was enchanted. She looked so alive, so filled with energy. He'd not seen this part of her before.

After she'd left the room, his hands strayed to the briefcase. He picked it up and gently shook it. Nothing rattled inside. What could she have gotten him that required an armed security guard?

He stood back puzzling his way through how he could open the briefcase. His breaking and entering skills were a little rusty, but he had all the right tools. He reached into his pocket and pulled out his Swiss army knife and studied the different accessories wondering which one he could use to open the briefcase. He finally decided on a long narrow tool. He inserted the end into the briefcase lock and tried to work it open. Nothing.

"Caught ya," Lily said from the doorway.

Marco jumped back, heat filling his face. "Just curious." He sounded like a peevish child.

She wagged a finger at him. "Wait until tomorrow."

Marco realized she'd deliberately left him alone with the mysterious briefcase. "You set me up."

She stood straight. "Yes, I did. Just wanted to see how you handle the pressure."

"You are worse than my mother." She had always set him up taking delight in catching him.

"I'll take that as a compliment. Okay, now get out of my kitchen. I have work to do." She shoved him toward the door.

Marco retreated to the office. He pulled out his sketchbook. He flipped it open to his Tiger Lily drawing and started sketching the panels and making notes on the story. The Adventures of Tiger Lily began to take shape.

He had heard the intercom beep and ignored it figuring it was another delivery. But Earl Jackson's voice boomed over the intercom and Lily buzzed him through the gate. Marco went back to his sketching, waiting for his father to arrive.

Earl Jackson was a tall, imposing man with graying hair, piercing brown eyes and an easy smile. After a career with the Phoenix Police Department, he'd moved on to acting. How the transition occurred, Marco was never certain. Just one day his father had announced his retirement from the force and the next day, he was cast as the police chief in a syndicated TV show filmed entirely on location in Phoenix.

Earl walked around the office, his face admiring. "Nice gig you have here." He picked up a Navaho pot and turned it over to read the designer's name. He returned the pot to its place on the shelf. He stood a moment in front of the huge salt-water aquarium and smiled as he watched the colorful fish swim back and forth. "Real nice gig. Connie and I looked at some property in this area a couple months ago. She wants a bigger house. I don't know why, with all you kids gone it's not like we need five bedrooms anymore."

Marco knew his mother was anticipating a house full of dozens of grandchildren spending the summer, but said nothing to his father. Earl would find out soon enough. "Thanks, dad. I have to admit I'm enjoying myself more than I thought I would. How's the surveillance going?"

Earl frowned. "I didn't like doing surveillance when I was getting paid for it."

Marco chuckled. "You're lying. You're thrilled. You're back in the saddle doing what you always loved doing, drinking stale coffee, eating donuts, smoking those smelly cigars, and trying to get the drop on the bad guy."

Earl sat down across from Marco. "Those were the days, my son. Those were the days." Earl's face turned soft with the strength of old memories.

Marco closed the sketchbook. "What's going on?"

"You have us watching the dullest man on the planet, or the sneakiest. So far this guy has gone to work, gone home, and gone to church."

"It's only been twenty-four hours. Give Sawyer some time to mess up. He'll make a move." He couldn't maintain this role for too much longer.

"He's too good to be true and that automatically makes him a suspect in my book. He hasn't done anything that seems out of the ordinary, but I've got a five-alarm suspicion going off in my gut."

Marco knew exactly what his father meant. "Who's helping you?"

"Some of my old cop buddies, a couple of the guys from the show who wanted some experience being real cops, and Elena." His father's face went stormy. "And let me take a moment to say, who the hell does she think she is taking my grandson on a stake-out?" Earl shook his head.

"Do you know she's getting her P.I. license?" Marco still couldn't believe Elena had decided on private investigating as a career choice.

"I know. I know. I don't have to like it. But babies do not belong on stake-outs."

"Dad, Daniel is probably just going to follow in the family footsteps. He may as well get an early start." Daniel wouldn't dare think of something else. Not and live. Jackson men were cops. Looks like North men were going to be cops, too, if Elena had any say in the matter. Since Daniel was already being indoctrinated, Marco figured Elena had his future already worked out.

"I just don't understand the modern woman," Earl said. "Your mom was content to stay home and be a wife and mother."

Marco laughed. His dad had blinders on when it came to his mom. "Why would she trade ruling the whole kingdom for serfdom in someone else's territory? Our home was command central. Why would she go out and work for someone else when she could make us work for her? Mom's a lot smarter than you or I will ever hope to be."

Earl chewed on the inside of his lip. "I never thought of it that way. How sad is it when the son has to give the father the lowdown on women?"

"I'm a man of the new millennium, I know these things." His mother had never been a traditional type of woman anyway. She'd started teaching him his lessons early.

Earl grinned. "Your mom likes Lily. Couldn't say enough good things about her."

Marco felt a softening in his heart. "So do I. Kind of hard not to." He liked every inch of her from the widow's peak at her hairline to her long delicate toes.

Earl leaned forward. "Got any questions? Need advice?"

Marco shook his head. "You were a lot more direct about my love life when I was younger. Why are you skirting the issue now?" In fact, he could remember being drilled by both his parents after every date in high school. His father had been relentless while his mother had watched with a knowing look in her eyes that told Marco one step out of line with a girl and she'd find her old wooden spoon and use it on his backside.

Earl chuckled. "When you were younger you were stupid."

"That didn't hurt my feelings."

Earl laughed. "Boys lead with their hormones. You're a man now. You should know how to use that brain you have between your ears."

"As opposed to other places."

"Yeah!" Earl nodded. "Back to Sawyer. Do you want us on his back, or give him some distance?"

While having his father and his friends watch Sawyer had been a brilliant idea, it did create some problems, like the fact they weren't cops any more. "Since you and your cronies only wear fake badges these days, keep the tail loose. I don't want him knowing we're watching. I'm hoping he'll make the right mistakes and that will allow me to nail him." Just the thought made Marco vibrate with anticipation.

"He's slick," Earl said, "and he's being very careful. A planner. I hate planners. They're hard to catch. They think everything through to the smallest detail and never leave anything to chance. This guy was in prison, wasn't he?"

"For awhile." Marco had decided not to tell his dad too much about Sawyer because he wanted Earl to see the man without a preconceived bias. If his feelings matched Marco, then Marco knew he was correct in his assessment of Sawyer.

"You might consider," Earl said, "taking the time to find out who

161

his roomie was. Guys learn a lot in prison and a lot of times their best teachers are their bunkmates."

Marco frowned. "Sawyer's been out three years."

"If he's been in the habit of confiding in his bunkie, he might still be confiding in him. Who knows what Sawyer learned to do during his incarceration."

Marco had heard his father say that over and over again during his years on the force. Some criminals did see the light and go straight, but most didn't. With experience, Marco had come to agree. He'd call Hunter and have her check on Sawyer's prison playmates.

Earl checked his watch. "I have to get going. I'm playing golf with Chief Sanchez this afternoon. He wants a photo op with a real live actor. Shows how liberal he is. You can do that when you're rich and retired." He shoved himself out of the chair.

Marco rose with him. "Thanks and go easy on the Chief. He's just doing his job."

"I know he is, but I don't like him. I'm working at getting Dawson in his shoes." Cher Dawson as chief. That was a frightening thought.

Lily stalked into the room. She smiled at Earl and then glared at Marco. "I was in the kitchen thinking, and I remember you telling me you have a twin brother. How come you're celebrating his birthday next month?"

Marco grinned. He'd been wondering when she'd ask. Everyone did sooner or later. They'd made that decision early on in their lives for a very specific reason. Besides not wanting to share their birthday, they loved all the extra presents. Since he was fifteen minutes older than Nick he got to choose which date he wanted.

She looked confused, her face all scrunched up in an adorable way. "You gonna tell me?"

Earl grinned. "Because sharing a birthday means only one cake.

Having two birthdays means two cakes. I'm the daddy. That's my rule."

Lily burst out laughing. "So this is a food issue?"

Marco held up his hand, one finger raised. "For dad it's always about the food, but Nick and I didn't like sharing. Two birthdays celebrated on two different days means more presents." He didn't care as much about the cake as he did the presents. He loved presents which shifted his mind back to the locked briefcase in the kitchen.

Earl put a hand on her shoulder. "It's all about Connie's Amaretto cake." He smacked his lips. "When you taste her Amaretto cake, trust me, you'll understand."

Lily shook her head. "You Jacksons are a very strange family."

"Yeah, but in a good way." Earl took Lily's hand and kissed it. "Promise you'll save a dance for an old man."

Lily giggled. "The second one. The first is for Marco." She gave Marco a flirtatious glance.

Marco's hand strayed toward Lily's hand. He curled his fingers around hers. His father could be a little too nosy.

His father gave him the thumbs up sign and headed for the door. Lily escorted him out. Alone, he called Hunter's cell phone.

"It's Saturday," she grumbled when she finally answered.

"I know. But crime doesn't take a day off. You should expect to be on call twenty-four/seven. You didn't call me with the results of the meeting with Sawyer's parole officer."

She sighed. "That was an exercise in futility."

"What do you mean?" Most times P O's cooperated with officials.

Hunter's voice was low and frustrated. "He played along, sort of, and he called Sawyer and arranged for him to come in on Monday. Leland Davenport and I are going to have a chat. But as far as I'm concerned, the parole officer thinks Sawyer walks on water, that he's the poster child for prison rehabilitation. What do I do next?"

Marco sat back in the chair and thought. "Two things. First, I've put together a surveillance team ...."

Her voice perked up. "How did you get Lieutenant Dawson to agree to that? Didn't she give you the 'no money in the budget' speech? I know Lily Alexander is her friend, but I can't see her approving all the overtime."

"This is lesson number one, Hunter. Make do with what you have, and I have a volunteer brigade."

"I'm lost here, Jackson." The frustration in her voice returned. "Sometimes I feel like everyone knows some great big secret that I don't."

Marco understood how she felt. His first day at Homicide had felt like he'd just entered clown alley. Nothing he had done was the right thing. Everyone had been so super critical of him, he'd thought about transferring out. But he'd learned. Hunter would learn, too. "My dad and some of his old cop buddies are revisiting their youth. They put together a surveillance team for me and Sawyer is under a twenty-four hour watch."

"Is that legal?" She sounded doubtful. "Would Chief Sanchez approve something like that?"

"Consider this more along the line of being creative and frugal. Besides, there isn't a cop who hasn't been on the force for the last thirty years that my dad doesn't know the dirt on. Chief Sanchez isn't going to blow any smoke up our behinds over this. Trust me."

"I trust you," Hunter said. "That's what I'm afraid of."

Marco grinned. She was learning. "Dawson told me to make a detective out of you and I'm teaching you all the tricks in my play book."

"Let me make a note on that," Hunter said, sarcastically. "While

I'm writing, I had an idea I wanted to run by you."

"What's your idea?" Good, he thought. She was taking charge of her end without his prompting. When he was through with her, she'd be a top-notch detective who would make Dawson proud.

"I was thinking about something you said about prison making the criminal better and badder. Sawyer had to learn his new tricks in prison. I found out he shared space with a man who was convicted of computer stalking and another guy who knows the ins and outs of identity theft. They were all released about the same time. After Davenport and I talk to Sawyer, I'm going to visit with the computer guy. I haven't tracked the other one down. He never met with his parole officer and hasn't been seen since. His parole officer thinks he's long gone with a brand-new identity."

"Hunter," Marco said with approval, "everyone thinks you're nothing but a pretty face. Now I know better and I'm delighted to make my acquaintance with your brain."

"From you," Hunter said, "that means a lot. You said you had two things to tell me."

"Never mind on the second."

"Then I'll see you tomorrow."

Marco was surprised. "You're coming to my party!"

"Elena invited me. I wouldn't miss your birthday party. Can I bring a date?"

"And here I was thinking of introducing you to one of my unmarried brothers."

"That's so sweet of you."

"You don't have a problem with inter-racial dating?" Giancarlo would like Hunter. He had a weakness for blondes and blondes had a weakness for him.

Hunter giggled. "I already have a date—Leland Davenport."

Now that surprised Marco. He wondered how her family would feel about her dating Leland Davenport. From all he'd heard and read about Hunter's parents, they wouldn't be too fond of her choice. She was in for a rough ride. "I've heard about Davenport. Dawson is impressed with the guy's record."

"Score one point for me. I'm going to make Lieutenant Dawson like me if it kills me." Hunter sounded wistful as though Lieutenant Dawson's opinion was that important.

Macro reassured her. "I don't think you'll have to work that hard." Dawson would never have allowed Hunter to stay in Cold Case if she hadn't thought Hunter would make the grade.

"I'll see you tomorrow."

"Good work, Hunter." He disconnected and walked out to the kitchen. "Lily, what did you get me for my birthday?"

"A box of rocks." She stood at the counter a smudge of flour on her cheek.

He started unbuttoning his shirt. "Let me show you how appreciative I am for some rocks."

She glanced at the clock. "It isn't even noon yet. Besides, I have so much to do for your party tomorrow."

He rubbed his hands together. "You can take a break." He grabbed her and swung her up into his arms.

—m—

Lily buried her face in Marco's neck as he pushed open her bedroom door. A warm shiver of desire ran her through at the touch of his skin against her face.

He laid her on the big bed. "You smell like vanilla." Marco stood and pulled off his shirt.

"From the cookies." Lily pushed herself up on her elbow. What a dumb thing to say, but her brain wasn't working quite right. With Marco's naked, muscular chest bared to her, her brain had just shut down.

"I like it. I want to eat you all up." He kissed her, nibbling her ear and then the corner of her mouth as his hands slid under her shirt.

Lily still couldn't believe a man like Marco Jackson, who could have any woman he wanted, would want her. She had to be dreaming. "This is so strange. I can't believe—"

Marco put a finger to her lips stopping her words. "Don't say it. Don't even think it."

Lily stilled his hand. "You make me feel so beautiful."

He bent over and planted a gentle kiss on her mouth. "You make me feel special."

"Thank you for making me feel normal."

He laughed, though his eyes were sad. "Normal's pretty boring. I like you just the way you are." He planted another kiss on her lips, then crawled on the bed to kneel next to her.

Lily smiled. "Me, too."

Marco began to unbutton her shirt. "Good. I don't want to think I wasted all this charm for no reason at all."

Lily sat up on the bed. "I haven't felt alive in years."

Marco cupped her chin. "You are special. Promise me you won't ever forget that."

"I promise I won't." She studied his eyes. In their brown depths she again saw that unnamed something and wondered what it was. She loved him so much. *If only she could have his love in return.* But she didn't want to tie him to her. She had way too much baggage.

His thumb glazed over her bottom lip. "Good."

"What have I done to earn your...respect?" This was not what she wanted, but she would have to accept it. He liked her. She knew that would never be enough. When he was gone and their affair was over, she would cherish the memory.

"You're you. That's enough." Marco leaned over and kissed her again.

The instant his mouth touched her, she lifted her arms and wound them around his neck, tasting his raw essence. Their tongues entangled and danced together. As his mouth traveled along her jaw, his hot breath fanned her cheek. What started as tenderness transformed to a dark, searching hunger. His hands moved over her body.

Lily couldn't get close enough. Marco's body was so hot and sleek. "Hurry, Marco, I need you to make love to me now."

"You have no patience."

She didn't have much time with him. Once Sawyer was caught, Marco would leave. She had to get everything she could as fast as possible. "And you do?" She loved the way his muscles tensed under her hands. The sound he made when their bodies came together drove her mad with longing. The smell of musk and sunlight clung to his skin.

"Tell me what you want" He nibbled at her neck. "I need to hear the words."

Tiny prickles of wanton desire filled her. She couldn't think, much less speak. All she wanted was for him to be inside her, filling her body, making love to her. She had no time for talking; her body demanded the satisfaction that only his body could bring.

"Tell me." His words cut into the haze of passion surrounding her.

"I—" She stopped, unable to form words as his hand skimmed over her breast. Her nipples ached and she arched her back to get more of his touch. "Marco you are torturing me."

"I want you to say the words!" Demand edged his command.

"Make love to me."

"Yes."

Her joy knew no bounds, yet he hadn't said the words she most wanted to hear. She bit her lip and took a deep breath.

He pushed her back onto the bed, nibbling at her taut nipples.

"Hurry," she said, "I need you. I'm begging."

His mouth moved down her stomach. He licked her, tickling at her navel.

"Stop tasting me like I'm a cookie." Lily slid down to the mattress, giving him access to her body. His hands roamed over her. She smiled as he slipped off her shoes and pants. A coolness danced over her naked skin, replaced by the heat of his mouth.

"We have all day." Marco trailed his lips over her breasts. His tongue made tiny circles around each nipple. His fingers slid between her thighs to create a whirl of desire deep inside her.

A strangled moan broke from her mouth.

Marco stripped off the rest of his clothes. Lily stared at him. He was so big and hard all over. She just loved the way he was made. He was the same color as the wild Tupelo honey she drizzled on her English muffins every morning. She wouldn't ask for anything else if she could wake up with him at her side for the rest of her life.

He covered her body with butterfly kisses. He sucked her toes. Lily laughed as his tongue slipped between them. She never dreamed that this kind of pleasure could be hers. She shuddered, as his lips worked their seductive magic. Marco massaged her calves, her hips, her thighs.

As his mouth caressed her stomach, he dipped his tongue in her navel. He swirled the velvet tip around her skin.

Marco tickled the curve of her breast. "Your skin is so soft, so

169

warm."

Lily burned on the inside. She burned on the outside. She could at least show him what he did to her. She could show him how much he needed her. "Make love to me," she moaned in a throaty growl she barely recognized as her own voice.

"You are such a pushy little thing." He flicked the pad of his thumb over her hardened nipple, rolled her over on her stomach. He kissed her shoulders and back. He nipped her buttocks and the back of her thighs. When he rolled her over to face him again, Lily thought she would die if he didn't take her soon.

Marco braced his hands against the mattress, as he hovered over her. Lily ran her fingers over his rippling muscles. She circled his waist with her legs and thrust her hips up to meet his hard penis. But he pulled away.

Marco slid to the side to lay stretched out next to her. He slipped a finger into her moist fold and began to caress her while his lips nibbled at her nipples. He blew on her hot skin.

He moved his finger inside her, slowly with long languid strokes that made her wriggle with passion. He brought her just to the point of climax, then slowed his movement to a leisurely stroke.

"Please!" she begged and shifted her body against him. The pleasure and pain of his touch sent her body soaring. "I want you."

"Play nice." He nuzzled her neck.

"Now dammit."

"Not yet." He kissed her again and inserted another finger inside her and moved it rapidly in and out until she thought she would die from the pleasure that built and built.

"You like to play games." She stiffened and gripped her legs tight. She did not understand how she could float on the point of total surrender and not climax. What kind of wicked game did he play with her? And why did she enjoy it so much?

He maneuvered his thumb to massage her tight, sensitive nub. He nibbled at her lips and neck. Lily thought she would come apart.

She attempted to lie back and enjoy his slow easy lovemaking, but her body had ideas of its own. She thrashed against his fingers trying to take them deeper. She pled and dug her nails in the broad expanse of his powerful shoulders.

His lips trailed lower. He laved her nipples, the tip of his tongue barely touching her skin. The heat engulfed in her, fierce and unchecked.

Slowly he suckled each breast drawing each nipple deep into his mouth. His fingers thrust hard inside her. A tightening spread across her belly.

His tempo increased and Lily stiffened near completion. Every inch of her body was on fire. She seemed suspended on a mountain ledge and she wanted to fall over. His fingers teased her. Her release shook her body to its core. She cried out and felt tears oozing out of the sides of her eyes.

Marco shifted to lie on top of her, his manhood hard against her belly, pulsating on her skin.

"Please!" Her demand raw. "Come inside. Fill me."

"Not yet."

"What are you doing to me?" Lily thought she would die. She needed him inside her.

"No games, Lily, I'm only making love with the most beautiful woman in Phoenix." Marco turned her over. Then he rained kisses all over her body. The texture of his mouth caressed her with the softness of a morning breeze.

He paused to explore the hollow between her shoulder blades and the small of her back. His fingertips grazed the curve of her hip and the rise of her buttocks. The tips of his fingers slid over her skin with no mercy. Her moans of pleasure died against her pillow.

Lily never dreamed her life would be waylaid by such joy. Her toes curled with every new sensation. She wanted to cry. She knew making love with him was sweet, but this torture was beyond all thought and reason. His mouth wreaked havoc on her flesh, from the nape of her neck to the soles of her feet. What evil seductive game did he play with her?

Marco nipped the back of her thigh. He played her body so masterfully. Giving her so much ecstasy, yet taking nothing for himself. She had no idea love was so selfless, so fulfilling. Or that she would crave it so much. All her life she dreamed she would find a man who was not afraid of what she was. "Let me love you."

He rolled her over and stroked her cheek. His tongue swirled around her lips. He ran a finger down her throat, between her breasts and across her stomach. He rolled over on her and she circled his body with her legs.

Fire and muscle greeted her as she rubbed against him. His manhood jutted tight against her thighs, and she was determined to have him inside of her. She wrestled to keep her legs around him. Marco laughed at her as he stretched her arms above her head, his fingers clamped around her wrists.

"You are wicked," she gasped.

"I do my best."

She struggled, trying to make him take her. "I'm getting frustrated here."

"We could wrestle." He ground his hips into hers.

Lily groaned. He used his body as an instrument of extortion. She was ready to pay any price to have him. "You can have anything, just do it."

The tip of his penis penetrated her by the smallest measure. She longed to take him fully inside, but his heavier weight restrained her. He closed his eyes, gritted his teeth, and withdrew slowly leaving her empty and wanting. "Tell me what you bought me?"

"Everything, except that." Not even his lovemaking would shake her secret loose.

"I'll have to re-think this then."

Lily grabbed his shoulders. She couldn't take much more of his teasing. "Make love to me. Please."

"You talked me into it." Marco pushed himself inside her with one powerful stroke.

A scream ripped from her lips. She had found heaven on earth. He filled every inch inside her and she felt herself stretch to accommodate him.

He moaned, buried so deep inside Lily knew he breeched her soul. He let go of her wrists and pushed himself upwards. Braced on his forearms, he began to slowly thrust into her.

She stroked his cheek, trailing her thumb to his lips. Marco sucked on her thumb. She caressed his other arm, feeling his muscles tense under her palm. His steady rhythm made her insane with passion. But he refused to increase his tempo until she wriggled beneath him and pleaded for release.

His strokes became more demanding and harder, grinding his hips against her. Sweat dripped off his skin melting their body's together.

Lily clawed his arms and dug her heels deep in his flesh. She gave everything of herself. With each powerful thrust he brought her closer to release. Spasms racked her as he continued to plunge deep inside her. When she thought she would die of the sheer pleasure of their act, he cried out her name and climaxed inside her. Her body joined his in climax. She felt transported with each powerful spasm.

Satiated, he collapsed, gathering her against his chest. She wept.

CHAPTER ELEVEN

Music blasted through the whole house. Lily felt pleased that all the Jackson males had been so impressed with her sound system. They couldn't compliment her enough.

Marco and his brothers had rearranged the furniture to make room for everyone. In the dining room, they'd pushed the massive table against one wall and lunch had been a buffet affair with the table decorated in the center with the huge Amaretto cake, a mountain of presents behind it.

She danced with Earl. He wasn't a great dancer, but he was enthusiastic. And considering her own lack of practice, that was okay with her.

The entire Jackson clan had descended on her at noon. Lily enjoyed the fact that they knew how to have fun. And even though her own parents had been loving and nurturing, they had been more reserved. The Jacksons laughed from their bellies and ate with their fingers.

Everyone was made to feel they belonged, including the people Marco worked with. No one was treated as an outsider.

Cher twirled around in the center of the living room holding Elena's baby.

Elena danced with her husband.

Lily didn't have everyone straight in her head, yet. She knew Nicolo, Marco's twin brother, only because he was a dead ringer for Marco.

Her gaze drifted back to Marco dancing with one of his nieces. He was enjoying himself so thoroughly that Lily was delighted. He had changed her and become so much a part of her life that she didn't know what would happen when Marco left. Nothing good ever lasted for her. What did she have to fill the emptiness? Two Bengal cats named Obi-Wan and Yoda, some fish and a career that delved into the sickness of the human soul.

"You're not concentrating, sweetie," Earl said as he caught her hand and twirled her around. "You just about jerked my arm out of its socket and I'm trying not to think about the pain." He swung her around.

"Sorry."

"That's okay. I can see you watching Marco. If you want to marry him, feel free to do so. I like you. And if you don't like him, I have others. If I say so myself, Jackson men make pretty good husbands."

She stared at him in surprise. "Thanks, Mr. Jackson, but I think Marco is supposed to do the asking."

"I'm the daddy. I make the rules."

She smiled at him. "No, you don't." She knew who made the rules for the family.

Earl's laugh was loud and filled with merriment. "I know. Connie is large and in charge, but she likes you, too."

He slowed, and she blew him a kiss. She would have preferred planting the kiss on his cheek, but the twelve-inch difference in their heights made that impossible.

The song ended. Connie stood in the center of the room and clapped her hands, yelling, "Cake."

"It's cake time," Earl looked delighted. He gave his wife a broad smile and Connie dimpled. She gave him a flirty glance and Earl looked like he would melt.

For a second, Lily was jealous of their love. "Is this why you had so many children, so you can eat cake?"

He grinned, his gaze never leaving his wife. "Among other reasons."

Lily could see the love in his eyes. Marco told her they'd been married forty-one years. The early years had been tough on them during a time when inter-racial marriages had been viewed with deep suspicion and intolerance. But they had triumphed. Their love had survived. Lily could only hope she would be as lucky.

As everyone trailed toward the dining room, Marco hung back catching Lily's hand. When no one was paying attention, he kissed her long and deep.

Her senses swirled. She felt as though she were melting against him, then he was jerked away from her by Cher's daughter. "Come on," Miranda Dawson-Broussard said, "Stop mooning over her, we want cake."

"And presents," Marco shouted.

"Cake," Earl replied.

"But grandpa," one of the little girls said.

"I'm an old man." Earl lifted the girl into his arms. "I have to eat tofu for lunch. I want my cake."

Connie shook her head. "My love. All you think about is your stomach."

Earl leered at her. "Not all the time."

Connie sighed. "Yes, and cigars." She caressed his cheek and then turned to the cake. "Cake, first."

Marco groaned. Lily patted his arm. "You'll get your turn."

Marco sent her a look that made her blood race. Heat curled inside of her as the memory of their wild lovemaking filled her mind.

Connie stood at the table, Elena and Lily helping. Connie lit the one large candle in the center of the cake; everyone started clapping, and singing happy birthday to Marco. When the last word died away Lily leaned toward Marco. "Why only one candle?"

Marco grinned. "Jackson lore has it that when Mom turned thirty-nine, she refused to put more than one candle on the cake. It's a favor she does for all of us."

"So that no one knows your age?"

He chuckled. "So Connie doesn't have to keep track of her age."

Connie cut the cake and the sweet aroma of the Amaretto filled the dining room. Elena started transferring slices to plates. She handed out plates to the younger Jacksons and ordered them outside onto the patio. When the room was cleared of all the children, the adults lined up for their slices. Elena and Lily handed them out and each person drifted into the living room and found a place a sit.

Marco was last in line. While he waited, he poked at two of the presents closest to him and Connie slapped his hand. "After cake."

"Can't I just open one of them now." His eyes danced with curiosity.

His mother slapped his hand again and gave him a fierce glare. "We will observe tradition."

Lily repressed a giggle. She'd never known anyone to enjoy a birthday so much. She usually just ignored her own birthday. What was another year?

"We need five more forks," Elena announced.

"I'll get them." Lily turned toward the kitchen. She grabbed them and started back to find Cher blocking her way.

Cher leaned in the doorway. "You haven't been an attentive friend lately."

"What's going on that requires my attention?"

"I think my best friend is in love and she's been keeping me in the dark."

Heat flooded Lily's cheeks. "You're so busy. You have a husband and a job."

"Number one." Cher held up a finger. "I always make time for you. Number two, your love life is with one of my detectives who not only works for me, but is also a friend."

"Other then some fun on the side, nothing is really happening."

"Don't lie. You look at him and your face lights up."

Lily shook her head. "Do you know what dating me is like? No dinners out. No football games. No picnics in the park. No weekends in Vegas. Talk about the old ball and chain, I personify it. That gets old pretty fast. Marco just doesn't realize yet that once he leaves, I won't be going with him."

"Maybe he's okay with the way things are."

"Would you be okay with who and what I am?"

"I've been your friend for a long time, Lily. You're worth it to me. Marco understands better than you think. He's not some party boy. He was built for home and hearth."

Lily didn't think so. "Men have expectations." She was exciting to Marco because she was the reason for his investigation. He really hadn't confronted her agoraphobia. Once Sawyer was gone and the threat ended, she'd still be housebound, and Marco didn't understand that, for her, life wouldn't change.

"Do you know what his expectations are?" Cher asked.

"Living in my house is like Disneyland for grownups. I have lots of toys. We have this exciting situation going on around us. When the investigation ends, what will be left?"

Cher shook her head. "What about conversation? Sex? Hobbies? Being a cop is hard considering what we face daily. Maybe he likes coming home where everything is clean and safe, and have someone around who understands who he is."

"You sound like he's popped the question."

"I'm getting you ready."

"You're insane. He drives a motorcycle and has a Clydesdale for a dog. He doodles." Marco was so filled with the energy of life, Lily felt like a shadow next to him.

Cher stared at her. "Doodles what?"

"I think he's writing and illustrating a comic book."

Cher burst out laughing. "Jackson writes comic books?"

Lily flicked her fingers against Cher's arm. "Don't laugh. He's a very good artist."

The laughter drained away. "I believe you. There are depths to Marco Jackson even he hasn't plundered."

"Why is it," Lily said, "that when you say things like that they always sound so dirty? Plundered!"

Cher shrugged. "It's my gift."

"You sound like your daughter."

"That's the problem with teenage daughters. No matter how you try to keep them on the straight and narrow, they end up changing you instead."

Cher linked arms with Lily, "We should get back to the party. Elena has been waiting for those forks long enough."

———※———

All the kids sat right in front of Marco on the floor. They loved presents as much as he did and he got enough gag gifts he could share them with his nieces and nephews. Behind them, all the adults sat on chairs, or stood in clusters watching him.

Marco rubbed his hands together. The mound in front of him was almost overwhelming. Two weeks ago he would have opened Nick's present first. Marco's twin was the only one of his siblings who knew about his secret love. Last year, Nick had given him a copy of Leonardo Da Vinci's sketchbook. Marco had loved the absolute mastery that Da Vinci had with line and the human body. Marco had tried to use some of the same techniques in his own artwork. But this year, he intended to open Lily's present first.

He rustled through the presents looking for Lily's. She sat on the floor cross-legged grinning at him. "Lily, where's my box of rocks?"

"I heard about you." She reached behind her back and drew out a slim box wrapped in paper decorated with little cowboys riding wooden rocking horses and a huge blue bow in the center. "But you have to wait a little bit longer." She tucked the gift back out of sight behind her back, a challenging look in her eyes.

Marco almost groaned.

"Here, Uncle Marco." One of his nephews handed him a box. "Open this one first."

Marco tore at the wrapping. No careful unveiling for him. He was greedy, he knew it. He opened a card and it was signed Giancarlo and the girls. The box was long and narrow. Before he opened it, he shook it. Something shifted inside. Marco opened the lid and held up a black and blue tie. "Look, G-man ties. From Giancarlo." Marco knotted the tie around his forehead like a bandana.

The next box was from Roberto's children. "You like it," they cried and crowded around him.

Opening the box, he found rawhide chews for Harley. Harley made out better then he did for most birthdays.

The next box was a sketching pad and charcoal pencils from Nick.

The fourth box seemed odd. It was wrapped in plain blue paper.

Usually his family went for really bright, weird papers. No bow, and no card. Mystery gift. He tore open the box and opened it.

Inside, on a bed of red fabric lay two skeleton hands entwined. Around the third finger of each bony hand were gold wedding bands.

"What is it," Roberto's son crowded Marco.

Marco didn't want to touch them. He shifted the red fabric aside and found a card. 'For the happy couple' Each letter cut from a magazine.

The hair on the back his neck rose. The kids surged forward to see. Marco closed the box and smiled at the children. "This isn't appropriate for family viewing." Marco stood and handed the closed box to his father. Lily frowned.

Earl glanced inside. He placed the box high on the top of a cabinet and nodded at Marco.

Marco returned to his seat, as he passed Lily he grabbed the box out of her hands.

She jumped to her feet. "Give it back."

Marco laughed. "I want to know what kind of rocks come in a briefcase, hand-cuffed to a security guard."

Connie clapped her hands and cried, "Jewelry."

"Down, Connie," Earl said. "This isn't your birthday."

Connie grinned saucily at him. "It's never too early to discuss your wife's needs."

Earl kissed her. "I've got your needs covered."

Connie burrowed against him.

Marco felt a moment of envy. He sat down and held Lily's gift high for everyone to see. He could see that Lily's eyes danced and she held her lips tight to keep from laughing.

Carefully, Marco shook the box. One of those quite presents. Marco slit the tape. He unwrapped it slowly.

"Hurry up," one of his nieces urged.

With the wrapping paper removed, he opened the lid. He flipped the lid to discover tissue paper held together with a gold foil sticker. He slit open the sticker.

Not one word sounded from the room. Even the kids seemed to be holding their breaths. They seemed to know that whatever was inside was important.

Marco pushed the tissue aside and stared. "Clutch my heart. I've died and gone to heaven."

"What is it?" Nick cried, crowding close.

Marco's other brothers leaned forward.

Marco held up the comic book encased in a protective plastic sleeve. "X-Men. Number one."

There seemed to be a collective intake of breath and then Giancarlo sighed. Marco lifted the comic book over his head. "I am now a god."

Lily jumped to her feet. "Happy Birthday."

Nick took her hand and held it to his lips. "You understand. Marry me."

An instant of rage pierced Marco. Lily belonged to him.

Connie yelled. "Please, don't say no." She put her hands together in prayer.

Marco loosened his grip on the comic book resisting the urge to beat his brother to a bloody pulp. He put the book down and stood. He sauntered over to Lily, dropped a hand on his brother's shoulder and pushed Nick away. Marco extended a hand to Lily, lifted her to her feet and kissed her in a way that let everyone know what his intentions were.

All the furniture had been returned to their original places. All the kids and their parents had left to go home. Marco held the box out in front of him as he sat down. Dawson, Hunter, Davenport, and his dad had stayed behind. Connie was in the kitchen cleaning up.

Marco pushed the box with its macabre contents to the center of the coffee table. Just looking at the box made his stomach clench. He opened it. "Everybody needs to take a look at this. But don't touch. Forensics is on its way to take the box."

He studied the bones with the gold rings. One hand was smaller and probably supposed to be a woman. A diamond ring interspersed with sapphires adorned the wedding finger in front of a gold wedding band with an ornate floral design engraved on the narrow surface. Small diamonds winked in the scrolls and curlicues.

"Is this box what's keeping me out of bed?" Cher Dawson asked with a yawn.

"Lieutenant," Marco said, "what's inside is going to blow the kink out of your hair."

Dawson's eyebrows rose as she peered at the skeleton hands. "Tell me they aren't real?"

Marco studied the shiny white bones. "I don't know." The bones were too shiny and too white. At first he'd thought Sawyer might have cut off Lily's parents' hands, but he realized that the joints were held together with metal clips of some kind. The same way the joints were held together of the skeleton that stood in his doctor's office. Marco didn't want to touch anything. He'd already touched the box. He'd kept the wrapping paper with it but had the feeling the paper was already compromised. Too many people had already touched the box.

Leland Davenport leaned over to look inside. Then Hunter and finally Earl Jackson. Each one leaned back their faces thoughtful.

"Whoever sent this, and I'm assuming it's Sawyer," Davenport said, "is one sick bastard."

"Can I see?" Lily sat against the corner of the sofa.

"No," Dawson said.

"Don't, Lily," Marco said caution in his tone. He wanted to protect her from the sickness of the gift.

Sawyer's campaign of terror was escalating. Why? Because Marco was around to protect her? He wished he knew. But he sensed that this little gift to him was somehow designed to do more than catch his attention. It was designed to let Lily know that no matter what precautions Marco took, Sawyer could still get to her.

Lily ignored Marco and stood to peek into the box. She turned grey, her eyes rolled slightly and she swayed. Marco grabbed her before she fell. He eased her back onto the sofa. She curled up, pulling her knees to her chest and covering her face with her hands.

"Lily?" Marco sat next to her, one hand on her shoulder. He could feel the tremors that shook her.

"The diamond ring." Her voice broke. "That was my mother engagement ring. I would recognize it anywhere. My father had the diamond specially cut for her and designed the setting himself. She was wearing it when she was buried." She turned to Marco. "Please, don't tell me Sawyer has dug up my parents. Did he cut off their hands?" She shuddered and tears fell from her eyes.

Dawson reached for her cell phone. "I'll have a squad car check it out." She dialed, spoke into the phone, and disconnected, her face grave.

"How did he get the rings? I had to have a closed casket for them. My mother's face was...." Lily's voice trailed away, the pain so deep she couldn't continue.

"I doubt that he dug up the grave. The bones look like the kind of bones you'd find at Halloween." Marco remembered that her mother had been shot in the head, point blank.

He felt sad that Lily was being forced to relive everything yet again and wished he didn't have to dredge up all the pain. All he wanted to do was take her in his arms and hold the world at bay. But he couldn't and he was powerless to make her stop hurting.

"I'm assuming the other ring is my father's. Can I get them back when the forensics department is done?"

"Yes," Dawson said. "But right now we have to figure out when the bodies were accessible for the rings to be taken."

Lily wiped her eyes of the tears gathering in the corners. "After the autopsy, my parents were taken to Tanner's Funeral Home and then to the Good Shepherd church." Her hands had gone cold and stiff, her face distant and sad.

"Did you go view the bodies?" Marco rubbed Lily's hands.

"No," she replied. "I couldn't. The funeral home asked me to choose burial clothes, and Cher took them for me."

Marco wanted to hold her, to soothe away her fears, but she had pulled tight inside herself. "So you don't know if they were actually buried with their rings."

"I saw the bodies," Dawson said, "but I don't remember the wedding rings. Sorry." She patted Lily's hand.

Marco understood. He squeezed Lily tight against him. Her trembling in her hands lessened. Seeing a friend's dead parents was a lot different than viewing a crime scene where recognizing details would break a case.

"Which means," Earl said, "that Sawyer probably had opportunity while the bodies were at the funeral home."

"How would he get into the funeral home?" Lily asked.

"Any number of ways," Earl said with a deep frown. "He could have posed as a grieving friend, even a possible customer and asked to see the facilities."

Hunter reached for her purse and took out her notepad, then flipped a few pages. "Sawyer is a big deal in his church. He handles a lot of funerals. I'd say he probably walked in claiming church business. I can find out what other funerals Tanner's was handling at the same time. Maybe we can connect one of them to Sawyer's church."

"Good," Marco said, "but I want to know how he knew about this party. The decision to move it from Elena's to here was only made a couple days ago."

Leland Davenport had loosened his tie. "The catering company."

"I did the cooking." Lily rubbed her eyes. "The party supplies were delivered from Home Bound, Inc."

"Explain to me how that works," Davenport said.

Lily twisted her fingers together. "I call Home Bound, Inc. and they make the arrangements."

"What is Home Bound, Inc?" Leland raised his eyebrows.

"A company designed to put home bound people in touch with local businesses. I've had an account with them for years."

"That doesn't explain how Sawyer found out about the change in location."

Lily shrugged. "The only other place I called was this comic book dealer in Florida for Marco's gift. I talked to Kevin Barnes. I know him from on-line."

Leland frowned. "Is Home Bound, Inc. located in Phoenix?"

"Their corporate offices are downtown," Lily said, "but they have offices in all the major cities in the country."

Marco sat back on the sofa. "Maybe, Sawyer has a link to them."

Hunter scribbled on her notepad. "I can try to track it down."

Marco nodded. "Take Sawyer's photo over to their offices and ask if anyone has ever seen him."

Hunter nodded.

"But how did the gift get into the house?" Marco asked.

Lily sat up straight. "It was in one of the boxes of party supplies. I didn't think anything of it because Home Bound, Inc. often sends thank you gifts like that. Part of their service. So I just added it to the pile."

"So," Leland Davenport mused, "there is a connection somewhere between Sawyer and Home Bound, Inc."

Lily seemed to shrink inside herself. "If that's true, then he knows everything about me."

"How so?" Davenport queried.

"I do everything through Home Bound, Inc. They are my Internet provider. I even do my banking through their website and pay my bills through their bill paying service. They are like a one-stop shopping mall. When I need something I just go to their website, or call them on the phone, and let them know what I need. They work it out, and take a commission. And I don't have to think about anything."

Hunter held up her hand. "One of Sawyer's cell mates was a computer hacker. Is it possible this guy taught Sawyer a few tricks about hacking into computers? If that's the case, then Sawyer can hack into one from anywhere."

Marco shuddered. Just the thought of that made his hands itch. "When I was in his house, I saw his office and he had a state-of-the-art computer."

"I can get a search warrant." Davenport reached into his pocket and drew out his cell phone.

Earl held up a hand. "Sawyer isn't hacking from his home. He's too smart for that. He's probably hidden a laptop in a place we'll never find and if you search his home you'll tip your hand and let him know that we're really on to him. All he has to do is reformat his hard drive and start over. Maybe the link is at his church offices?"

"So what do we do?" Marco asked his father. "Everything we have right now is circumstantial."

Earl replied. "Even smart criminals make mistakes. He'll make one and we'll pounce on him."

"But he hasn't made a mistake yet," Dawson said.

Earl gestured at Lily. "We have his ace in the hole."

Marco put a protective arm around Lily. "We're not using Lily as bait to draw this guy into the open." She had already been in that bastard's power once. No one was taking Lily away from him.

Earl shook his head. "I didn't mean it that way. What's Sawyer's one weakness? Lily. Has anyone done a profile on this guy?"

Hunter reached into her purse. "I brought his psych report from prison to give to Marco."

"What did you find out?" Marco asked.

"The prison psychologist felt that Sawyer is a high-functioning sociopath. Which means, he can function in society and present a facade that allows him to blend in and even form short-term relationships, but he has little self-control over his impulses. He is highly intelligent, knows the difference between right and wrong, but is disdainful of social rules. He feels that he is intellectually superior to society and therefore the rules don't apply to him."

"That's classic," Marco replied. "Most sociopaths feel and act the same way. What's different about Sawyer?"

Hunter rifled through the folder. "The one different thing is his need to be nurtured. Most sociopaths don't give up control of themselves, or their situations, but Sawyer is looking for the perfect family.

The psychologist believes that Sawyer believes, if he finds the perfect family with the perfect, care-giving mother, all his problems will go away."

"Which supports something Lily said," Marco said, "that he kidnaps the women, auditions them, and when they don't live up to his standards, he disposes of them."

Dawson paced around the room. "He just didn't wake up and decide to be a psycho."

Marco had been thinking the same thing. "Which doesn't tell us why he wants Lily so badly." Because Sawyer was twisted in some way.

"Unfinished business," Cher replied. "She was his one failure. She got away before he could decide whether or not she was the one who had the ability to nurture him according to his needs."

"I didn't know what his needs were," Lily murmured.

Marco rubbed his temple. This investigation was giving him a headache. Despite the preponderance of circumstantial evidence, they had nothing really concrete. "I want to know every move Sawyer has made since the second he was conceived."

Hunter flipped open her notebook. "I'm working on that. When I pulled his sheet, I discovered that he had a juvenile record."

"Why didn't you say something already," Marco asked.

"Because I didn't know if that information would lead anywhere, and I didn't want to get anyone's hopes up. Because the records are sealed, I thought I'd try contacting the guy who arrested him, but so far no luck. The cop who arrested him is retired in Mexico and I haven't been able to track him down, not even through his pension."

Lily shifted away from Marco. "I always thought Sawyer acted like he knew what he was doing. Cher, if you think Sawyer has abducted other women to play house with, then maybe we should be looking at missing women in Phoenix."

Dawson shrugged. "I have no idea how many women have disappeared in Phoenix in the last year. Most women reported missing eventually show up."

Dead or alive, Marco thought with a frown. He and Lily had started down this path before, but had been distracted by the break-in at Natalie's apartment. So many other things had happened since then, he'd put the idea on the back burner. "How many haven't been found?"

"I'll check into that," Hunter said.

"Hunter," Marco said, "you can't do the entire case. Besides, you're pulling Sawyer in tomorrow for a parole check. We don't want to make him more suspicious than he already is. Dad, tomorrow, you come make Lily blueberry pancakes for breakfast and I'll check with missing persons."

"I have my contact," Lily offered.

"I remember. Give me the name and I'll start with him." Marco turned back to Hunter. "Did you talk to Sawyer's wife?"

Hunter shook her head. "According to her boss, Mrs. Sawyer decided to visit her mother in Tampa. Gave me the number. I called and she answered, but she refused to talk and I couldn't get her tell me when she was returning."

"Think she left him?" Dawson asked.

"I can find out. Any money in the budget for me to fly to Tampa?" Hunter looked hopeful.

"Not in this lifetime," Dawson said with a laugh. "I'll call a friend in Tampa and see if he can get in touch with her."

The discussion trailed off when the forensics team arrived to take the gruesome gift. Marco explained how the gift had been handled and gave them the wrapping paper as well.

With the party officially ended, everyone left, leaving Marco alone with Lily who continued to sit on the sofa looking like a frightened child.

"I'm going to get him for you." He sat next to her and drew her into his arms.

"I know," she replied as she cuddled into the protection of his arms. "I know."

CHAPTER TWELVE

Beatrix Hunter stood in the interview room with Joe Sawyer. Up close and personal, he made her skin crawl. She wondered if Leland Davenport was affected the same way even though he had spent the last hour behind the two-way mirror in the next-door room observing.

"I hope you're satisfied, Detective." Sawyer's voice held a mild taunt.

She walked over to him and straightened the collar of his shirt and brushed imaginary lint off his shoulder. "Do you know why I brought you in here, Sawyer?"

"You think I'm being a bad boy again."

She shook her head. "No. I brought you in here simply because I could. Our little session has made my entire week."

"How so?"

"I get to screw with your mind." She smacked him lightly on the chin.

"Didn't work," Sawyer said with a leer. "I have your number, lady cop. If you hassle me, I'll file a complaint."

"Do that." Hunter smiled. "You be careful out there."

"Are you saying I can go?" He frowned and gave her a suspicious look.

She nodded. "Just remember to behave yourself now."

Sawyer scurried away after a piercing last look at the mirror.

"What the hell was that?" Leland demanded as she emerged into the hall. He stood in the center of the hallway waiting for her.

"Psychological warfare."

"What do you think you are, the NSA?"

She headed toward the elevator. "It occurred to me that by calling him in and roughing him up a little, we may have sown a few seeds. Now he'll wonder if he's done something and if we're watching him."

"Frankly, if I never have to do this again will be too soon."

She laughed. "Didn't enjoy the strip search, did you?" She had to admit, she was happy she didn't have to witness it.

"So what have we learned from this tawdry little exercise?"

"You sound like such a snob." He was a man after her own heart.

"Thank you."

The elevator opened. "We learned something more important than you know."

Politely, he waited for her to precede him. He raised an eyebrow and Beatrix' heart went into overdrive. He looked so cute and boyish. "Mr. Sawyer has no body hair."

"And that means?"

"Not only does he have no body hair, he wears a wig. A good wig, but ...."

"How did you spot that?"

She pointed to her eyes. "After so many years of commando grooming lessons from my mother, one learns to spot things like that."

"When are you going to explain what that means?"

"That man has gone to a great deal of trouble to insure that he leaves no DNA behind anywhere."

They stepped out into the lobby. "Now I'm suspicious."

"I'm earning my paycheck." She pushed open the door and stepped out into hot morning air. Traffic was snarled on the street. A fire hydrant shot water into the air spraying Beatrix with a fine mist. A fire truck was parked at the end of the street and two firemen worked to turn the hydrant off. "What do you say I buy you lunch and then we can go to Tucson and talk to that computer geek?"

"Deal."

Waving goodbye to Natalie, Lily touched the computer screen and it went blank. Thank God for technology. Home Bound, Inc. had set up a DSL line and a security camera in Natalie's hospital room that was linked directly to Lily's DSL line and her own security camera so that she and Natalie could see each other and talk, or rather type, any time they wanted. Knowing that Natalie was safe was very important to Lily.

Natalie was able to type with one only finger and in two days had been able to tell Lily that she remembered little of the attack. The doctor said she was probably blocking everything. She would remember eventually, but needed time. Lily didn't want her to remember.

She hated seeing her friend in such pain. She knew how deep it went. Lily remembered the first full-blown anxiety attack after her rescue. She'd been standing in the drug store and the feel of the walls closing in had left her unable to breathe. She had stood in the aisle and tried not to scream, not to draw attention to herself. The walls had gone in and out of focus until she'd been unable to stand. When her mother finally found her, Lily had been only moments away from a total emotional breakdown.

Marco had put a security guard inside Natalie's room. The guard seemed competent and Natalie had told Lily she felt safe. But Lily wouldn't stop worrying until Natalie was out of the hospital and safely sequestered in her mother's home in Flagstaff.

Lily left the office and walked down the long hall to the living room. Harley was sprawled all over the leather sofa and Lily burst out laughing. Her two cats lay on the dog. Yoda played with on of Harley's paws and Obi-Wan groomed Harley's ears.

Earl entered holding a soda in one hand. "You can't get too angry at the big lug, can you?" Harley opened an eye and gazed at Earl before going back to sleep.

Some watchdog she was. "Harley is sweet," Lily admitted. As Earl passed, she removed the soda from his hands. "Connie told me to watch you. She said no sodas."

"It's diet." Earl grimaced. "She can't argue with a diet drink."

Lily shook her head. It just amazed her how much Marco looked like his dad. They were both so tall and handsome. In twenty years Marco would look just like him. "You can have juice."

"I didn't see any juice." He gave her a wide-eyed innocent look that said he hadn't looked too hard.

"That was the glass pitcher with the orange stuff in it, right in front of the six-pack of sodas." Next time, Lily would hide the sodas and make sure the juice was in plain sight. But then she figured he'd find another excuse.

"So that's what that was. All that orange brightness blinded me."

Lily tapped him on the arm. "I like you, Earl Jackson." Earl had a dazzling smile she rarely saw on Marco who, she realized needed to smile more.

Earl grinned at her. "I like you too, Lily Alexander."

"So what are we gonna talk about?" She headed toward the kitchen to return the soda. She wasn't a big soda drinker. The six-pack was left over from the party.

"I was hoping you'd show me the media room again."

"Don't you have one like that?"

He shrugged. "Connie won't let me. She said if my chair was too comfortable and the screen was too big, I'd never come out."

She chuckled. "She has a lot of rules." After replacing the soda back in the refrigerator, she led the way to the media room. Marco would need the same kind of rules when he got married, she thought to herself. Her chest tightened. How she wanted to be the person in his life making those rules and enforcing them.

"I thought," Earl said, "if I married an Italian woman my life would be filled with pasta and wine. Instead, my life is full of rules and tofu shakes." He sighed and gave her a lop-sided grin.

"You need rules." She opened the doors to the media room and flipped on the light.

"But I need a day off occasionally." He tapped his chest. "Good for the soul."

"Do you really want to watch TV? There's nothing but trashy talk shows on."

"I like trash.

Lily rolled her eyes. Like father like son. She'd caught Marco watching wrestling the other night. "Why am I not surprised?"

"How about a movie instead. I saw yesterday you have The Dirty Dozen movie. Let's watch it."

"I'll bet you've seen that movie three hundred and seventy-two times."

"Close."

"I'd rather talk," Lily said as she sat on her recliner. She patted the recliner next to her. "You sit here."

"Makes me nervous when a woman says she wants to talk."

Lily smiled at him. "I promise to be interesting so you won't be bored."

"What do you want to talk about?"

"Did you know that Marco likes to draw?"

Earl nodded. "When he was a kid, he always had a sketch book around. But nothing ever came of it."

"Au contraire, my friend." She reached into her pocket and handed him a folded sheet of paper. "Tell me what you think?"

Earl unfolded the paper. "This is you. My son drew this! He's more talented than I thought."

"Yes, he is."

Earl glared at her. "You think I tried to stop my son from pursuing an art career?"

Lily remembered how his face lit up when he got the sketchpad from his brother. She wanted Marco to be happy. He needed to create. "What was the gift you gave Marco when he was four years old?" Marco had told her his delight at the gift, but also the unspoken decision that he was now expected to be a cop.

Earl frowned. "A badge and a toy gun. So he could play cop. I gave the same thing to all my kids, even Elena. I wanted them to be proud of me. I wanted them to respect the law and what I did. I didn't think I was being a bad father."

She held up a hand. "Calm down, Earl. You're a fabulous father. I've met your children and your grandchildren. They're happy. They're sane. They're law-abiding. You think Connie's a bulldozer. Look at you. You just have fur-covered wheels."

"Not one of my kids was made to feel that they couldn't pursue other interests if they so chose."

"Earl," Lily touched his hand, "you are such a sweet man, but you have this incredible talent to make people want to please you. You have no idea how much I want to give you the soda, but I'm more afraid of Connie than I am of you. Marco feels the same way. He wanted to please you, just like all your other children."

Earl pouted. "That's not fair. First you say something nice about me, then you hit me across the face. I'm a tyrant, but I'm nice about it."

"Yes," Lily said.

He laughed. "How do we fix this?"

"You mean how do you make Marco quit the police department and become a comic book artist?"

"I guess."

"Has it occurred to you that maybe he can do both."

"You're so smart. What do you want me to do?"

Lily grinned. "Give him a little nudge. Let him know that if he chooses to change careers, he won't disappoint you."

Earl's eyes narrowed. "How come you're so smart?"

"I watch a lot of daytime TV."

Earl gave her the once over stare. "You wouldn't worry about my son being happy if you didn't care for him."

Lily's stomach knotted. "I care." *More than I should.* Earl steepled his long fingers under his chin. "So now that we've figured out Marco, how can I help you?"

"Help me with what?"

"Lily, you're a beautiful woman. You need to get out of the house."

Lily repressed a shudder. "I'd love to, but I can't. Trust me."

"Marco said you weren't always like this."

"That was different."

"How different?"

Lily took a deep breath. "Going out has never been easy for me. My parents wouldn't let me give in to my fears, but after the attack, I found it harder and harder to leave. I feel safe here. I know where everything is."

"Marco says Sawyer broke in and killed your parents."

"But now I have a big wall, big locks and a big gun. And a big Cocker Spaniel masquerading as a Great Dane."

Earl chuckled. "Don't let Harley's easy-going nature fool you. Four months ago one of Angelo's kids was playing in the front yard and one of my neighbors' crazy pit bulls escaped and went straight for the baby. Harley took that bruiser down like it was nothing. That dog is mild-mannered and sweet as the day is long, but if something threatens anyone she loves, she's a terror. I'd trust the littlest of my grand-kids to that dog." Suddenly he swung around and gazed at her with new interest. "How did you get licensed for a firearm, young lady?"

"I have connections in law enforcement on the city, state and federal levels. Being a true crime writer, I meet a lot of interesting people on both sides of the badge."

"My son had better grab you up quick."

Lily giggled. More out of embarrassment then anything else. Then she felt ridiculous because giggling was so high-schoolish. "Why would Marco want me?" She had to admit he was a terrific lover, even though she wasn't the most experienced person in the world. And he was a slob. But then her father hadn't been the neatest person in the world. She could live with that.

"Didn't you know I hand-pick all my future daughters-in-law?"

She felt so complimented. "You're kidding, aren't you?"

He shook his head, still grinning. "My sons all have nice little Connie juniors. If I have to suffer, so do they."

"Suffering, my left pinkie." She had seen how Angelo and Roberto had doted on their wives.

"I taught my sons the most important thing about marriage?"

"And that is?" she asked.

"The woman's always right. No matter what. Silence for a man is the better part of valor."

Lily grinned. "You're a smart guy."

"Yes, I am. So let's watch the new X-Men movie."

―――∿――――

Marco sat at Lily's desk, two stacks of file folders in front of him wondering where to start. Who knew so many young women could go missing in one city in the course of three years?

"What do you have?" Lily sat at Natalie's desk and flipped through the stack.

He smiled. He really liked working with her as if they were partners. "Missing women who turned up dead." He pointed at one stack. "And missing women who never turned up." He rested a hand on the second stack.

Lily glanced at him. "How did you manage to steal these files from the station?"

He liked the way she always questioned him. There was no way he'd ever get anything past her. Hell just being around her forced him to be at the top of his game. "I didn't steal anything. I'm borrowing. Missing persons is one of the busiest divisions in the city. I say I'm here to help and they say what can they do to expedite matters. They even helped me carry the boxes down to my car. Who says service is dead? Besides, your contact was very informative."

"Don't that beat all?" Lily said as she scanned the contents of the open folder. "I just had a thought."

"You're cute when you think." He wiggled his eyebrows and inclined his head toward the bedroom.

Lily rolled her eyes. "Later, Stud."

His bottom lip poked out. "I'm all ears."

She was so tempted to give into him. "Sawyer is a predator and predators stake out a territory where the feeding is good and easy. The easier the better."

"True."

"Because Sawyer picked me, we know he's not into hookers. Which we know is the easiest prey of all."

God he loved the way her mind worked. This is the kind of woman every cop needed. Someone who truly understood their job and could help. "True."

"Narrow this down to the local universities."

Marco frowned. "Why?"

"My third book was about Quinn Riley Dalton. And he preyed on college girls at the UCLA and USC campuses. He even skipped over to Loyola Marymount, which was his big mistake. College women on campus are hard to keep track of. One woman goes missing and someone else says she dropped out. No one calls home to check. The school has eighteen thousand other students to keep track of. Who's going to miss one homesick girl? I was a college girl, and so was the other girl, Leanne Cook, who disappeared from my campus and turned up dead. Narrow your focus to women missing from universities."

Marco studied her. Her dark eyes were shining with passion. He could feel the excitement radiating off her. It was intoxicating. "Now that's why they pay you the big bucks."

"So true."

"You go, girl." Marco started flipping through the files. Some he could automatically discard because they were outside the profile.

Lily slapped the desk with her palms. "Finally, I'm starting to feel like I'm participating instead of playing the victim."

Marco grinned at her. "You weren't reacting like a victim, but a normal person with something to fear."

Relief flooded her face. "I may not live, breathe, and sleep this stuff the way you do, but I know criminals. They've talked to me because they think I'm going to make them famous. Sawyer doesn't want fame. He just wants to go about his 'job' of making my life a living hell. He's low-key. That's why he's so good at stalking me."

"Killing your parents was not low-key."

"He wasn't out to make a point, or do something flashy. I'm sure in his mind he was doing my dad a favor by killing him. After all, my dad has less the than two years to live. And killing my mom, well, they were devoted to each other. Why not die together? That's pretty damn romantic and that's pretty much what the cops saw, too. No one wanted to dig deeper. On any given day, how many homicides did you have sitting on your desk?" Just talking about her parent's murder in such a rational manner brought back all the pain. But the pain didn't seem to be as sharp as it had been in the past. Maybe because she now had someone in her life who understood.

He shrugged. "Four or five in different stages."

"And when you went out to a slam-bam easy case, didn't you close the book and move on."

"I had to, but we've had this talk before"

"Exactly," Lily said.

Good, he could stop feeling guilty about how the department had rushed through her parent's case. "I'm glad to know you're not upset with the police."

"I write about cops, I know the reality of the job. And the reality is too much to do and not enough time, personnel or money to help. I understood why Detective Innis put the case to bed. Because I was personally involved, I was still angry."

Marco and Lily spent the next two hours separating the possibles from the not-possibles and were able to eliminate ninety percent of the missing women. And when he had finally reassembled things, Marco stared at what he had. And what he had was an interesting collection of fourteen women reported missing from the various campuses in Phoenix and the surrounding areas.

"What do you think Sawyer really wanted from you?" Marco asked, hating to think about what went on in that twisted piece of mind.

Lily stopped reading. "I think he wanted me to be the Leave It To Beaver mom. What's her name?"

"June Cleaver."

"Right. He would watch me vacuum wearing high-heels, a fake pearl choker, and those stupid fifties dresses. I had to iron his clothes, cook meals for him, and treat him like he was king of the hill."

Marco couldn't see Lily in that kind of role. Who would want a woman who was just above a dog fetching his slippers?

"He even wanted me to bake him cookies."

Marco frowned. Something tickled the back of his head. He grabbed the stack of files containing the murdered college girls. He searched through the short stack and found the folder he wanted.

"What's the matter?" Lily asked.

"Pearls," he muttered, "Pearls." He extracted the file and handed it to Lily. "Take a look at that."

Lily glanced through the file and the photos of the dead woman. Her eyes went wide. "She's wearing my pearls."

CHAPTER THIRTEEN

The woman lay on the sand, her eyes closed and her hands outstretched. Around her neck was the pearl choker Lily had been forced to wear. She also wore a plain blue shirtwaist dress that Lily recognized. In fact she resembled Lily, with a petite body, chocolate brown face and dark curly hair.

"She's wearing my dress." Lily felt sick. She started to shake. The tremors began in her hands and then radiated up and down her arms until she had to drop the file and clasp her hands together to stop their shaking. She glanced at the date. The woman had been killed a week after Lily had gotten away from Sawyer, the day before he'd been arrested. "Sawyer killed this woman."

Marco stared at the photo and then at his hands. He wiped his palms on the sides of his pants. "Are you sure?"

She opened her eyes and studied the photo again. "I'm certain. Sawyer killed her. I can feel it. You can, too. I can see it in your eyes." Had he done so because Lily had escaped? She closed her eyes. Had she been the cause of this woman's death simply because she'd gotten away and frustrated Sawyer so much he'd walked right out and kidnapped another woman? The tremors vibrated through her whole body and she fought the sense of being out of focus that signaled a panic attack.

Marco reached out and touched her hand.

Electric pulses sprinted up Lily's arm. For a second, she managed to put aside her fears and forget that a madman wanted her dead. Why couldn't every moment be like this forever? Just Marco and Lily and nothing outside to intrude.

Marco's cell phone rang breaking their bond. He withdrew his fingers and answered. He listened.

Lily picked up the report. The young woman had been a student at Phoenix City College. All the terror, all the horror of that girl's death left Lily gasping. She knew what that poor girl had gone through.

Lily remembered the first time she'd made cookies for Sawyer, and in her nervousness, she'd burned them. He'd been so angry with her she'd thought he would kill her right then, but he'd gone away and come back a few minutes later all smiles. If Lily had not been so frightened she would have made a run for it then, but she hadn't because she'd been too afraid.

The girl's body had been found by hikers who'd been searching for a little-known canyon that contained ancient Anasazi ruins. She hadn't been dead for more than a day. Lily wondered how many other women, women no one knew about, Sawyer had killed.

She half-listened to Marco talk on the phone as she relived her time in the shack. The police had searched for that shack, but never found it. But they hadn't been able to backtrack her. The dry desert sand hadn't held her footprints and they had no idea which direction she'd traveled from once she'd escaped. She wondered if Sawyer had had other bodies stashed around the shack. Other women who hadn't made the grade.

The criminal mind shouldn't shock her, but Sawyer's did. She couldn't put herself in his mind; figure out what he was thinking, why he was thinking it. Maybe, because she was too close. But he'd wanted something from her. Something from the dead girl in the photo. *Dammit, Lily*, she told herself, *stop thinking like a victim. You know crime, you know criminals.* What did he want? What was his psychodrama and why the hell was she the lead actress in it?

Marco disconnected and put his phone away. "That was Hunter. She's been busy on completing the background check on Sawyer."

"What did she find?"

"The standard issue abused child, alcoholic father, hooker mother. Blah! Blah! Blah! One interesting thing though. Hunter talked to a neighbor who lived next door to Sawyer when he was a kid, and she said when his mom was turning tricks, she'd lock him in a closet with the TV. She said she would hear TV reruns blasting away all day."

"The perfect mother. The perfect wife." Everything clicked into place. She sorted through the flood of ideas.

"What?"

"The perfect wife. I told you he was auditioning me. He's looking for the perfect mother. The June Cleaver clone who is nurturing and loving. Who bakes cookies and dresses in pretty clothes. Who takes care of him?"

Marco stared her thoughtfully. "Now that's different from the run-of-the-mill serial killer. And he kills when the audition goes wrong because the ideal is somehow contaminated."

"That's why he never tried to touch me or rape me." Lily had always puzzled over the lack of sexual advances on Sawyer's part. Whoever he thought she should be, she had to be pure and untainted.

Marco opened his notebook and started to doodle. His pencil moved furiously over the white paper. "But now he wants to kill you."

"Kill me or finish the audition. How did his mother die?"

"According to Hunter, mom just disappeared."

Lily found herself nodding. Everything made sense now. In a way she almost felt sorry for Sawyer. "I think Sawyer wants me back because in his mind I abandoned him and demolished his dream. Now he has to finish what he started." Marco had been right when he'd said unfinished business.

Marco nodded, his pencil flying over the paper. "Let's take this to its logical conclusion. We know you escaped and by doing so pissed him off. You thought he was going to kill you that last night. Does he still want to kill you, or does he want something else?"

"He wants to kill me because I'm contaminated in some way. The interview ended when I ran. I don't care what he wants with me anymore, he's not getting me." She closed her eyes and tried to control the terror. Stop being a victim, she scolded herself. Breath in. Breath out. Concentrate on something else. The fear will pass. She wasn't a victim; she was Tiger Lily in control of her destiny.

"If you want to be safe you need to leave this house."

Lily's blood ran cold. She thought she would shatter. Then she started to sweat. She took a long, steadying breath. "You don't understand. I can't walk out of this house. If I do, I feel like I'm going to die. There's no logic in agoraphobia. I can't be a normal person just because you say so. I know I probably frustrate you. If I could, I'd be on my way to Alaska, getting as far from Sawyer as possible. I can't, Marco. I can't."

"When you're sick, you go to the doctor."

Lily shrugged. "When I'm sick, the doctor comes to me."

Marco allowed a small grin. "Point taken, but that's not what I mean. You seek help."

Lily had no ready answer. When her parents had been alive, they'd supported her and kept her going. But with them gone, she didn't have to put herself into situations that made her anxious and she was relieved.

She understood that she was lost. But she didn't know how to find herself. She also knew that her fears were not the delusions of a weary mind. "I..." her words trailed off.

"I know the big, bad world out there isn't something you can control. Hiding in here isn't going to solve anything."

"I have everything I need."

"That's the problem. You have everything you need."

Lily stood and stalked over to him. "You don't have the right to sit in judgment on me, Marco Jackson. You're the one who doesn't have the guts to tell your own father you want to be an artist."

Marco chuckled. "We're having our first fight?"

She stopped, surprised at his comment. He was not taking her seriously and for a second she wanted to smack him. But he was right. "I think so."

"You're right." Marco held up a finger. "But, number one, I have been working on my career as an artist, maybe not as quickly as you think I should. But if you ask anyone in my family, I do things my way and at my own speed. And number two, I have a life, a dog, a demanding career, and a family who takes up a lot of my time. And I'm not ready to give up any of those relationships to pursue a personal pipe dream." He planted his hands on the top of the desk and leaned across it. "That's how my father taught me to be a man. You have to take care of everyone else before you worry about yourself."

"Don't be bringing your dad into this." Marco wasn't being fair. Opening a door and walking outside wasn't going to prove anything. With enough anti-anxiety drugs, she could take a vacation in Nepal. She just didn't like the idea of taking chemicals when she could simply re-arrange her life to make things easy for herself. She'd had an online friend who took pills to get herself out of the house and ended up taking pills to remember to take pills. If things didn't work themselves out naturally, they wouldn't work out. "Listen, I'm a useful person. I teach Internet classes for the police academy. I've helped the police anytime they called. I find justice for people. Does it matter if I do my job in this house, or in an office in downtown Phoenix?"

Marco suddenly frowned. "Office in downtown Phoenix!" He pulled his phone of his pocket. "Hold that thought."

"What are you doing?" She almost stamped her foot. They were having an argument and she didn't like being cut off in the middle of her point.

Again he held up a finger. "Don't make me lose this thought." He dialed, and said, "Whitaker, I need some information." He paused, listening. "Yeah, the Sawyer case." He listened again, then went on, "Sawyer works for a janitorial service. I want to know what buildings they clean." He disconnected and put the phone away.

"Why do you want to know all that?"

"In a minute. First, we are finishing this argument."

"We're not finishing this argument. I'm not going to speak to you anymore. You either tell me what that phone call was about, or I'm leaving." She folded her arms across her chest and stuck out her chin.

"Oh really?" His voice held a teasing tone.

She nodded, refusing to be tricked into answering.

He ran a finger down her shoulder. "Can we still have sex?"

She scowled at him, pressing her lips together to keep the words unsaid.

Marco grinned in delight. "I'm taking that as a yes. I'm all right with that because you do tend to be noisy." He tilted his head at her, his eyes narrowing and his lips quivering with suppressed laughter.

She scrunched up her face resisting. *Don't say anything, Lily.* She picked up one of the file folders, smacked him on top of the head and stalked out to the kitchen.

She opened the dishwasher and started unloading it, trying not to smack plates down on the counter. He was the most frustrating man she'd ever known. Not that she'd known many, but the few she did know were tame compared to Marco.

Marco followed and came up behind to kiss her on the back of her neck. He nuzzled her ear gently and she felt a surge of desire for him. Just the thought of her nights with him sent her pulses soaring. The feel of his hands on her skin almost brought a sigh of contentment.

He turned her around and kissed her. "Stay in the house. Get out of the house. I don't care. I want you safe, but I want you just the way you are."

"I'm afraid."

"I know," he whispered.

"Not just of Sawyer, but of going outside. Of life." Because bad things happened to her when she went outside her house. Not even her fear of Sawyer could force her to leave. Just the memory of the panic attacks sent her into a spiral of paralyzing fear. The room tilted on its axis and she found herself clinging to Marco when she didn't want to cling because she wanted to be strong.

"How do we make you unafraid?" Marco's arms tightened around her.

"I don't know." His touch felt so good around her. She leaned back against his chest. She felt safe right here, with Marco holding her. She didn't need the world when she had him. But a small voice nagged at her, what would she do when he left? What would she do when he grew tired of dealing with the irrational elements of her agoraphobia?

"I'll tell you about the phone call." He held out the lure like holding out a carrot.

"All right, I'm listening."

He leaned against the counter keeping her safe against him. "The comment you made about office buildings. My mind had been mulling over things while we were talking, and I kept thinking about Sawyer, he seems to know a great deal about you. He even knew how to get his bizarre gift to me without making us suspicious. I started thinking about Home Bound, Inc. which has an office downtown."

"In the Ramsey building."

"Right. I kept trying to figure out how Sawyer would know so much, then it hit me, he's a janitor. Janitors clean offices. Could he be cleaning up at Home Bound, Inc? If he is, he'd have access to their files."

Lily frowned. "Home Bound, Inc. does everything through their computers. They don't have files that people can actually read because they are very conscious of security. They have people's entire lives in their databases."

"When I was in Sawyer's house the other day, he had a pretty sophisticated computer set up, and Hunter commented that one of his cell mates at state was some computer geek who had the stones to crack the CIA computers."

"When did you find this out?" Had he been keeping secrets from her? Wasn't she a partner?

"Hunter called earlier this afternoon. That girl has a nose that could sniff out a trail in a rainstorm." He kissed the top of Lily's head. "This guy had turned his life around and is now on the FBI payroll. According to Hunter, he was anxious to cooperate."

"So you're thinking that this guy taught Sawyer how to hack into a computer? That's something to think about."

"He taught Sawyer something." Marco's cell phone rang and he answered. He listened for a few seconds, then disconnected. "That was Whitaker. Sawyer works for the janitorial service who just happens to clean the Ramsey building, which just happens to house the corporate offices of Home Bound, Inc. which makes a guy think."

If Sawyer was as competent as Marco seemed to think, the scope of the man's attacks took on new meaning. "That dirty bastard," Lily said. "I wonder if he's terrorizing anyone else the same way he's terrorizing me?"

"I don't think so. Currently, you seem to be his target *du jour*. After all, you're the one who got away. I think you did more than ruin something for Sawyer. You rocked his little world. He thought he had complete control of you and you proved him wrong."

Marco slid his arms around her. She closed her eyes and breathed in his scent, a mixture of plain old soap and something lemony. "I'm heartbroken. He's ruined a lot of things for me." She thought about her parents. Maybe they hadn't done her a favor by shielding her the way they had, but they had always had her welfare in mind. They had understood her and were patient with her. Never condemning her, yet never allowing her to give in to her fears. With their deaths, Sawyer wiped out her support system.

"You ruined his fantasy," Marco continued, "You out-smarted him. By escaping, you canceled the TV show."

"Shame on me." Maybe this whole nightmare would end soon. "Do you have enough to get a search warrant?"

Marco gave an evil little smile. "Sawyer's on parole. I can search his house any time, just because I want to."

"Why don't you?" Her mind screamed that they should arrest him.

"Because we're still in the dating phase."

"The dating phase?" Lily asked curiously.

Marco nodded. "Right now, Sawyer thinks he's the smart one. He knows how to work the system. I could arrest him, but I want more. I want him tied up in a knot so that he has no wriggle room, because when I arrest him, it will be for multiple homicide with a sentence of lethal injection. End of problem."

"Explain the dating phase."

"I make a move. Sawyer makes a move. Maybe I'm going out on a limb, but I think Sawyer thinks when I arrived here last week I came with the intention of talking to you about your parents. He was out there taking photos of you, probably right on the street, and I just happened to come along. He did some digging and found out who I was. If he's as good as I think he is, hacking into the police computers would be a piece of cake. He got mad and sent you the heart as a warning to make you back off. Then I moved in and Natalie got beat up. Then I visited him at his house and the hands came. Hunter pulled him in this morning. She made some interesting discoveries. He has shaved everything off his body hair and wears a wig."

Lily knew why. "Because hair has DNA and his DNA is on file because he was in prison." She shuddered. Marco's arms tightened. She allowed herself to be lulled back to her safe place.

"Well hello, Miss Smarty Pants." Marco patted her on the head.

Lily pushed his hands away and stepped back. "So you're telling me that if Hunter paid him a visit today, then we should be expecting a counterattack soon." She waited for the terror to rise, but all she felt was a distant breathlessness. Knowing the future took away some of her anxiety.

"Yep! But what? I already have a twenty-four/seven tail on Sawyer. If anything happens, we'll have some warning."

I hope, Lily thought. "Basically, we're just sitting here and waiting."

He tilted his head toward the bedroom and touched her arm. "We don't have to sit and wait. There are other things we can do."

He gave her a seductive grin that just about knocked her socks right off.

"You are always thinking below your belt." *Just like a man*, she added to herself.

"Hey, I'm half Italian here and bilingual in the language of love. Come along, my little biscotti." He took her hand and started leading her toward the hallway to the bedroom.

When Lily didn't move, he stopped.

"I have a better idea. Have you ever seen my Jacuzzi?" She felt deliciously naughty. Her parents had installed the Jacuzzi as a way to relax her. Little did they know that she had just come up with a new use for it.

With one eyebrow upraised, he said, "Let me get my swim fins."

She leered at him. "Trust me. You don't need them."

CHAPTER FOURTEEN

The phone rang. Marco forced himself through the deep layers of sleep and reached out to grab the cordless out of the cradle before the shrill sound woke Lily.

"Hello," he said.

"Is this Marco Jackson?" a strange voice asked.

Marco rubbed sleep from his eyes. He could hear odd, crackling sounds in the background. "Yeah. Who are you?"

"This is Neal," the man paused. "You know, your next door neighbor."

For a second, Marco couldn't think which neighbor, then he remembered that he'd given Neal a key and asked him to pick up his mail and keep an eye on the house. "What's up, Neal?"

"I don't know how to tell you this, man, but your house is on fire."

Marco sat up. "Oh, shit!"

Neal said, "I called the fire department and they should be here in another minute. Gladys has a hose and is squirting water on the flames, but it's not having much effect. I think you'd better get here, fast."

Marco hung up the phone and turned on the lamp. He shook Lily. She struggled to wake up, glanced at the clock and said grumpily. "It's two a.m., Marco."

Marco pushed the blanket back. "I've got to go. My house is on fire."

"Your house." Lily jumped out of bed. "How can your house be on fire?"

"I don't know." He searched for his clothes. He reached for the phone and dialed his dad. No answer. Then he remembered that his parents had decided to go to Laughlin for a few days. His brothers had all returned to their respective homes. Dawson? No, she'd gone to Los Angeles for a meeting. He dialed Elena's home. No answer. Where the hell was she? He tried her cell phone and when she answered all he could hear was a massive roar in the background.

"Where are you?" Marco growled, tapping his fingers impatiently against the back of the phone.

"I'm at Logan Airport in Boston."

"What the hell are you doing there?"

"I'm ovulating. I came to jump my husband."

He didn't need to know that. "I've gotta go."

He disconnected her in mid-word. Who to call? He couldn't leave Lily alone. Greyhorse? Maybe. Whitaker? Only as a last resort.

"Why are you calling all these people?" Lily had wrapped the sheet around her and had picked up his jeans from her settee and tossed them on the bed.

"I can't leave you alone."

"Sure you can. I have Harley and a big gun." She opened the bed-side table and drew out her Glock. "I'll be fine."

"No. Sawyer started this fire."

"Then he's probably done all he intended to do tonight. This is just another part of his campaign. Remember. You said you make a move and then he makes a move. Don't worry about me. Go."

But he was worried. He dialed Hunter. Beatrix answered on the first ring. Marco quickly outlined the problem.

"I'm leaving right now, but the drive out to Lily's is almost an hour from my house."

"Drive fast."

"That is fast."

"Drive faster."

"I'll be there."

Marco hung up and sat on the bed to pull on his jeans. "Stay in this room. Don't open the door. Don't do anything. If you hear anything, you call the cops." He opened the bedroom door and whistled for Harley. Harley trotted down the long hallway and entered the bedroom to sniff at Marco's shoes and then plop herself down in front of Lily. "Keep Harley with you at all times."

"I'll be fine." Lily kissed him.

Marco checked the house before he left, and headed out to his motorcycle. He didn't feel right about leaving Lily, but he needed to check his house and see if he could save anything.

He pulled out through the gate and paused to make sure the gate closed behind him and then he roared down the street anxious to get to his home.

Lily locked the bedroom door. Harley had positioned herself on the rug in front of the fireplace and fallen asleep, her gentle snores a soothing sound.

Too nervous to sleep, Lily sat in the chair in front of the fireplace, and with her Glock cradled in her lap she leaned her head back and tried to relax.

The phone rang and Lily jumped up to answer it. "Marco?"

"Hello, Lily." Sawyer's voice was barely above a whisper.

Lily's fingers tightened on the phone. "What do you want?"

Harley stirred and jumped to her feet. She sniffed the air, padded to the door and scratched at the wood. Then she jumped up, whining, juggling the door latch. Terror rose in Lily. She could hardly breath.

Sawyer's voice was like sandpaper on wood. "It's time for you to go home, Lily."

A huge tremor shook her. Where was he? "If you want me, you come in here and get me."

Sawyer laughed. "I've already got you, Lily. Your boyfriend can't stop me. All those men he had on my doorstep can't stop me. No one can stop me. I am God, Lily."

Her fingers went numb. She could barely hold the phone still against her ear. "I can kill you."

Again he laughed. "I just want to take care of you, Lily. I love you." His laughter grew louder and harsher. He disconnected.

Lily froze. She checked her gun and the safety was off. She was ready for anything.

The lights went out. She clutched the phone, remembering Marco's instructions. She dialed 9-1-1, but the phone was dead. No electricity, no cordless phone. But in her office, she had a regular desk phone that didn't depend on electricity. She would have to open the door.

Was he inside the house? Outside the house? Where? Harley whined again and Lily patted the dog's massive head. She wanted to hang on to Harley, but she needed to get to a working phone.

Her hand hovered over the doorknob. Paralyzed, her feet felt like lead. She had to get to a phone.

She gripped the doorknob and twisted it open. Even before she had the door completely open, Harley pushed past her and galloped down the hallway toward the living room barking madly. *That's it, Harley, go get him, girl.*

Lily tiptoed the other way to her office, the darkness almost as frightening as Sawyer. Harley went silent, then started barking again. A scream reverberated through the house. The sounds of a struggle echoed through the house. Lily could hear the heavy thuds of Harley's paws, then a gunshot, and then silence. Lily froze again, unable to step forward. Harley whined.

She couldn't breathe. Her head spun, as she stared horrified toward the front of the house. He'd shot Harley.

"Lily," came a throaty, raspy whispery. "I killed the dog, Lily. You're next."

Kill him, she urged herself. She clutched the Glock, but her fingers were cramped. Kill him. Kill him. She couldn't.

Lily pressed herself against the wall, her whole body trembling. Go toward the office, she ordered her powerless feet. There's a phone. Help is only three numbers away. She managed to move along the wall and realized her clothing scraped against the plaster. She stood straight. He didn't know where she was.

A door opened at the end of the hall. Lily saw Sawyer's faint shadow. Then the door closed. She crouched. He couldn't see her if she could make herself smaller.

Her mind was transported back to her flight so many years ago. She'd escaped then, and she'd escape now. She inched forward and slipped on a rug. She caught her balance.

"Where are you, Lily?"

Her heart pounded so loudly, she knew Sawyer could hear her. He opened the door to a closet. Lily inched forward again, feeling with her feet. She only had twenty feet to go.

Another whimper came from the living room. Harley was still

alive.

Sawyer was getting closer. He came to the locked door of the garage and jiggled the handle. A shot fired and Lily saw the flash. He wrenched open the door and stepped through.

"Are you in here, Lily?"

A scream started building in her throat. She couldn't give in to her panic. She slid further down the hall trying to make herself invisible. Then she ran.

She reached her office, flung open the door and just as she reached for the phone, Sawyer grabbed her and jerked her back. Her Glock jerked out of her hands and slid across the floor. Lily was amazed it didn't go off. Her moment of indecision would now cost her her future.

"Hello, Lily." His voice was iced cold, expressionless. "Going somewhere?"

He ran his fingers down the side of her neck and she shook with revulsion.

A frail moon shone through the bank of windows that illuminated her office. Sawyer's eyes reflected the light. He was bald and dressed in a dark jumpsuit. Lily wrenched herself free. "No." She inched toward her desk.

"You're not a nice girl anymore." He shook his head. "I had high hopes for you."

"I never was a nice girl." She took another tiny step back. The gun in his hand wavered.

"I know that now. I should have killed you. You were just like all the others."

"All the others?" Her voice trembled and she hated herself for her weakness. But she hoped to keep him talking.

"They're all dead. You're the only one who didn't die. I've come to remedy that little annoyance."

"Why did you kill my parents?" The room whirled. She had to focus on him; she couldn't lose this game. Little by little, she grabbed the mad edges of her fear and tucked them away in the back of her mind.

"Because you needed them. I wanted you to need me, but then you took in that cop." Suddenly, his voice sounded almost conversational as though they were having a companionable cup of coffee at the local Starbucks.

She reached for the phone. If she were going to die, she wasn't going tamely. But Sawyer grabbed her arm and pulled her back.

"No. No. No." He shook a finger, his eyes still gleaming, reflecting the light from the windows.

A car drove down the street. Halogen street lights cast muted haloes over the floor of her office.

"How did you escape your handlers?" Lily asked. Her Glock was cold against the edge of her big toe. If only she could distract him enough to get it. Her fear was under control now. She was calm, resolved. She gulped air, amazed that she could face mortality so easily.

"They're pretty stupid," Sawyer boasted. "They think I'm at work in the Cross building tonight. They parked outside and I went out through the parking garage. I always keep spare clothes there and a place to stash my wig. All in all it was easy." He snapped his fingers. "They never even saw me leave. Who would be looking for a bald man? I'm assuming they're cops. I could have told you, Lily, that the cops are no match for me. If they couldn't find the evidence to prove I killed your parents, they'll never find the evidence to prove I killed you."

"You're going to kill me." She created and discarded a half dozen schemes to distract him. She had to get the Glock.

"Of course, I'm going to kill you. I've waited long enough."

She stretched out her hand toward the desk, and Sawyer hit her. She fell down and groped on the floor for the Glock, her fingers brushing against the handle. "You know what the problem with you is?"

"What?" he asked in a condescending tone.

"You talk too much." She grabbed the Glock and fired.

Sawyer swayed, staring at her. "You missed."

She fired a second time. She had no idea if she'd hit him, but he slumped slowly to the floor.

"Lily," he repeated.

"Die!" she screamed.

He sprawled on the carpet. Lily pulled herself to her feet and raced for her desk to yank open the bottom drawer. She pulled out her flashlight and shone it at Sawyer.

He stared back at her. "You shot me." Blood pooled around him. He closed his eyes.

For a second, she forced deep breaths into her lungs. The room stopped whirling. On the desk were Marco's handcuffs. She opened them, and quickly put one bracelet on Sawyer, and dragged him toward the desk. Then she slid the chain around the leg of her desk, and then attached the other bracelet to his hand. She didn't know if he were dead or not, but she wasn't taking any chances. She pushed his gun as far away as she could with her foot.

She straightened, reached for the phone and dialed 9-1-1. The dispatcher took all the information. Then she dialed Marco, but he didn't answer. With the roar of his motorcycle and his helmet cutting off the sound, he probably couldn't hear his phone. She reached his voice mail and told him what had happened and that she was taking

Harley to the vet.

She checked Sawyer one last time, staying as far from him as she could, running the beam of her flashlight over him. He breathed shallowly and his face had gone pale.

Lily raced out of the office and headed for the living room, the beam of her flashlight bouncing off the walls. She thought about looking for the breaker box but Lily wasn't certain where the box was. She didn't want to waste the time when Harley could be dying.

Harley lay in the center of the living room on her side. Blood oozed in a sullen rivulet down her side. Lily fell down next to her and listened. Harley whimpered and tried to get to her feet. But her hind legs wouldn't obey.

Lily stroked the dog's silky muzzle. "Stay."

Lily glanced around the living room. An afghan had been tossed over a corner chair. She grabbed the afghan and spread it out on the floor. She rolled Harley onto the afghan. "Hang in there, girl." She thought about calling the vet to come to her, but she didn't know if there would be enough time. Even in the few minutes since Harley had been shot, her breathing had gone more shallow than before.

Lily dragged the afghan across the wood floor toward the garage. She pulled the dog toward the car, and opened the door. Lily coaxed Harley to her feet and as the dog struggled to climb into the back seat of the Volvo, Lily pushed. With Harley stretched out on the back seat, Lily wrapped the afghan around her and ran back into the house to get the car keys.

Lily entered her office. Sawyer lay where she had left him. His eyes flickered open briefly.

Lily circled him, keeping as far from him as possible. She opened the center drawer in her desk and removed the car keys. She couldn't leave without telling the cops were she was. She grabbed a post-it note and wrote, "Dog shot. At vet on Central. Keys and guns in frig." She tacked the post-it note on Sawyer's forehead and then added a piece of tape to it to keep him from shaking it off. She set the flashlight down on the desk and trained it to shine on the sidewall showing Sawyer in the reflected light.

She picked up his gun and ran to the kitchen to put the guns and the handcuff keys in the refrigerator and fled back to the garage. She had to figure out how to disengage the automatic garage door opener. She yanked on the cord that took the opener off the track. She heaved the door up and the garage moved upward.

Without another thought, she got into the car.

Harley cried.

"I'll save you, Harley." Lily started the car and backed out into the night.

———ᘒ———

Marco's hands sweated and the back of his neck tingled. The hell with his house. He couldn't do anything to stop the fire and the fire department would take care of it. He pulled the motorcycle to the side and dug his cell phone out of his pocket and dialed Lily. The phone showed a missed message alert. He dialed his voice mail and heard Lily's voice telling him Sawyer hurt Harley and that he had to come home.

Marco dialed the station and talked to the cop on duty.

"We just got a call to dispatch units to that address. They are on their way," the cop said.

Marco was stupid. He should never have left Lily alone despite her assurances she'd be all right. Nothing in his house was worth her life. Nothing was worth losing the one woman he loved beyond all measure.

Yeah, he could admit that he loved her. Though he'd been fighting that idea.

He turned the motorcycle around and headed back toward Lily's.

The house was dark. The front gate wide open. Marco's heart turned to lead. Lily! He parked the bike at the front door. The door was open. He drew his gun and crouched. In the distance, he could hear the sounds of sirens. The cops were on their way, but he couldn't wait. If Lily were still inside, he needed to save her.

He slid into the entry hall. He could smell the coppery aroma of blood. Whose blood?

He eased down the hallway and looked into the living room. The night-lights Lily had positioned throughout the room were all out. No electricity. As his eyes adjusted to the darkness, he could see the room was empty. The smell of blood was strong here. *Had Sawyer shot Lily and taken her body? Where was Harley?*

He slipped down the hall. The doors lining the hall were open. Each room dark. The throw rugs on the wood floors were askew as though someone had hastily pushed them aside.

The garage door hung open. Marco glanced inside and saw that the car was gone. *Had Sawyer taken Lily?* A hole opened inside his soul. He turned back into the house. He was a cop; he had to be thorough. He checked the next door. It was a closet. The darkness was smothering.

He should check the breaker, but he hesitated. If Sawyer was still loose in the house, he would have the advantage.

Where was Lily? He wanted to call out, but he didn't want to alert Sawyer. If she were hiding, he could give away her position if she answered.

He crept down the hall checking each open door, and finding an empty room, an empty closet. The sirens were closer. He heard a groan from somewhere and stopped to listen. The groan didn't repeat. When he finally pushed open the office door, and the smell of blood hit him.

A flashlight had been left on the desk sending a beam of light to one wall. Just enough light for Marco to see Sawyer stretched out on the floor, his arms over his head and something blue on his forehead. A trickle of blood oozed from a wound in his hip.

Sawyer groaned. Marco approached cautiously, until he saw Sawyer's hand was handcuffed to the leg of the desk, and the blue something on his forehead was a post-it note. He picked up the flashlight and read the short message Lily had written. Harley was shot. She was safe. She was at the vet.

Marco started laughing.

Sawyer opened his eyes and glared at him. "You have to help me."

Marco squatted down. "You burned my house, you shot my dog and you tried to kill my woman. And you think I'm going to mosey on over there and call 9-1-1 to save your sorry ass."

Sawyer's eyes went wide. "You're a cop."

Marco slapped Sawyer lightly on the face. "I have to take care of my dog and my woman."

He stood just as the sounds of squealing brakes sounded outside. Marco put his gun away and fumbled for his badge. He pinned the badge on his jacket.

He heard a woman's voice. "This is Phoenix P.D. Come out of the house with your hands raised, you're surrounded."

"Hunter," he called, "the place is secure. See if you can find the breaker box and turn on the electricity."

"Okay," Hunter called.

Marco waited impatiently. He didn't want to leave the scene, but he had to check on Lily and Harley.

A few seconds later, the lights popped on. The hall was still dark, Marco flipped the switch and light flooded it. Then he walked down the hall and turned the lights on in every room so that when the rest of the posse arrived, they could see what they were doing and not shoot him or Hunter. In the living room he found a puddle of blood that was smeared across the wood floor as though something had been dragged through it.

Hunter entered through the front door. "Where's Lily?"

"At the emergency vet on Central."

Hunter's eyes went wide. "What happened?"

"Sawyer is handcuffed to Lily's desk. He's bleeding, so we'd better call an ambulance."

More cop cars pulled through the gate and squealed to a stop at the front door. Marco wanted to leap on his motorcycle and head after Lily, but someone had to explain the situation.

"Go," Hunter said, "I'll take care of everything." She flipped open her badge wallet and held it over her head as cops opened car doors and stepped out. "Hunter," she called, "Cold Case Unit. The house is secure."

Marco showed his badge to the approaching cops. "I've got another call." He pointed at Hunter standing by the front door. "She will explain everything." He straddled his motorcycle, the motor roared to life, and he left.

The vet's office was tucked into a strip mall. The Volvo was parked in a handicapped spot, and Marco pulled in right next to it.

When he entered the waiting room he found Lily pacing back and forth. She was covered in blood and for a moment Marco thought it was hers.

"Lily."

She threw herself in his arms. "I'm sorry. I couldn't protect Harley."

"Lily ..."

"I told the vet you would need the bullet as evidence."

"Lily ..."

"I know you told me to stay in the bedroom, but Harley got away. I shot Sawyer, but I couldn't kill him. I tried. He was bleeding, you need to call an ambulance for him."

He grabbed her by the shoulders. "Lily, do you know what you've done?"

She covered her mouth with her fingers. "Oh no. I left the scene of a crime."

"Lily," he almost laughed. "You're getting warmer."

"What are you talking about?" She frowned.

"You left the house."

She stared at him. "I did, didn't I? I didn't once think about that, I was worried Harley would die."

Marco pulled her into his arms. "I love you. But you scared the shit out of me."

"I didn't mean to do that. But Harley was bleeding and I didn't know what to do except get her here."

He kissed her.

For a moment, she stood rigid in his arms, and then her mouth softened and she swayed into him. "We have to get married. I love you. My dog loves you. My family loves you."

"You love me!"

"Like I'm going crazy in my head." Until he'd almost lost her, he hadn't known how much he loved her.

"I love you, too," she said. Then her face changed. "But, my trip to the vet may be nothing more than a fluke. I may never leave again."

"Then I'll always know where you are." He grinned, happiness spiraling through him. She loved him, too. They could make this marriage work despite the obstacles.

A warning look came into her face. "I'm not going to be the 'little woman.' I'm going to nag you about your writing career."

"Technically, you are a little woman. You're just barely bigger than a midget. And you can nag me all you want. Just as long as you love me forever."

"What about children?"

"I want children. Don't you?"

A door opened and a man in surgical garb came out, stripping rubber gloves off his hands. "Your dog is going to be fine. Nothing vital was hit. The bullet lodged in a rib and I saved it. I tried to be very careful in removing it, so I don't think she's even going to have a scar. The main thing I'm concerned about is that I found blood around her mouth. She attacked someone?"

"That's my girl," Marco said. "She's protecting mama."

The vet frowned. "I took bite impressions because I have to report the incident to animal control. You might want to talk to your breeder and your regular vet and have them give affidavits as to the temperament of your dog. And I can tell you; she was well-behaved even though she was in pain. I will also make a note of it in her file."

"The man who shot my dog has enough to worry about."

The vet nodded, "Get the documentation, just to be on the safe side."

"Can we see her?" Lily asked.

The vet shook his head. "She's groggy and pumped up full of pain-killers. I want to keep her for observation for a day. But you can spend a couple minutes with her."

Harley's stumpy tail wagged when Marco bent down to open the cage and pet her. Lily knelt down next to her and kissed her nose. Her big eyes closed and she relaxed. Marco patted her for a few seconds and then drew Lily up. "We need to get back to the house."

Outside, Lily handed him the keys to the Volvo. "You'd better drive, I don't think I can." The keys jingled in her trembling fingers.

"The adrenaline rush is wearing off." Marco took the keys. He'd worry about the motorcycle later.

When he pulled into the drive, the house was ablaze with light. Cop cars and an ambulance were parked outside. A few neighbors, roused by the commotion, stood on the sidewalk watching.

The minute Lily stepped out of the car, Marco could see all the cops were ready to converge on her.

Marco stopped them. "She needs to change her clothes, first. Lily, go change and bring everything back. The crime scene guys are going to want your clothes."

She nodded. Beatrix Hunter stepped forward to accompany her to her bedroom.

Leland Davenport stepped out of Lily's office, a frown on his face. "You're just the person I want to see."

Marco caught a glimpse of the emergency medical team, bending over Sawyer.

"Do you know," Davenport said, "you violated every rule in regards to crime scene procedures? You left the scene of the crime. You ...."

Marco held up his hand. "The scene was secure. Hunter arrived before I left, and Lily was already gone so I couldn't do anything about her decision to leave. And frankly, I had to take care of both my woman and my dog. So if you want to roast my chestnuts, Mr. County Attorney Davenport, you just go right ahead. I had priorities."

"I'm not upset. I just wanted you to know."

"Consider me informed."

The EMTs had gotten Sawyer on a gurney, and as he was wheeled past Marco he sneered. "I'm going to sue you and the whole damn department. Your dog bit me."

"So what." Lily shrugged.

Hunter walked out of the office. "I just talked to the tech guys. They have Sawyer's computer."

Sawyer looked panicked. "You can't take my stuff without my permission."

Leland Davenport leaned over him. "You have violated your parole, Mr. Sawyer. You were caught carrying a gun. You invaded this woman's home. Everything you own is subject to search and seizure. I look forward to another strip search."

Hunter waved her hands. "I have more. I have more."

Davenport glanced at her. "Tell me later. Let's get out of the way and let these good people take Mr. Sawyer to the hospital for treatment."

The crime scene team arrived and Hunter took charge of them.

Lily returned wearing jeans and a white t-shirt. She handed Hunter a grocery bag with her clothes. Her eyes looked bruised. She yawned, exhausted. Marco told Davenport that he would take Lily to the media room and keep her out of the way.

CHAPTER FIFTEEN

Lily didn't intend to fall asleep. But the minute Marco made her sit down in the recliner, her whole body relaxed and she found her eyelids too heavy to keep open.

When she awoke, the house was quiet and Marco was asleep in the recliner next to her. She wanted to wake him and ask what had happened, but he looked so tired that she didn't have the heart to disturb him just yet.

She decided to make him breakfast. But as she walked through the house she found evidence of the night's activities. Blood everywhere. On the walls, on the floor. Fingerprint powder, shoe prints. Her house was a mess. Her fingers itched to call her cleaning crew, but she didn't know if she should. She would have to ask Marco when he woke up.

She entered the kitchen and was pleased to know that very little damage had occurred to it. She set about gathering the supplies for breakfast, though a quick glance at the clock told her lunch would be a better idea. She'd been asleep for nearly seven hours, yet she didn't feel rested. Her whole body felt out of sync.

Marco's cell phone rang and she heard him answer it. She continued with making breakfast. She couldn't believe he loved her. She loved him, too, but she worried that if she married him, he'd lose patience with her. Living with an agoraphobic wasn't going to be easy.

She vaguely listened to the distant sounds of Marco's voice as he talked on the phone while she stared at her kitchen. Her prison. She'd created it herself. She had to do something to tear down the walls. She wasn't going to marry Marco unless she could come to him as a whole woman.

She went to her office and flipped through the Rolodex. Natalie had found a behavioral therapist who specialized in agoraphobia. Lily had resisted calling the woman because she'd been happy with the way things were. But not any more. Something had to change.

Before she could call, Marco came to the door. "What are you doing?"

"Redefining my personal goals." She took the card out of the Rolodex.

"That means?"

"I can't marry you the way I am." The road ahead frightened her. Yet she couldn't go back, now.

He took a step into the room, his face showing surprise. "Lily, I love you the way you are."

"That's not good enough for me."

"I don't understand."

She showed him the Rolodex card.

He took the card and said, "Who the hell is Dr. Mary Knowles?"

"The person who is going to help me become the woman I want to be–a woman who can get married and have a life."

"You don't have to do this for me."

She touched his arm. "I have to do it for me. You want children. Someone has to take them to school, take them to soccer practice and ballet lessons."

"My sons aren't taking ballet lessons."

"Put your macho away," Lily said with a grin, "our children will be whoever they want to be, but first they need a mother who can be a mother."

"I can help."

"I need to take the first steps on my own."

"What are you saying?"

"Marco, when you told me you loved me last night, I felt such joy, such a sense of completeness, I knew I had to do something that wouldn't jeopardize all that. I know you love me and will do anything to help me, but I've always had a support system to help me out when I needed it. What I'm saying is that I need you to leave."

Marco shook his head. I'm not leaving."

"Yes, you are. Just long enough to let me get all my ducks in a row." She had major decisions to make and she needed to be able to make them without people hovering around her. Having people waiting to catch her if she fell was a two-edged sword. Recent events had crystallized a growing sense that she needed to make a major change in her life.

"I read up on agoraphobia," Marco said. "You could spend years in therapy. I can't wait that long."

She put a hand on his chest. "You won't have to wait that long, I promise. Just a few days."

"Lily, I love you."

"I love you too, Marco, but I need to do this by myself. Don't make it harder."

"Can I bring Harley to stay with you? I'll feel better."

That sounded good. "I would love to have Harley."

"And then I can visit her."

She stroked his cheek. "You can visit her."

He kissed her, his lips soft on hers, filled with promise, filled with love. For him, she could do anything.

New York City, Madison Square Garden

Marco couldn't believe he'd actually made it to the Westminster dog trials.

Sawyer's trial had run two extra weeks and Marco thought he might miss being the show. Leland Davenport had refused to take any chances with the trial. He had been able to link Sawyer to the deaths of several other women, the homeless man, as well as Lily's parents. Sawyer was going away for a very long time.

Joe Sawyer had thought himself invulnerable, but he'd made one vital mistake. He'd chosen Lily and she'd brought him down. Marco was so proud of her, especially the day she'd testified. She'd fought her panic and with her testimony hammered the final nail into Sawyer's coffin.

Marco watched as the seven dogs that had won best of group began to circle the ring. Harley trotted after a Maltese and an Airedale Terrier.

She strutted as only a Great Dane could strut. Marco chewed on his thumbnail focusing on her. The dog was in top form. The vet had taken extra pains with her gunshot wound and not even a hint of a scar marred her beautiful coat. Her ears were erect and her posture perfect, Champion Harley Davidson Jackson was in her element. His baby had charmed every judge. He could hardly take his eyes off her.

A stinging slap hit his arm. He jerked upright. His mother cast a sidelong glance. "Hi, mom."

She'd made it. He'd worried when her plane was late.

She bent over and kissed him. "Stop worrying," she said, "I made a special offering to Saint Francis of Assisi."

Marco smiled. The patron saint of animals. Only his mother. Harley was taking her turn around the ring. Applause rang out. Harley was the crowd favorite.

His mother brushed past him to sit on his other side. Only then did Marco notice that she wasn't alone. Lily sat next to him. His heart raced. She looked good.

She smiled. "How is our girl doing?"

Marco could barely contain the joy he felt just looking at her. "You came."

"Sorry to be late. It took me a couple of tries to get on the plane. But your mom was very patient with me."

"It's okay. I didn't think you'd come." He was totally awed that she was even here. Not only had she left her home, but she'd taken a plane to come to New York. Though she was nervous, she'd managed to keep her fear under control.

"I'm okay. I have my doctor's cell, home, office and even her mother's number. If I get into trouble I'm not alone." Lily glanced at Connie who nodded encouragingly at her, an approving light in her eyes.

Marco grasped her hand. "You'll never be alone again." He was never going to let that happen. She was his. He'd been waiting so long for this moment, he wondered how she felt about eloping to Niagara Falls. He didn't think he could wait for a formal wedding to be organized.

She put her fingers to her lips. "The judge is going to make his choice."

Without looking at the judge, Marco said, "Harley's going to win." Then the suspense crawled through him, and he glanced at the ring to watch the judge walk down the line of dogs. After several hesitations, the judge pointed at Harley. A roar went through the crowd.

Harley had triumphed. She accepted the accolades with royal dignity.

Marco jumped up. Lily did to. They embraced. "That's my girl,"

he said. He meant both of them.

Lily broke away. "You have to go down to the floor."

Marco grabbed her hand and started pulling her with him. "I don't want to leave you."

"This is your moment."

Marco shook his head. "No, every moment from here on is our moment." He fumbled with his briefcase on the floor and popped it open. He pulled out an envelope. "This is for you."

He waited while she opened it carefully. She pulled out the advance copy of Marco's graphic novel, The Adventures of Tiger Lily. She took a deep breath, her eyes widening. "You didn't tell me you'd even submitted it."

"I didn't want to spoil the surprise."

The loud speaker called his name and Marco glanced at the ring. "We have to go. The judges are waiting for us."

A slight fear showed in her eyes and then was gone. "I can do this." She smiled; one hand curled tightly around his while she held the graphic novel to her chest with the other. She mouthed the words I love you.

He kissed her.

He didn't know he could be so happy. His future stretched out in front of him and he was certain he would always be happy with her despite the barriers of her fears. They would have their ups and downs, but he understood that Lily's progress would be made in baby steps. And he would always be around to support her.

Together they walked to the victory circle to share the moment.

AUTHOR BIOGRAPHY

Born in Boston, Mass. **J.M. Jefferies** attended college at UCR. Her occupation is a writer of romance and suspense. She has spent some of her free time traveling all over Europe and the U.S. Read more at **www.jmjeffries.com**.

THE WEDDING GOWN
BY DYANNE DAVIS

CHAPTER ONE

Wedding gown for sale. Cheap. Brand new, never worn. Reason: Potential groom turned out to be a two--timing jackass!!!

Keefe read the notice posted in the laundry room, amusement creasing his handsome face. He wondered for a moment if this was a joke. He glanced casually once again at the notice and saw what he'd missed initially, an e-mail address. He knew instantly that the woman was serious.

Cheap, he thought, wondering how cheap it would be. Some people thought five thousand dollars for a gown was cheap. He wasn't one of them. Of course his sister would think his even considering buying her a second hand gown would be cheap, meaning him not the gown.

And she would consider it used, worn or not. He could just hear her scolding voice now. "But Keefe, you promised. Why do I have to buy a gown someone else chose? It's bad luck, Keefe. Did you ever think of that?"

Just to be sure, Keefe read the notice once more. The potential bridegroom was a "two-timing jackass." Well, that couldn't be because of the gown, he assured himself as he pulled a pencil from behind his ear and scribbled down the e-mail address. It was at least worth looking into.

"What are you doing?"

"Excuse me?" Keefe answered turning to confront the hostile voice.

"I said, what are you doing?"

Damn, she's fine, he thought to himself as he eyed the woman standing before him. His eyes were drawn to her breasts and stayed a second or two longer than was decent. He was aware of that. And if he weren't, the glare the woman shot him from her brown eyes reminded him of that fact in a hurry.

"I was reading the notice about the wedding gown. Why? Is there something wrong with that?"

"That notice is for a wedding gown, a woman's wedding gown."

Keefe took a step back better to peruse the woman looking at him with such disdain. Having done that, he began inventorying himself, making it obvious what he was doing. It was clear what the woman standing before him had just implied.

His eyes flicked over his attire, jeans and a tee shirt. Nothing about his clothes implied he would be into wearing women's attire. He continued scrutinizing: tool-belt around his waist, hammer on the counter near him with a half box of penny nails spilled out in varying spots. Just as he thought, everything about him appeared to be in order.

"Excuse me, miss, but is there something about me or my demeanor?" He raised an eyebrow, daring her to answer before he even finished the question. "Is there something about me that would have you questioning my manhood before you've even introduced yourself to me?"

"You're looking at a notice to buy a wedding gown."

"And that fact alone tells you what? That I want it for myself?"

"Well, it tells me one of two things. Either you're gay, or you're a cheap bastard who wants to buy his girlfriend this gown because he thinks he can get a bargain."

The woman was beginning to irk him. Fine or not, he wasn't in the mood to charm a man-hating female. Nope, too many women in the world that loved men for him to go to such trouble.

"Why is what I do or read any of your business?" He watched as the woman's eyes lifted. He saw her blink as though she hadn't expected him to say anything.

"It's my gown," she answered at last.

"Oh."

He wanted to apologize, to tell her he was sorry things hadn't worked out for her, to tell her not to become bitter, but while he was contemplating how to begin, the woman turned and walked out of the laundry room, leaving him standing with what he knew was a stupid expression on his face. Damn, he hadn't even gotten the woman's name.

You do have her e-mail address, his subconscious screamed at him, so make use of that.

***

"I don't want a gown someone else picked out, Keefe. You promised to help me with this wedding. You made the offer to buy the gown, now you're trying to back out."

Just as he'd expected, his little sister was not taking to this idea very well. Hell, he'd tried presenting this to her as a good opportunity, but now he was feeling every bit as stubborn as she was.

"I'm not made of money, Mia."

"You're not broke either, but you're always poor mouthing. God, Keefe, when you die you can't take it with you."

245

"At the rate that you're going if I don't die soon there will be nothing left to take."

"Forget it, Keefe, I'll buy my own gown. Just forget it."

The pounding sensation began in his temples. Women. Sometimes he thought the world would be better off without them. They always wanted something from you; usually it was your money. For women everything came with a price tag. If you had enough money you could buy them what they wanted and perhaps receive some momentary peace.

"Is it because you think I have money that you won't even look at the gown?"

"No. It's because you made me a promise."

"Asking you to take a look at the gown isn't breaking my promise. You don't know how much the gown is selling for or whether you'll see it and fall in love with it. It was just an idea. You don't have to bite my head off. I swear, you women, you want one thing: a man to spend his money on you."

He wished he could take back the words but it was too late. The sudden chill in the room was evident of that fact.

"I'm sorry, Mia."

"Forget it, Keefe. I don't want you to buy my gown, not now."

"I shouldn't have said that. I was thinking about Mom and Treece. I didn't mean to compare you to them. I really didn't."

"But you did. So you must think that about me too. Anyway, give me the e-mail address, Keefe. I'll contact the woman with the gown and make an appointment to see it. But if I like the gown, I'll buy it myself."

"No, forget it. It was a bad idea. Let's go to some of those bridal shops you wanted to go to."

"Look, Kee, don't try to humor me. I don't want your help, not any longer."

"I want to help," Keefe pleaded, wishing for once he'd not allowed his relationship with women to color his conversation with his sister. She was the only female in the entire universe who didn't want anything from him. The only one he could trust.

Hell, the whole thing had been his idea from the beginning. He'd coerced her into allowing him to help with the expenses. The only thing she'd asked of him was that he walk her down the aisle. Now he'd probably screwed that up as well.

"Mia, I really am sorry."

"I know you are, but I won't have you putting me in the same category as you do all women. Give me the address."

He dipped his hand into his pocket, his eyes never leaving his sister's face, a face so like his own: pecan coloring, dark brown eyes fringed by a massive amount of black lashes, usually smiling eyes now marred by the sparkling of tears. He couldn't believe he'd been the one to put them in her eyes.

"Mia, please."

"No," she answered as she took the paper from his outstretched hand and headed to the corner to turn on her computer. She typed in a few words, then sent the message off, leaving the speaker on.

"It's going to take time to hear from her," Keefe offered. "You may as well try a few shops while you wait for her to get back to you."

His sister merely arched her brows in a derisive manner, dismissing him. For twenty minutes he fiddled with his fingers, wondering how on earth he could possibly make things right.

"You've got mail."

His eyes turned toward the sound of the speaker. His gut told him it was the wedding gown woman. His sister headed for the computer, then called out to him, "It's her." To his surprise, he felt a little excitement. Then, reluctantly, he admitted to himself that he'd had ulterior motives in getting his sister involved with the owner of the dress.

"What did she say?" Keefe badgered. "Has she sold the dress?" For a moment he thought she wasn't going to answer.

"She told me if I'm interested to give her my number and she'll call me. She also wanted to know how I found out about it. Don't you think that's a little strange? I mean, you did say she had a notice in the laundry room of your building. Why is she being so paranoid? How does she think I got her e-mail address?"

Keefe cringed inwardly at his sister's analyzing look, wishing she didn't know him so well.

"I talked to her for a few minutes. For some strange reason she took an instant dislike to me. I don't think you should mention me. Just tell her that a friend of yours who was in the building saw the notice and gave you the information."

"So you want me to lie?"

"Not lie. I do consider myself your friend."

"Hrrump. That's splitting hairs, you're my brother."

"What? You don't consider me to be your friend?" Keefe teased, sensing his sister's mood was lightening and she was no longer angry.

"You're my best friend, Keefe," she smiled broadly, "and I think I'm your only friend. I'm the only person alive who can stand your pompous behind." With a flourish Mia typed in her phone number and the half-truth that a friend had given her the information about the gown.

Less than five minutes passed before the phone rang. The caller ID flashed "unknown caller." Keefe and his sister both smiled at the extent the woman was going to in order to maintain her privacy.

"Hello, this is Ashleigh Johnson. Is this Mia?"

"Yes it is. Thanks for calling back so quickly. Listen, I'm sorry to hear that things didn't go so well for you. I'm a little curious, though, about why you posted the ad."

Keefe heard the laughter, even from where he was sitting. He turned his head in his sister's direction. Surely this laughing from the other end of the phone couldn't be the same surly woman he'd met. This woman sounded downright pleasant. This woman was one he'd want to meet, especially since he already knew how she looked.

He felt the beginning of a bulge that embarrassed the hell out of him. How the hell had he allowed that to happen and in the presence of his little sister?

He walked away, wanting to hear the rest of the conversation, but knowing his ardor demanded he go somewhere and cool off a bit, forget about the woman on the phone, forget about the lush round behind and the firm breasts that he could see his lips clinging to even now.

Stop it, Keefe, his inner voice scolded. That's not the way to get rid of a hard-on.

"Okay, big brother, I'm going to go and take a look at the gown," Mia yelled to him.

"You don't have to do that. I'm sorry I said anything. I'll buy you whatever gown you want."

"No, Keefe, the woman sounds interesting, I want to meet her. I want to know how she put you in her web so quickly."

"What the hell are you talking about...no one has me anywhere. You're crazy."

Keefe was sputtering; he backed away from his sister. "Leave me out of this. You want the gown, go look at it."

"So... Is she cute?"

"Cute is what you are." Keefe smiled into Mia's eyes, then laughed. "Okay, yes, she's beautiful, but I've never seen a woman with so much attitude."

"Who do you think you're fooling, Kee? You're interested in the woman.

"What are you talking about? I talked to the woman all of five minutes. I don't even know if I like her, let alone want to date her."

"Please, Keefe, you're protesting a bit too much. I know the signs. You don't fall often but I think you're almost there."

"All I said was…"

"I know what I said and how you said it. I also saw your eyes light up. That's interested."

"Who's the oldest here?" Keefe smiled again at his sister, glad to have this woman on his side. He knew he could always depend on her. She would have his back at all times.

He hugged her close. The two of them against the world. They had each other, always had, and always would. She was the only woman who'd never lied to him.

Still, he wanted more, for both of them. The odds of finding it weren't good. Look at the divorce rate. Hell, why was he thinking of divorce? The gown, he realized. That dammed wedding gown had him going way past the wedding day straight to divorce court.

"What's her name?" he asked.

"Ashleigh Johnson."

"When are you going over?"

"I told her I could be there in a couple of hours. She's having a group of her friends over. She said they're going to have a cleansing and said I could participate if I wanted."

"A cleansing?" Keefe frowned, wondering what the hell he was getting his sister involved in.

2003 Publication Schedule

January	Twist of Fate Beverly Clark 1-58571-084-9	Ebony Butterfly II Delilah Dawson 1-58571-086-5
February	Fragment in the Sand Annetta P. Lee 1-58571-097-0	Fate Pamela Leigh Starr 1-58571-115-2
March	One Day At A Time Bella McFarland 1-58571-099-7	Unbreak my Heart Dar Tomlinson 1-58571-101-2
April	At Last Lisa G. Riley 1-58571-093-8	Brown Sugar Diaries & Other Sexy Tales Delores Bundy & Cole Riley 1-58571-091-1
May	Three Wishes Seressia Glass 1-58571-092-X	Acquisitions Kimberley White 1-58571-095-4
June	When Dreams A Float Dorothy Elizabeth Love 1-58571-104-7	Revelations Cheris F. Hodges 1-58571-085-7
July	The Color of Trouble Dyanne Davis 1-58571-096-2	Someone To Love Alicia Wiggins 1-58571-098-9
August	Object Of His Desire A. C. Arthur 1-58571-094-6	Hart & Soul Angie Daniels 1-58571-087-3
September	Erotic Anthology Assorted 1-58571-113-6	A Lark on the Wing Phyliss Hamilton 1-58571-105-5

Other Genesis Press, Inc. Titles

Gentle Yearning	Rochelle Alers	$10.95
Glory of Love	Sinclair LeBeau	$10.95
Heartbeat	Stephanie Bedwell-Grime	$8.95
Illusions	Pamela Leigh Starr	$8.95
Indiscretions	Donna Hill	$8.95
Interlude	Donna Hill	$8.95
Intimate Intentions	Angie Daniels	$8.95
Kiss or Keep	Debra Phillips	$8.95
Love Always	Mildred E. Riley	$10.95
Love Unveiled	Gloria Greene	$10.95
Love's Deception	Charlene Berry	$10.95
Mae's Promise	Melody Walcott	$8.95
Meant to Be	Jeanne Sumerix	$8.95
Midnight Clear	Leslie Esdaile	$10.95
(Anthology)	Gwynne Forster	
	Carmen Green	
	Monica Jackson	
Midnight Magic	Gwynne Forster	$8.95
Midnight Peril	Vicki Andrews	$10.95
My Buffalo Soldier	Barbara B. K. Reeves	$8.95
Naked Soul	Gwynne Forster	$8.95
No Regrets	Mildred E. Riley	$8.95
Nowhere to Run	Gay G. Gunn	$10.95
Passion	T.T. Henderson	$10.95
Past Promises	Jahmel West	$8.95
Path of Fire	T.T. Henderson	$8.95
Picture Perfect	Reon Carter	$8.95
Pride & Joi	Gay G. Gunn	$8.95
Quiet Storm	Donna Hill	$8.95
Reckless Surrender	Rochelle Alers	$8.95
Rendezvous with Fate	Jeanne Sumerix	$8.95

Rivers of the Soul	Leslie Esdaile	$8.95
Rooms of the Heart	Donna Hill	$8.95
Shades of Desire	Monica White	$8.95
Sin	Crystal Rhodes	$8.95
So Amazing	Sinclair LeBeau	$8.95
Somebody's Someone	Sinclair LeBeau	$8.95
Soul to Soul	Donna Hill	$8.95
Still Waters Run Deep	Leslie Esdaile	$8.95
Subtle Secrets	Wanda Y. Thomas	$8.95
Sweet Tomorrows	Kimberly White	$8.95
The Price of Love	Sinclair LeBeau	$8.95
The Reluctant Captive	Joyce Jackson	$8.95
The Missing Link	Charlyne Dickerson	$8.95
Tomorrow's Promise	Leslie Esdaile	$8.95
Truly Inseperable	Wanda Y. Thomas	$8.95
Unconditional Love	Alicia Wiggins	$8.95
Whispers in the Night	Dorothy Elizabeth Love	$8.95
Whispers in the Sand	LaFlorya Gauthier	$10.95
Yesterday is Gone	Beverly Clark	$8.95
Yesterday's Dreams, Tomorrow's Promises	Reon Laudat	$8.95
Your Precious Love	Sinclair LeBeau	$8.95

Subscribe Today
to
Blackboard Times

*The African-American
Entertainment Magazine*

*Get the latest in book reviews, author interviews, book ranking,
hottest and latest tv shows, theater listing and more . . .*

*Coming in September
blackboardtimes.com*

Order Form

Mail to: Genesis Press, Inc.

1213 Hwy 45 N
Columbus, MS 39705

Name _____

Address _____

City/State _____ Zip _____

Telephone _____

Ship to (if different from above)

Name _____

Address _____

City/State _____ Zip _____

Telephone _____

Credit Card Information

Credit Card # _____ ☐ Visa   ☐ Mastercard

Expiration Date (mm/yy) _____ ☐ AmEx   ☐ Discover

Qty.	Author	Title	Price	Total

Use this order form, or call 1-888-INDIGO-1		
Total for books		_____
Shipping and handling: $5 first two books, $1 each additional book		
Total S & H		_____
Total amount enclosed		_____

Mississippi residents add 7% sales tax